I0772380

GRANTED

GRANTED

KATHRYN
HOLZMAN

Picaflor Press

*If you were fortunate enough to be born into a family whose an-
cestors directly benefited from genocide and/or slavery, maybe you
think the more you don't know, the more innocent you can stay…
Follow it back and you might find your line paved with gold or
beset with traps.*

There, There, by Tommy Orange, 2019.

CHAPTER ONE

Abduction

Nictaux, Nova Scotia, May 1761

I held on to my brother William, ahead of me in the saddle, for dear life. A thick woolen blanket padded the horse's bony back, but not nearly enough. Ahead of us, a convoy of parishioners, adults in the lead and children in the rear, followed a narrow path along the Gasperaux River as it snaked toward the Bay of Fundy, its water as red as bricks. By the time we arrived at the beach, my legs were like those of a newborn calf, my blood curdled, and my bottom surely bruised as blue as a berry. I slid off the horse, only to have my knees buckle beneath me.

"Lucy," William said, "you clumsy girl. He offered me his hand, but the other children laughed. We were here to witness my father's baptism, but I, his sinful daughter, had landed in the sand face-first.

The rest of the congregation, in immaculate white finery, tied their horses to tree trunks. The younger children jumped from the backs of ox-carts, stretching their limbs on the beach. Girls shook out their braids and straightened their ribbons and bows. Their mothers, in stiff white aprons and tidy caps, attempted to rein them in.

I ducked behind a bush to relieve myself, catch my breath, and regain my composure. That's when I saw him. Behind the thorny berry bushes, an Indian boy watched silently as the congregation spread across the red sand beach. He wore buckskin, his fringed seams as weathered as the earth and clay. The oaks' shade camouflaged him, but our eyes locked. I recognized him. This was the boy who had approached me in my father's field, clutching a game he called Waltes. Like me, he must have traveled forty miles to arrive here.

Did he recognize me? A blank mask replaced the cautious smile I remembered.

The crowd gathered around the minister from Wolfville, a pompous fellow whose face was pitted with smallpox scars. Father, towering above the solicitous pastor, held my stepmother Salome's hand. The man was shorter than Father by a head and resembled a toad.

The minister cleared his throat.

"This morning, the Baptist Church welcomes Nathaniel and Salome Parker."

I hung behind the crowd, one eye on my father, whose baptism the congregation had come to witness, and the other on the dark-skinned boy.

The waves from the bay slapped the shore. Under the minister's stern gaze, the chattering crowd formed a semi-circle facing the sea, their backs to the children. In front of me, a young girl I knew from Sunday school hopped first on one foot and then the other, trying to see over the adults' heads. When she could not, she turned away from the baptism, alert for other diversions. I wondered if she saw him, if she would sound an alarm. But then the young boy at her side tickled her. They tittered and began sparring. Their tussle evoked a sharp rebuke from the children's mother. All eyes once again focused on Father.

In the bushes, the boy was as still as a deer sniffing a hunter's scent.

"Do you, Nathaniel Parker, recognize this sanctified church as essential to the work of conversion and to the advancement of the causes of God?" The pastor from Wolfville addressed my father but looked out at the congregation.

Father looked over his head. "I am prepared to accept with gratitude membership in the Church."

"Amen." The congregants raised their arms and eyes to the heavens. I followed their example, but with my fingers crossed.

In the shadows, the Indian boy edged closer. His leather moccasins muffled his cautious footsteps. He skirted the towering pines far from the crowd as if looking for a clean line of sight. At the far side of the field, he crouched behind a large granite rock.

Then my father headed out into the open water of the bay. Salome and the minister from Wolfville followed him, tiptoeing gingerly into the icy water. My stepmother lifted her long white skirt, showing ankles as pink as a newborn. With a brief prayer, the minister began. We watched him etch an invisible cross on Father's forehead. His white robes floating on the water, he cupped a hand over Father's scalp and dunked his head into the breaking waves.

A chorus of hallelujahs rose from the crowd, echoed by the excited cries of gulls. The boy startled and disappeared behind the rock. Father burst from the water, blinking and spitting.

Next, the minister pushed Salome's head under the water. For a moment, I held my breath, hoping she might drown. But she emerged, sodden, hugging herself to shield her body, her mouth a determined line on her reddened face. She crossed her arms in front of her, but I saw the swell of her belly. I stared, unable to hide my astonishment. A bump strained against the shivering white fabric of her dress. The women smiled and exchanged knowing glances. Father took off his jacket and wrapped it around her. Then he joined the men on shore. They closed their prayer books and congratulated him.

It was over. Children pushed and shoved, resuming their play. Little girls rolled in the grass, their white Sunday dresses sullied by the porous red mud. The men turned their gazes to the horizon.

I squirmed as the women clustered around Salome. She answered their solicitous inquiries with the same cold, stoic smile she often directed at me.

The men mounted their horses. After one last race the length of the beach, the younger children returned to climb into the oxcarts, making beds in the hay.

William had already mounted his horse. "Lucy," he said, "wouldn't you be more comfortable joining the others in the cart?" As much as I hated Salome's progeny, I nodded yes. My bottom hurt, and my legs were tired. I wanted to stick out my tongue as I climbed in, but I resisted. Grandmother Hardy taught me you catch more flies with honey than vinegar. Ma Salome and her brats were vinegar for sure; I intended to be the honey. Besides, I could nap in the oxcart.

That's when I remembered the boy. As the cart joined the line of departing parishioners, I scanned the undergrowth, but he had disappeared.

The women doubled up on their horses, smoothed their rumpled skirts, and tied their caps tighter for warmth. Salome was the last person to mount her steed. Her wet, white skirt clung to her thighs. She wore my father's jacket, but the grimace on her face betrayed her discomfort. She rode alone, though a woman from the congregation attempted to pull up beside her.

The assembly ascended the path. Out of the corner of my eye, I imagined a muscular shadow following us.

Salome spurred her horse forward, passing the oxcarts and the chattering women. She craned her neck.

My stepsister stabbed me with her elbow.

"Is that my mother?" she asked. "Calling out in the distance?"

It was hard to hear over the noisy clomp of horse hooves.

"Nathaniel," I thought I heard Ma Salome call. "Nathaniel, where are you?"

In the alarm that spread like fire after we realized Father had disappeared, I completely forgot the boy who had been lurking in the shadows.

●●●

Amen. Even Meuse recognized that word. He had learned it in the French church. It often echoed in the Acadian mission his family once attended but now stood in ruins. But these people were not French. And they were not Catholic. They were New Englanders who had recently resettled in the Kespukwik Valley. They were not his friends.

Meuse stalked the men along the dirt path that paralleled the river, hiding behind the reeds, where the congregation could neither see nor hear him. Their horses pranced, mirroring their riders' excitement. Their voices echoed through the pines, drowning out the birds' twilight chorus. Meuse proceeded unnoticed.

Although he did not understand English, he could spot Elders when he saw them. He recognized the respect the short man wearing robes showed the taller man whom he addressed as "Parker," and that man's easy acceptance of the crowd's attention. The boy concluded the congregants had gathered this day in recognition of this Parker's high status in their tribe.

Meuse watched the tall man's every move, waiting for him to be separated from his companions. Then he heard the woman calling "Nathaniel." He heard the uncertainty in her voice.

The timing was perfect. The sun had descended below the horizon. The lingering light faded fast, the rosy hue on the horizon hardly noticeable between the trunks of the trees.

"Nathaniel," she called out.

The man called "Parker" turned around, listening. Meuse crouched in the reeds, out of his sight.

"Salome?" Parker said. "Is that you?"

Perhaps she answered, but the distance muffled her voice.

The other men continued down the path. Meuse watched the tall man halt his horse, pause for a second, listen, and then turn his horse around, trotting back on the trail before reining in his steed to wait for the woman to catch up with him.

This was the moment. Without hesitation, Meuse grabbed the reins of Parker's horse and swung himself up behind him, counting on the element of surprise. He grabbed a handful of the white man's dirty blond hair and pulled his head back, stretching the tendons in his neck, his Adam's apple like a frog struggling beneath taut pink skin. Meuse clamped a hand over his mouth and nose, denying him a voice and air to breathe. Parker struggled to free himself, but Meuse's hold was firm. He used his shin to pin Parker's thigh to the leather of his saddle as securely as rope encircles a stallion's neck to break him. He yanked the reins and steered the horse off the beaten trail toward the narrower path worn by deer and other animals of the forest. When he could no longer see the river, he pulled up on the reins, and the horse halted. There, he bound the man's fists behind his back with a strap of sinew. Parker struggled, but Meuse twisted the strap until he bit his tongue and grimaced with pain. Meuse's strength and determination quickly subdued the man's futile attempts to twist himself free.

"*Silence*," he spat, knowing the English-speaking man would understand this French word. Summoning a fierce expression, he pantomimed scalping his captive, pulling a fistful of Parker's hair as he drew a jagged fingernail across his forehead. He avoided looking into the man's eyes but smelled his fear. Stuffing the white man's mouth with an old bandanna, Meuse tied another over his eyes, nose, and mouth and knotted it behind his neck. Blind and mute, his captive struggled to speak, but soon abandoned the effort.

Meuse bound Parker's right ankle with the end of a short rope he passed under the horse's belly. He tied the other end to the man's left ankle. Now the white man could not escape. His horse shifted restlessly but waited for Meuse to finish his task. In the distance, the woman called again, her voice more urgent now. Fused to his captive on the back of the horse, Meuse steered the steed away from her, away from the voices of the children and the distant clatter of hooves, far away from the white men's settlements. Meuse had traveled through these woods since he was a boy. In the dark, he followed animal trails, his prisoner pinned in front of him, skin against skin, captive embraced by captor. The man smelled like the sea, his hair still wet from the baptism, his clothes damp, his skin cold and clammy.

By the time the northern star appeared in the night sky, they had reached the canoe Meuse had stowed in the marshland. Meuse let out a sigh of relief. Untying the ropes that bound the man's ankles to the horse, he tugged Parker from the horse until the man lay limp and helpless in the dirt. Meuse inhaled deeply, steeling himself. He could only hope his body, only recently beginning to resemble that of a man, would be equal to the task ahead. Could he trust the newly discovered knot of muscle in his biceps to be strong enough to carry his captive? Could he depend on these legs, longer every day, to support both of their weight?

Meuse spat on Parker before lifting him. Summoning a grown man's strength and a hunter's determination, he tossed his captive over his shoulder like a lifeless pelt and carried him to the canoe. With surprising ease, he loaded him in like cargo.

If only his cousins could see him now, as strong as any man. A warrior. When Parker struggled, Meuse jerked his bound hands behind his back, inflicting as much pain as possible. When he kicked, Meuse re-bound his feet and forced him to his knees. Meuse retrieved the oars from their hiding place in the undergrowth and pulled the boat into shallow water. With bound hands behind him, the white man knelt in the front like a bowsprit facing the dark river. Meuse pushed off from the shore with his oar. His strokes were deft and sure. Soon, this pasty man would understand what his people had taken from Meuse and his family. From the Mi'kmaq. From a land that was not his.

•••

Kejimkujik, Nova Scotia

Meuse pulled the canoe ashore where the Mersey River flowed into Kejimkujik Lake, close to the site of his tribe's deserted winter camp. Loosening the ties on Parker's ankles, he pointed to a field at the edge of the forest. He nudged his captive forward with his foot. A circle of stones marked the tribe's fire pit, left cold when the tribe had traveled to their summer camp. There, he pushed Parker to the ground and retightened the sinew that bound him. Then, as the white man watched, he gathered twigs and fallen branches and sparked a fire in the pit.

When the flames were bright, he swept a clearing for a wigwam. Using green saplings as poles, he spread them wide at the bottom and tied them together with split spruce root at their peak. He made a hoop of moosewood, which he placed under the top to brace the shelter. After testing its stability, he covered it with birch bark.

The moon was high in the sky by the time he finished. The fire he had built smoldered.

He pushed his captive into the wigwam and then returned to the fire. The summer night was warm, and the surrounding forest filled with the rustling of small animals. By the light of the moon, he lit a bundle of white sage with a smoldering twig and cupped his hands to direct the smoke over his head. Looking up at the sky, he gave thanks for the gift of life. He asked forgiveness for taking the lives of animals, birds, trees, and fish, as his father had taught him. He washed first his mouth, then his eyes, and finally his weary heart, with the healing smoke.

In the murky light of the fire, the blue eyes blinked. It didn't matter to Meuse that the man didn't understand a word he said. He had something he needed to say.

"This is how it is done," he said to his captive, buoyed by the smell of smoke and the light of the moon. He placed a pile of heated stones in the center of the wigwam. The man cowered in the darkness of the shelter. His eyes, squinting against the smoke, showed a startle of fear. "My father was younger than you when he died," Meuse said. "The British forces slew him on the Isthmus of Chignecto, a narrow strip of land separating the French Beaubassin colony from Canada's mainland. In Mi'kmaq, we call this strip of land *Siknikt* or drainage place, because this is where low-lying marshes and tidal bores return water to the sea. My father faced down foreign invaders like you to protect our land."

Meuse described his father, a brave *smáknisk* called into battle.

"On a late spring evening in 1755, Father Le Loutre received a warning. French sentinels had spied British vessels approaching Cape Maringouin, the spit of land separating the Beaubassin Channel from Chipoudy Bay. By sunset, Yankee militia and British forces disembarked and set up an encampment. Responding to the call across the river, several hundred Acadian men, along with loyal Mi'kmaq and Maliseet Indians, took up defensive positions along the crest of the dikes. Soon, the roar of cannons filled the air. Lethal sprays of small iron balls blasted French gunners. The British ascended Beauséjour Ridge, firing at the defenders, who pulled back to the cover of the forest canopy and finally retreated to the fort. The battle lasted only forty-five minutes. My father was one of seven warriors killed."

The British raised their flag in Butte à Roger, a mile to the southeast. Le Loutre ordered the destruction of the fort, torching it shortly after sunset.

"Father Le Loutre asked for our help, and we gave it to him in good faith. Prior to retreating, Mi'kmaq and Maliseet warriors joined forces and killed three Englishmen."

The white man shook his head. Perhaps to deny culpability, but more likely because he could not understand the strange words, spoken quickly and with passion. Meuse ignored him. He knew the colonists from Massachusetts had arrived to these lands later, after his father had already died. But they had reaped the benefits of his father's ignoble death. "The warriors carried my father's body to this spot. They laid him where you cower now, on a soft bed of seaweed."

For this vision, he had brought Parker to this outpost where the lake met the forest.

"Where were you?" he asked the white man. "Waiting to take their place? Preparing to occupy a house the British stole from an Acadian family? What gives you the right?" He spat again in Parker's face.

Now the prisoner was still, his skin flushed with fear.

"My father was not afraid like you are now," Meuse told him, his voice rising, cracking. Yesterday he had the treble voice of a boy, but today he spoke like a man, angry that this coward benefited from his father's misfortune. "My father stood with those Acadians. The Mi'kmaq, side by side with the French, faced your countrymen, daring them to cross into our land. But even with reinforcements, the English soldiers outnumbered the proud and defiant men who fought with Father Le Loutre. They burned the village of Beaubassin so that the British could not establish a fort there and claim land that did not belong to them. Instead, they gave it to you. To the New Englanders."

Parker closed his eyes, which were irritated by the smoke. Tears ran down his cheeks; his white skin was flushed from the stone's heat. When he inhaled, the gag over his mouth formed an empty well. When he breathed out, a sob escaped. With each action, Meuse tried to dispel the negative energy in the smoky darkness, to rid the air of this man's impurities.

With his captive as his witness, he performed four rounds of prayer as he had seen his Elders do. He gave thanks to the seven levels of creation.

With the seven hot rocks, he honored the seven regional families. He braided the sweet grass of Mother Earth and set it on fire, offering smoke to the seven sacred directions.

The Elders had taught him that each generation was responsible for the next seven. That each generation must be a caretaker of Mother Earth, of the plants, the animals, and the minerals. As Meuse held up his offerings, he did not move. He avoided Parker's frightened gaze, the sight of his wrists bound tightly, a red ring of irritation spreading from his ankles up his legs.

"This," he said, "is how my Elders taught me to honor all creation. This is who we are."

Quiet now. The power was in his hands. A wave of serenity swept over him. Like his mother, he was beautiful. Like his father, he was the strongest of men.

At last, he was not afraid.

• • •

Parker's ankles and wrists were tied with animal sinew. He was curled like a fetus on the dirt floor of a primitive wigwam in the middle of the forest. Parker watched the savage, an adolescent, half-naked, with mud smeared on his arms and legs. If he were patient, the boy would fall asleep. Then Parker could loosen the ties that bound his wrists. *All I need is a moment of weakness.* An experienced military man, Parker would re-assert his superiority when that moment arrived. He was confident that by the time his compatriots came to his rescue, he would have already vanquished the enemy. Governor Cornwallis forewarned the new settlers: the countryside was rife with savages who did not wish them well. This boy was young and foolish, his brown limbs were muscular but too skinny to be much of a threat. His feet were bare, his hair greasy and uncombed. He sat on his heels like a toad, speaking the guttural language of the local natives. The intensity of the boy's harangue was persistent, the flash of his black eyes indignant. He knew Parker did not understand a word he said. The boy would never get away with such a foolish stunt.

Dear Lord, Parker prayed, *why on this day of all days have you tested me?*

Parker, a righteous man, thought of Salome, abandoned on the road from the Gaspereaux Valley to Annapolis. The baptism had been Salome's idea. With a view to their spiritual benefit, she had encouraged him to leave his Congregational roots behind. She introduced him to thirteen neighbors in Annapolis: They were Planters, as the newly arrived New Englanders now called themselves, who were forming a Baptist parish, a satellite to the thriving congregation in Wolfville.

"They need guidance," she had said. "A strong leader like you could be their pastor." Flattered, Parker had agreed to convert, and the pastor in Wolfville had taken him under his wing. Now Parker was baptized, and he could be ordained.

His life had never been easy. He had served the Lord with loyalty and dedication, not to mention a determination to succeed. Like his father before him, everything Parker earned, he earned with honest labor. Every hardship he suffered, and there had been many, he survived through perseverance.

Now, despite it all, he was at the mercy of a heathen. As a boy at his father's side, Parker had witnessed an Algonquian Indian who refused to convert being burned at the stake. His father responded to his son's horror by explaining that the settlers had a moral duty to God to use whatever tools they had in their arsenal to bring Christianity to an un-tamed land.

The air in the wigwam was thick with smoke. Hours passed; night became day. The boy's speech slowed to a weary whisper. In the lulls between his incomprehensible ravings, his eyes lost focus. At these times, the boy's countenance softened as if he had purged himself of some great anger. He appeared younger, vulnerable. Parker watched this transformation with curiosity, seeing in the boy's expression a familiar piety, one he himself experienced when overcome by God's glory.

Did he notice a resemblance to his youngest son, William, at a moment of redemption? When, humbled by a belting but wiser for it, the child understood his father's lessons? A moment of illumination. Perhaps, if he could understand the boy's words, a dialogue could take place. They might, for a moment, bridge the infinite space between them.

But as quickly as these thoughts occurred to Parker, he dismissed them. He was a captive in mortal danger for his life. Since his arrival in Nova Scotia, the local papers had been filled with hair-raising accounts of the Indians' brutality. The struggle to bring civilization to Nova Scotia was a task he had willingly assumed. This was no time for sympathy. This young boy, as innocent as he might appear in his conviction and weariness, could kill him at any time. Like the other heathens of his tribe, given the opportunity, he would slaughter Parker's family without compunction. Cut the baby from Salome's belly. Leave his children orphans in a strange land.

The passion he sensed in the boy's eyes was deviltry. Nothing more.

Parker was hungry. He needed to piss. His anger at his helplessness consumed him. He tried once more, without success, to loosen his bonds. His head ached. His legs cramped. He regarded the boy with fury. *He will never get away with this.* The first chance he got, he would wrestle the bastard to the floor and choke him, using nothing but his bare hands if need be.

CHAPTER TWO

The Baptists

Westborough, Massachusetts, July 1759

Father came home last night.

All day, I waited for him by the window, expecting a soldier. I figured I would know Father by his uniform, but when he walked up the path to our front door, he wore a tailcoat, breeches, and a jaunty three-sided hat. I would have recognized him anywhere.

He hugged Mother so hard his hat fell off, and I was afraid he might crush her. Then he shook William's and Nat's hands. Finally, he turned to me. "Lucy, how you have grown!" He swung me around until I was so dizzy I fell to the floor.

We had been expecting him for days. Mother had heard from the women in her sewing circle that his Massachusetts regiment had returned after the capture of Louisbourg. Serving under Brigadier General James

Wolfe, the Massachusetts regiment had scaled the cliffs of Cape Breton and defeated the French forces.

My brother William asked about the battle.

Father was still wearing his coat. He told us Commander Wolfe and several of his compatriots had been fatally wounded during the battle. "Maggie, dear," he said to Mother, "you remember my good friend and fellow soldier, Ezekiel Cleveland? He perished beside me, right there on the battlefield."

"That poor man. May God grant him peace," Mother said. "His wife must be devastated."

"That day was the last I will ever wear a soldier's uniform," Father said.

All of Father's elation at having arrived home dried up when he told us about his friend. We were still standing in the entryway. I held onto his hand, but he didn't seem to notice. "I will never forget the dying man's last words: 'Please, I beg of you, look after my wife Salome and my two children when I am gone.'"

"I'm sure you will," Mother said, taking his coat.

I tugged his hand to get his attention. When he looked down, he seemed surprised to see me. But my gesture returned him to the room.

"Let's not talk about that now. You do not know how much I have looked forward to this moment." He embraced Mother again. "How delicate and precious you are, my sweet," he said. She looked up at him, her green eyes aglow. We children clustered around them, a family once more. Mother wiped a tear from her cheek, and we took turns bringing him up to date. Nat told him that in the hope of one day becoming a magistrate, he had a clerkship in the governor's office, drafting statutes that could apply the word of God to the governing of men. William, always his favorite, showed him his new Bible. When it was my turn, my mind went totally blank. Me, who always has something to say! He took my hand and said he hardly recognized me. Well, no wonder. "I grew six inches while you were away," I bragged. "I'm not little anymore." He laughed and agreed with me.

William and Nat begged him to tell them more about the siege. Mother hung up his coat, and he settled into his armchair, which Mother had re-centered across from the hearth. We sat at his feet. Mother puttered at the hearth, and he told us the rest of the story.

"A boatload of us discovered a rocky inlet protected from French fire and secured a beachhead. When the rest of the division followed us there, the French retreated to their fortress. They say the battle was the feather that broke the horse's back," he said, "but I'll spare you the gory details. Suffice it to say that, as a result, the French surrendered their territory across Atlantic Canada. The British forces hailed us as heroes."

My father, a hero. I couldn't wait to tell Louisa, my best friend. She thinks the sun rises and falls on her father, but had he won a war?

"In recognition of our successful campaign, the local government offered us land grants in the new English colony."

"Land grants?" Nat said. "Where?"

"In a valley they call Annapolis. On the Bay of Fundy."

Mother had finished pouring tea and was warming supper on the hearth. She turned, her eyes filled with alarm.

"A generous gesture," she said. "But Massachusetts will always be our home."

"And I am happy to be here," he replied. "All I want now is a warm meal with my family. We'll have plenty of time to discuss the future."

• • •

The winter after Father came home was as cold as a witch's tit. Storm after storm rolled through with rain, sleet, and dark clouds threatening snow. Even though Mother forbid me to utter this phrase in her presence, it was surely my favorite. I overheard William tell Nat that in Salem, during the 1600s, witches were portrayed as old hags. Ever since, the expression has come in handy during very cold weather because it alludes to their icy blood and wrinkly skin. Not that there were witches here, fifty miles west of Salem. But the phrase stuck in my head. Apart from the thrill of hearing the word "tit" emerge from my brother's mouth, I wondered if the witches they hanged in Salem were not hags but simply girls like me doing their best to survive the frigid season.

Mother spent most mornings embroidering linens, keeping an eye on me as I worked on my spinning, reeling off skeins of yarn. Even Mother admitted my output was impressive. More than enough for a pair of stockings.

Mother believed I had to be protected from the world. Fortunately, William was my tutor, supplementing Mother's limited reading and writing lessons with lectures on politics and philosophy. All I had to do was flutter my eyelashes and ask him to tell me a story, and he was off describing an Indian raid on a distant settlement or the drumbeat of revolution that was all the talk in Boston. When I wrinkled my nose with displeasure, he'd say, "Don't be a witch." Sometimes I did it on purpose, just so he would describe the trials of those poor girls possessed by the devil.

I shuddered to think of them hanging on the gallows.

Every winter day was the same: cold and damp. Finally, one day over lunch, William and Nat announced their intention of joining Grandfather Hardy for a meeting at the Congregational Church. Father was away in Boston to receive the report from a fellow member of the congregation who had recently sailed on a government ship to study the topography and soil in Annapolis. Seeing an opportunity to escape, I asked Mother if I might join the boys. At first, she hesitated, but William said a meeting might be just what the poor girl (me) needed.

Mother sighed as she stacked the dirty dishes. "I suppose an outing will do her good."

I immediately asked to be excused. At last, I could wear my hairpiece, the heddus I kept in my dresser drawer.

By two in the afternoon, I was snuggled up next to Nat in the back of Grandpa Hardy's chaise. William sat up front with Grandpa and discussed the upcoming voyage, while I peered out the window at the sideways rain. I held my head up high, careful not to disturb my precious heddus. Nat called it a red cow tail, but the heddus roll was a mixture of that and horsehair—coarse and scratchy—and a little human hair of a yellowish hue. All I knew for sure was that the barber carded it together and twisted it up before showing me how to tuck it under my cap with yellow ribbons complementing the yellowish hair. My scalp itched, ached, and burned, but I wasn't about to let that show.

Bouncing over the rutted road in the chaise, I felt quite the stylish lady with my fancy new hairpiece. That and my yellow coat, black bib, and apron, not to mention my pompadour shoes and the very handsome heart-shaped locket that was a birthday gift from my mother.

Grandpa Hardy dropped us off at the meetinghouse before tying up the horses. We ran in, shaking off the wind and rain, and huddled together on the pew for warmth. I twisted around to see who else was there and was pleased to see several of the girls from my Sunday school class. I waved, hoping they'd notice my hair and locket.

Mr. Beacon began his sermon by asking: "What is beauty?" I shifted, certain he addressed me and my yellow hair.

"Holiness," he answered himself, followed by a significant pause. He looked right at me, but I pretended not to notice. "My dear young friends," he said, "you like to be thought of as beautiful, but let me tell ye, you'll never be truly beautiful 'til you are glorious within."

I scratched my head when no one was looking. The deacon's message was obvious. I might sit here in this drafty church despite the weather, but that would not be near enough to save me. He continued: "Without holiness, beauty is a deformity. You are all over black and defiled."

That's when the Salem witch trials came to mind. But he was talking about Betty. William nodded in agreement as he spoke. According to my brother, everyone in town had been talking about Betty. Now Mr. Beacon said, in a thunderous voice, "The way of sin is downhill. When persons get into that way, they are not easily stopped."

Betty Smith, with her long dark curls and thick eyelashes, was the prettiest girl in Westborough, although her father was a drunk and her mother afraid to stand up to him. The boys pretended not to notice when she walked into the butcher shop, but I saw them sneaking looks when she turned her back. Even Nat had whistled underneath his breath when she passed by. But Mr. Beacon saw things differently. According to him, the girl's long hair was a wile of the devil. No wonder the constable carted Betty off to the jail last month for stealing apples from the fruit cart.

Mr. Beacon's voice boomed through the hall, and I slid lower in my seat. "If you are not glorious, you are ugly and loathsome, and if you die in this condition, you will dwell in hell with ugly devils to eternity."

Of all days to wear my heddus roll! If I could have ripped the whole twisted thing off, I would have. Instead, I clasped my hands in my lap and cast my eyes down with what I hoped appeared to be pious devotion. While William watched Mr. Beacon with serious admiration, I pretended to pray. When the meeting ended at last, I was the first out the door, avoiding my friends. How I wished I had stayed home with Mother or that she was at my side. Mother would surely have dismissed the deacon's sermon as easily as she did Father's incessant preaching, smiling sweetly and saying: "Let your conscience be your guide."

Grandpa dropped us at our front door and headed off to town, promising to see us soon. As we peeled off our wet coats, Mother noticed my wretched hair and burst out laughing.

"What have we here?" she asked, offering to comb out my hair before we sat down for dinner. I didn't answer and instead ran up the stairs to my chamber. I put the heddus away in a box and hid it under my bed. When I returned downstairs, Mother brushed out my hair and massaged my itchy scalp. She told me I was beautiful just as I am.

I was mulling over Betty's predicament. Was the girl bad because of her beauty or as the result of her difficult circumstance? The deacon would have me believe my heddus would "head" me right to hell, but I fingered Ma's locket, as handsome as it was harmless.

Mother said beauty had nothing to do with sin. Betty's beauty, which she didn't deny, was only skin deep. Her naughtiness came from deep inside her, she said, a hunger that begged for attention, a gaping hole the lack of proper guidance had never healed.

William didn't agree. He said that was a crock. "Sin is sin, and we are all born with it." Many a gentlewoman radiated the blessed beauty of maternal grace, but if granted too much importance, it is a symptom of something not right.

Over dinner, Ma said we were spending too much time on idle gossip. No one mentioned my heddus roll again. Instead, Father monopolized the conversation, reporting that Benjamin Franklin and a company in Philadelphia had hired surveyors to travel to Nova Scotia. Their report back described seven rivers that emptied their waters into a large basin. On the banks of each, there was an abundance of fertile soil.

"Lush forests cover the rolling hills. The Acadians planted apple trees during their time on the land, and in a few months, they will bud. The grass on the dikes will turn green, and the uplands will be ready for the plow." With a copy of the report in hand, land agents in Boston were now recruiting settlers.

"Dear ones," he said. "The first families have been cleared to leave."

At that, my brothers hooted. Ma said nothing, continuing to pick at the stew gelling on her plate.

• • •

At supper the next night, Father broached the topic of the land grant once more. "There is an urgent need for English-speaking settlers to move to Nova Scotia."

Mother looked up from the soup she was ladling. Her jaw twitched as if there was something she wanted to say.

Father had just returned from one of his regular meetings with the men from his regiment. In between dollops of soup, he explained that the British in Nova Scotia were struggling to establish a local democratic government. Given Nova Scotia's widely dispersed population, they were finding it hard to establish a community.

"If they are to secure the victory we fought so hard to win, they need people to work the land they commandeered. Those who are best qualified to do so are we New Englanders."

"I'm sure that is true," Mother said. "But you have acres of land here that need your attention."

"Not half as many as my father had."

Two generations ago, Grandfather arrived from England as a lowly servant to John Winthrop, an English Puritan lawyer and one of the founding fathers of the Massachusetts Bay Colony. Mr. Winthrop rewarded my grandfather for his lifetime of service with a small grant of sixteen acres. My father and uncles divided this acreage among them.

"The best farming lands in New England are all taken now." My father chewed on his bread, choosing his words carefully.

William and Nat listened attentively. Neither of them ever took a shine to farming. I knew this, but did my father? Since he'd come home, they had joined him in the fields only when they couldn't come up with a credible excuse.

"With hard work and faith in the Lord, my father planted these fields while Indians still roamed the colonies," Father said. "But with each generation, we divide the plot among more sons."

He directed his comments at Mother. "There is not enough land for Nat and William to provide for their future families, not to mention the many cousins who also have a claim. If we are to continue to thrive, we need to look elsewhere. That has always been our way."

Mother heard him out, patient as always. When he finished, she put down her spoon.

"Darling, I have an announcement of my own." She paused, swallowing hard. "I am expecting a child. So certainly, you will understand, now is not the time."

She looked up at Father, a blush climbing from up her neck.

When he said nothing, I blurted out: "I hope it is a girl!"

Nat and I sat out on the porch in our Sunday clothes, waiting for Grandfather to pick up the family for church. Father paced the fields, planning which crops he would sow in the spring.

"He's done this so many times," Nat said. "It's a thankless task, and now he's getting restless."

My brother was right, because when we rode home from Sunday services, Father told Mother he had decided.

"This is an opportunity I cannot refuse. The new British government in Nova Scotia offered us land. They will even pay for our passage."

I was all ears. My brothers shifted in their seats.

Mother remained speechless. Father added that he was seriously weighing the possibility of entering the ministry. "In Nova Scotia," he said, "the government allows congregations to build their own meetinghouses and choose their own members. I can still farm but also answer to a higher calling."

Finished, he waited to hear what Mother had to say.

Which was nothing. My brothers and I sat behind them in the chaise's rear seat, and I could see the muscles in my mother's shoulders tighten.

Nat spoke up first when it was clear she would not. "Will the new settlers require solicitors?"

William jumped in. "The prospect of a new beginning…"

"But, William," Mother said, engaged at last, "what about your education? It would grieve me in my grave if you withdrew from your books. That would be the way to be good at nothing at all."

I didn't weigh in. Nobody mentioned the baby on the way.

Father reassured Nat that the provincial government functioned like those of New England, so he would have no difficulty finding a clerkship.

William said he would pray on it.

Mother asked Father to stop the buggy. She was going to be sick.

After praying on it, William decided the land grant was God's will. He had been standing at Father's side at church singing "We Gather Together" when the revelation came to him. A new sense of responsibility inspired him. He, too, wanted to spread enlightenment to the new world.

Mother sighed when he made his announcement, rubbing her hand over her belly. She and Father argued over supper.

"Massachusetts is our home," she said. This time she did not hold her words back. "This is where we raised our children. Our parents are growing old here and will need our support."

"Massachusetts is not the peaceful community you portray it to be," Father said, his tone patient but determined. "Members of the Continental Army are questioning who they are fighting for, the new colonies or Britain? A gentleman from Boston named Samuel Adams spoke recently in town, filling our boys' ears with dreams of revolution. The last thing I want is for my sons to follow me into battle. Little Lucy is vulnerable to the worldly temptations that surround her. This land grant will allow our family to sidestep simmering discord."

I smarted at the "Little Lucy" part. I wasn't little, and I could hold my own against evil, despite my flirtation with the heddus. Didn't Father see that? If all he desired was peace, why then was he always armed and ready? He pulled a flier from Governor William Shirley from his waistcoat pocket and set it down on the table. With a dismissive sniff, Mother pushed it away. Out of the corner of my eye, I read

Shirley's Great Plan, an advertisement recruiting six thousand settlers to move to Nova Scotia.

The time has come for people to cultivate not only the lands made vacant by the removal of the Acadian French but other parts of the valuable province.

As we finished our meal, Father laid out his arguments. If you ask me, they were quite persuasive. He said this was a once-in-a-lifetime opportunity requiring all the skills he had learned in battle. He had seen his compatriots die; now, he longed to serve them. He saved the best for last. "Think of our unborn child," he said. "Where might they flourish?"

Yes, he had planned the assault. Grandfather and Grandmother Hardy arrived in time for dessert and announced that Father had persuaded them to join our family in the new territories. His own parents had also agreed to emigrate. Together, we would be a convivial community of friends and family up north.

He had made up his mind. The change would benefit us all. Six nephews would divide up the farmland we left behind in Massachusetts. In Nova Scotia, we would grow corn, wheat, rye, barley, oats, hemp, and flax. According to Father, the fields awaited us, also orchards and gardens.

He assured my mother the family would live in a Christian community that shared her values.

Mother cocked her head and then rubbed her lips together as if tasting all he had said. "How can I deny you?" she said with a sigh. Like the French, she could not stand up to him. Mother was no match for Father's enthusiasm and persistence, especially in her condition.

Father promised her he would become a selfless pastor. All of our lives would be better for the change.

In front of us all, Mother placed his hand on her stomach and let him feel the baby kick.

"In the morning," Father said, "I will arrange our passage."

• • •

My dearest and beloved sister Caroline,
I hope this letter finds you in good health and that the Boston winter has

not been unbearably harsh. I find it hard to imagine my little sister working in gray and dreary Boston. But I recognize the value of your work as a midwife and understand that many women value your training, and it provides you with great satisfaction.

As you may have already heard, Nathaniel will sail in April on the first voyage of the Charming Molly, headed for Nova Scotia with thirty-one men from Massachusetts aboard. Most of the men plan to leave their wives and families in Massachusetts until they can prepare living quarters for them. Like these families, we will soon follow Nathaniel to a new home. I am writing you in the hope you will join us on the upcoming journey. It would lighten my heart considerably to have another woman at my side. As you know, I am with child, and the prospect of giving birth in a new colony is worrisome. Nathaniel has suggested that your skills as a midwife might ease my concern. They would also be of great value to the other colonists who are moving North in substantial numbers.

Dare I ask so much of you? Without Nathaniel's goading, I wouldn't dare. But this is my query: Are you interested in the prospect of a new life in a country offering limitless possibilities?

Nathaniel says that Nova Scotia has room for all.

Military Governor Lawrence of Nova Scotia offered Nathaniel a free land grant as a reward for his military service. They have granted him seven hectares of arable land, thirty-four more of mowing, twenty in pasture, and nine hundred and eighteen in woods. Nathaniel sat the children down and told them that in Nova Scotia our family would prosper and lead a peaceful life. Under the beneficent eyes of God, he said, we would begin anew.

I have reconciled myself to the change in our circumstances, trusting in Nathaniel's account of the new land. He describes a spacious farmhouse, an apple orchard right outside our front door. Dear sister, picture me making pies for our parents who live down the lane as I nurse the new baby, a sister I hope for Lucy. If only you would join us!

We will travel by water instead of over rough country. The government of Nova Scotia will pay for our passage. Nathaniel assures me we will not be alone. A community—others from Massachusetts, New Hampshire, and Connecticut—will join us soon.

I can only hope that you will accept this entreaty as a symptom of my condition, an earnest desire born of my gratefulness to so faithful a sister as yourself for all your surpassing affections both to me and mine.

Dearest one, you can only imagine how much courage it has taken to write this letter. And how very much I hope its contents will intrigue you. Who knows? A dashing young colonist who longs for an ambitious (and beautiful) young woman who has never in her life turned down a challenge might await you in Nova Scotia!

I wait for your reply with bated breath, knowing that if you were to accompany us, I would rejoice in our reunion and look forward to a shared life of discovery and, dare I say it, adventure.

Your obliged and affectionate sister and friend,
Maggie

CHAPTER THREE

The Mi'kmaq

Kejimkujik Lake, Nova Scotia, October 1759

Downwind, Meuse spotted moose tracks in the red mud along the river. With one hand, Uncle Gehne lifted a shelf of antlers high above his head. With the other, he clutched a birch-bark cone. He blew into the cone, imitating the mating call of a bull moose. Meuse's grandfather, Elder Peregrine Thomas, and his many uncles and cousins listened for a response.

The brisk November day didn't require snowshoes. Beneath his moccasins, the first winter snow was soft. The sun was low above the horizon.

Cousin Francis walked in front of Meuse as they hunted for the remaining deadfall traps in the dark stands of evergreens. Meuse's mother, Anne, and the women of the family were hard at work curing meat for the long, cold winter to come. Meuse's assignment was to hunt ruffed grouse. The young male birds, reddish brown with black ruffs around their neck, gathered in temporary, loose flocks in the fall. An easy target, Francis told him. Over the summer, Francis had grown taller and more muscular. His voice was deeper. Tendons twitched impatiently below his skin. When girls passed, even those ten years his senior, he leered. Meuse listened for the flutter of grouse wings thumping against feathered breasts. When he detected the loud drumming sound of the mating call, he joined the other boys of the tribe chasing the birds, competing to be the first to snare one with a pole and leather noose, jostling for position and pushing each other aside.

Meuse honored his father by using his surname, but after his father's death, Gehne had taken him and his mother Anne in; the two families became one. His cousin Francis, like most of the children in their tribe, went by his French baptismal name, given to him by the missionaries in Father Le Loutre's church. The two boys were cousins as every boy in the hunting party was a cousin, brothers as every boy in the tribe was part of the same family. Gehne, whose own wife died giving birth to their third child, treated Meuse as a son. Gehne was the family's *sagamore*, the son of a powerful Elder. The tribe had named him their chief and the leader of their family. In exchange for his shelter, Anne took over the traditional woman's role, providing a life-giver's perspective when Gehne faced important decisions. At his side, Francis and Meuse had learned to hunt and fish. Until the boys married, Gehne promised to protect them, guide them, and provide them with everything they needed.

Everything the men hunted today would be food for all.

Meuse was no longer at Francis's side. He could hardly see his cousin, only the dust kicked up behind him as he ran off into the distance.

Francis ran faster than all the other boys in their family group, calling out in his schoolboy French: *Vite, alors!* Hurry! He had learned French in the Capuchin School in Port Royal. Port Royal adjoined their summer hunting grounds, and the previous year, the Acadians had invited several of the tribe's boys to join their children at the school. While Meuse had missed his mother's gentle instruction, Francis had mixed with the Acadian children and now showed off his French for the other boys' admiration.

Meuse could not keep up with his cousin, but at least today he was lucky. In his haste, he stumbled on a family of grouse hiding in the grass. By the time he returned to the aunties, he carried three fowl, fat from the summer grasses, tied to a stick.

His mother congratulated him on his hunting skills. Francis, returning empty-handed, overheard the compliment and scoffed. Anne turned her attention back to the pelt of a deer, scraping it clean to prepare for drying. "Today, we have hunted with love in our hearts, treated our prey with respect," she said. "Nothing you killed today will go to waste. Not the grouse, not the bones of the deer. We will harvest everything and put it all to good use." What they did not use themselves, they would share with others.

Pride in the day's success filled Meuse with warmth, just as the weak sun warmed the stones on the ground. He shuffled his feet, hungry for a taste of fresh meat. But the day's hunt was not over.

A lovelorn cry filled the woods. In the distance, he heard a bull moose reply to his uncle's call. Despite the rumbling of his stomach, Meuse shivered with anticipation.

"Do you hear it?" he asked Francis. His voice cracked, starting low and then reverting to boyish uncertainty.

"Of course, I hear it," Francis replied, his voice deep and impatient.

The dogs barked. In preparation for the hunt, Peregrine Thomas had not fed the dogs for several days. At the sound of the moose call, the pack headed off into the woods, snapping and jostling for position. The men followed, clasping their bows, arrows at the ready. To Meuse's surprise, Francis joined the men. Uncle Gehne handed his son a spear as they headed off in pursuit of their prey. They left Meuse behind with the younger cousins.

Francis planned to study English next so that the tribe could trade more successfully with the colonists arriving from New England. Everything came easily to Francis—languages, hunting, love. One year older than Meuse, his lead increased by the moment. His feet flew over the muddy terrain.

This morning, Francis had confided to Meuse that he was in love. Perhaps that explained his swiftness. The object of his affections was a French girl he had met at the mission, a Mademoiselle Lisette LaFleur. When he confessed her name, his eyes brightened. LaFleur, he said, meant flower. With that admission, he had darted out in front of Meuse, fueled by passion, leaving the younger boy behind.

Francis grinned broadly as he ran to catch up with the men. The girl cousins watched him go, giggling. He was as tall as his father now, his legs even longer, and he stood straighter. His stride was confident; he played to the audience.

An arrow easily pierced deerskin, but a moose's hide was tough; an arrow would not bring the large animal down. When the dogs surrounded the moose, a hunter would need to aim a spear with precision. If Francis's aim was off, the moose would escape with his spirit intact, and it would deny them one final winter feast. They would have to subsist on the meat they had dried while the crickets cried.

The dogs barked louder now, in active pursuit. Their yipping filled the air as women and children listened to the hunt. The men had headed the moose toward their camp so that the women would not have to travel so far to bring the carcass back. Francis led the hunt, ready for his first kill. This was a momentous development, the object of their excited chatter. A boy who killed a moose became a man.

Meuse, left behind, could only imagine the pursuit. The heat of battle. The crack of twigs as the massive moose fled through the thick forest. The frenetic dogs' thirst for blood. The men watching as Francis took the lead, spear in hand, every muscle taut. The bellowing of the beast as his weapon pierced the heart. The thud as the animal fell to the ground, his blood pooling among the pine needles.

Francis a man? Meuse's heart must have skipped a beat at this unexpected turn. His awe mixed with gnawing jealousy. Standing among the children, he flexed his fists, cracked his knuckles. He couldn't help but resent his exclusion from the company of men.

Francis's younger sister Mimi sidled up to him, her long braids swinging as she walked. Her cheeks were pink with excitement. "Soon my brother can ask his mademoiselle to marry him," she whispered.

Startled, Meuse looked at her in surprise. They were the same age, but Mimi, like her brother, had grown tall over the summer. Her braids reached to her waist, and her eyes were bright. Her body was no longer girlish, and she had recently sprouted breasts. "The French girl?" he asked.

She nodded.

As Mimi described her brother's courtship, Meuse's eyes were drawn to her body. His exasperation at her brother's secrecy churned up feelings he struggled to ignore. Unlike her brother, Mimi believed in the traditional ways. Uncle Gehne had raised Francis, Mimi, and Meuse as a family, but this summer he felt drawn to her in a new, confusing way.

It would be another year before the Elders handed him the spear as they had Francis today. Today, he was only a spectator, despite the excited pounding of his heart. The satisfaction he felt when he caught the grouse was gone. His own success paled next to Francis's willful ambition.

Mimi and Meuse stood side by side, spectators and nothing more. Soon they heard the men shout with joy. The dogs quieted. The silence confirmed they had slain the moose. Meuse could only imagine Francis's exaltation the moment he had slashed the bull moose's stomach. The cavalier toss of his head as he fed the guts to the dogs, a reward for their worthy efforts.

The men emerged from the forest, laughing and slapping each other on the back. Francis, in the middle of their joyful circle, did not bother to acknowledge Meuse and Mimi standing at the edge of the clearing. The women followed the men, ready to harvest every piece of the moose.

Mimi beamed at the sight of her brother, his arms stained with blood.

• • •

"Soon we will prepare the *cacamo*," Mimi said.

Moose butter. A great delicacy. Once the women collected the bones of the moose, they would pound them with rock, reduce them to powder. Boil the powder until grease rose to the top of the water. "If I am lucky," she said, "they will let me collect the fat with a wooden spoon."

Long after they had devoured the moose meat, the cacamo would provide fuel for the long winter.

And they would credit Francis with the day's bounty.

Meuse shuffled his feet. The late-day sun shined on Francis. Meuse stood in his mother's shadow, a fatherless boy once again, invisible among the children.

Mimi left to follow the others, eager to see if Francis appeared different now. Meuse refused to join her, choosing instead to help the women scrape feathers off the grouse. As they worked, his mind wandered. Would Francis really marry an Acadian? If so, would she join their family, or would his cousin live among the foreigners? But his questions would not be answered that day. His Elders surrounded Francis. Meuse could not catch his eye.

The women had hours of work ahead of them. His mother asked him to head back to stoke the fire. He handed her his grouse, slender and unimpressive. "The earth is bountiful today," she said, adding it to the pile of birds.

Uncle Gehne came up behind him as he slouched back toward the camp. The older man put a comforting arm around his shoulder. "Your father would be happy this day," he said. Meuse, embarrassed, hoped Gehne had not sensed his jealousy.

Gehne poked him in the ribs. "The competition to be the best hunter, the best leader, the best fisherman keeps our larders full. Rejoice today in your cousin's success. One day, you too will slaughter a moose."

At Gehne's side, he joined others around the communal fire.

Mimi, sitting among the aunties roasting the grouse, pointed at Meuse. The aunties laughed, sharing a joke he could not hear.

He blushed.

His uncle nodded, unable to keep an impish smile from spreading across his face. Laugh lines crinkled next to his eyes. The winter would be long, dark, and cold. Many nights spent inside shelters warmed only by stones from the community fire. Protected by the skins of moose and caribou, covered by wool blankets from local trading posts. But tonight, the moon was bright, the men drunk with victory. Francis danced in a joyful circle, slapping his drum louder than any grouse ever beat its wings. His dance was a celebration they all shared. He led the line of dancers, confident in his physical prowess. Proof of his endurance. The women cleaned the bull moose by the light of the large bonfire. In the shadows, the boys played ball. The aroma of roasting meat filled the night air. Meuse's stomach growled with hunger.

"Our countryside, blessed by the Great Spirit, is generous," Uncle

Gehne said, holding up an offering of tobacco. "Today, our bellies are full, and our hearts are grateful."

The community celebration lasted late into the evening. Woodsmoke peppered the crisp night air. Meuse dozed by the fire as his uncles and aunties danced, the urgent rhythm of the drums permeating his dreams. But when his uncle thanked the Great Spirit a second time, his words roused Meuse from his stupor. The Elders were prodding his cousin. Mocking him as he pranced around the fire with the pelt of a deer draped over his shoulder. Meuse stewed: When would he distinguish himself from his many cousins? Why did his Elders see only the brightest stars in a sky full of stars?

His uncle amused the Elders around the fire by poking Francis with the tip of a white birch branch, forcing him to remain on his feet long after the young man's energy had lagged. The Elders laughed at the exhausted boy struggling to keep up with the women, whose steps remained strong and rhythmic.

Uncle Gehne had taught them that a young man must earn the esteem of his people. He must show bravery but must also be generous and hospitable. He must remain unpretentious and humble, even at moments of great courage. For this reason, his cousin was now the victim of his uncle's teasing jabs. The final lesson of the long day was humility.

Every one of us, his uncle had said. Meuse mulled over Gehne's words. All his life he had been told that the Great Spirit gave each member of the family a special gift. Meuse had lost a father, but Gehne had taken him in. With patience and good humor, he had taught Meuse the skills required to become a valued member of the tribe. But today it had become clear: Meuse was skilled but undistinguished. Not yet a successful hunter, he chafed at his invisibility. When would the Elders recognize his special talents? He could navigate the streams of Kejimkujik on his own. He had crossed the Bay of Fundy without a compass, trusting the sun and his instincts for guidance. Now he longed for the Great Spirit to show him his path.

The time for childish games was over.

•••

Meuse, dozing in front of the fire, woke to the clatter of horse hooves. The hoarse caw of a raven sounded a warning. The blue jays screamed an alarm. From out of the curtain of the velvet black night, two horses appeared, approaching the tribal camp. On their backs, Meuse discerned a disheveled man, a stern-faced woman, and two sweaty children dressed in Acadian garb.

The man called out in French, his voice frantic and breathless. *"Ils nous ont chassés de chez nous."*

Like the other men around the fire, Meuse turned to Francis to interpret. But even with his poor mastery of the foreign language, the alarm on the visitors' faces told him these people were in trouble.

"They have chased us from our houses." Francis translated the man's words. With an exclamation of surprise, he leapt up and approached the Acadian family. "Lisette, is that you? *Pourquoi es-tu ici?*" This greeting Meuse understood. He studied the young girl's face and thought it was familiar. Then he recognized her as a classmate from the Acadian mission.

The young girl answered Francis with a torrent of incomprehensible French. A steady flow of tears swallowed her strange words.

"The British have confiscated her father's house," Francis reported to the tribe. "They ordered the family to report to Annapolis for deportation."

But Francis was not through.

"The English plundered the French homes, smashing furniture and pottery about the cart paths. Cattle still grazed the wheat fields and pigs rooted in the garden, but by nightfall, the English had burned the LaFleur's house to the ground. Nothing remained for them to salvage."

The Elders passed this story, one to the next. It made its way around the circle. As each person learned of the Acadians' plight, their expressions softened, their initial alarm melting into sympathetic nods. When the story had completed its travels, Gehne stood up and approached the man, raising his hand in greeting.

"They fled here and are asking us for protection," Francis translated, adding, "Lisette is a classmate of mine." Francis spoke faster now, emboldened by his pivotal role in the drama. "Her father has been promised work on the dikes, but until he can secure a job in Grand-Pré, he seeks a place to shelter his family."

The uncles nodded at the strange man, signaled their understanding, and then spoke among themselves. The family remained on their horses, dark rings around their eyes, their clothes dusty and worn. Sensing their plight, Anne beckoned to the woman, who climbed down from her horse after a moment's hesitation.

"Meuse," Gehne said, "these horses need water. Take them down to the river and tie them up."

Meuse was loath to leave, but he took the horses' reins after a sideways glance at the girl's familiar face. *Lisette*, he thought. He remembered her now. This was the girl Mimi had told him her brother intended to marry. Now she appeared here in their camp with her entire family in tow. What had already been an eventful day had taken an unexpected turn. He patted down the nervous horses, attempting to reassure them.

Heading down the well-worn path toward the nearby stream, grateful for the guiding light of the moon, he heard Gehne say, *"Smaqa'si etuk nike'."* Sit down. You are welcome.

By the time Meuse had tied up the horses and returned to his seat by the fire, the Acadian family sat among the tribe. The man, who had introduced himself as Louis LaFleur, warmed his hands over the flames as he described his escape. Francis translated. In a mesmerizing call and response, they described the horrors that had taken place that day in Port Royal. Families, husbands, wives, and their children, had been dragged, kicking and screaming, from their houses when they refused to pledge allegiance to the Crown.

Lisette's father called the displacement he had suffered the *Grand Dérangement* (The Great Upheaval). "Our entire nation is being ripped by ruffians from the land we love and cherish. You are our only hope. But to save our necks, we have refused to fight against friends who have worked beside us on this land." As Francis translated his words, the man looked each of the uncles in the eye. "As I see it, this land is not ours. It is yours. But you have let us live peacefully among you all these years. Your tribe was here long before our Champlain arrived, but unlike the British, you welcomed us. Together, our communities thrived. Now the rangers have chased us from our houses. I ask only that you help me protect my family until I can locate a safe place for us to live."

Meuse listened to the family's sad story, thinking *but our home is the earth, not the structure we erect to shelter ourselves from the elements.*

Francis explained that Lisette's father had worked for many years on the dikes, where he was held in high esteem. The successful function of the dikes was necessary if the newcomers were to cultivate the land. The new government knew this, and he hoped his family would be given refuge in Grand-Pré. In the meantime, he asked if the tribe would take his family in. "A few days," he assured them. "I would be grateful."

Seated next to Francis, Lisette drew her shawl around her delicate shoulders. Francis smoothed the shawl, treating her with a tenderness that surprised Meuse. Meuse watched his cousin's gesture warily, remembering Mimi's words. Now that Francis had slain a moose, he had the tribe's blessing to take a wife. Was this protective gesture that of a man claiming a wife? When Lisette's family left for Grand-Pré, would Francis accompany them? Or would Lisette remain behind? Would they ask this delicate white girl to join their family and learn their ways?

If Uncle Gehne gave Francis his blessing to marry, Meuse might be about to lose the companionship of his closest friend and ally. Jealousy sprouted inside his chest like a spring bud about to bloom. He could not take his eyes off this girl, so slight, so shy.

During the time Francis and he had attended the Acadian school, Meuse had recognized Lisette only by her book smarts, which intimidated him. His cousin, however, had insisted she was the prettiest girl in their class. One spring afternoon, instead of frolicking with the other boys in the schoolyard, Francis had invited Meuse to join him after class. When they entered the schoolyard, Lisette had been waiting for them, holding the reins of two saddled horses. Together, the three of them had ridden through budding spring fields until they arrived at a white farmhouse. In an open field of newly planted corn, Francis had told him this was Lisette's family home. Tongue-tied, Meuse watched as Francis sat down next to the girl and attempted to teach her the dice game of Waltes. The freckled girl had proved herself a quick study, throwing the dice with enthusiasm. Teasing, she had threatened to beat Francis at a game he had played at every tribal gathering since he was a boy. As usual,

Meuse remained a spectator. It had never occurred to Meuse then that Francis thought of their fellow student as anything more than a potential companion. Instead, he had viewed the outing as another example of Francis's daring.

How wrong he had been.

As usual, Meuse had remained a spectator, no longer comfortable on land he had once considered belonging to all.

He replayed this scene in his mind now, as the tribe listened to Francis translate the story of the family's expulsion. He considered the implications of his uncle's blessing. His cousin's new rank threatened to tear his family apart just as surely as the British forces had torn the Acadian community asunder.

If only his cousin had never attended the Acadian school. If only he had never met his mademoiselle. Now, in their time of need, Lisette and her family had joined them, leaving behind the white farmhouse and fleeing into the wilderness he knew so well in search of the tribe's protection. *What will become of that field now?* he wondered. *Who will plant it and collect the corn at the end of the summer?*

The possibilities that occurred to him were alarming. What would become of Lisette's family? Would Francis, having set his sights on marrying her, choose to follow the family if Lisette's father found refuge working the dikes?

Francis flopped down next to Meuse, nudging him over to make room and then spreading his legs wide. Closer to the fire, the smoke stung Meuse's eyes, and his head throbbed with the possibilities, even as his eyelids drooped after the long and eventful day. Finally, his mother stood up, gesturing to the LaFleurs to follow her, gathering bedding and pointing to a wigwam where the family could sleep. Following her example, one by one, the women and children settled for the night.

• • •

Outside, around the fire, the old men talked into the night.

Beside Meuse, his cousin yawned and stretched out his legs. Francis was strong and virile. His confidence never flagged. This is why they celebrated him. Now that Francis was a man, would he abandon his family, abandon Mimi and Meuse, leave his tribe?

Like Francis, Meuse longed to become a warrior, a *smáknisk* like his father. But he feared he would never be as tall as Francis. In their games, he would always come in second. His uncle's lessons held him back. When would he be able to shake the submissive role of a younger brother? He was no longer content to follow his cousin and celebrate his victories.

Around the smoking fire, the Elders talked in low voices. Meuse shifted closer to the fire so that he could hear them.

There were rumors, they said, that their summer hunting grounds had come under siege. Only a few of the Acadians remained in the Annapolis Valley, those few whose skills on the dikes were of value to the British. The new British governor had charged the remaining French settlers exorbitant fees to remain in houses where they had lived and farmed for generations. When they could not pay, soldiers with fire sticks routed them out of their homes. But now, the soldiers were also chasing the Mi'kmaq from towns where they had previously traded with impunity. The British, having defeated the French, regarded the Mi'kmaq with disdain. "Savages," they called them: a word spit more often than spoken.

"I hear the Maliseet chief offered to sign a treaty with Cornwallis," the revered Elder Peregrine Thomas said, puffing on his pipe. With his long gray hair and the tobacco smoke surrounding him, his words seemed to emerge from a dark cloud.

The others nodded and sighed.

"How foolish," said John Baptiste, who claimed to be older than one hundred years. "Now the British feel they have the right to rule our lands unconditionally."

Old Joe, who had no teeth, responded, "The rivers we fish are no longer safe. The forests where we hunt hide bounty hunters looking for an easy kill. Even Father Le Loutre cannot help us now."

Recent marriages between Mi'kmaq and French citizens had put all in jeopardy, Old Joe added. In the silence that followed, he chewed on his gums.

Meuse was awake now, even if Francis was not. As he listened to the Elders' conversation, he wondered if Francis heard their words. Knowing Francis, he would pursue his mademoiselle regardless of the consequences.

But the British were not only taking the Acadians' houses. They were also giving away the tribe's hunting grounds to men from the Massachusetts Bay Colony. Surveyors, devils with papers in hand, claimed the land belonged to the British.

"The newcomers have no desire for our friendship," Peregrine Thomas said. For many years, his fellow warriors had returned from trading expeditions to the thirteen colonies telling stories of the slaughter of local tribes, of tribal members sold into slavery, and of bounties offered for the scalps of women and children. "We have seen the cruelty of these men in their own lands," Jean Baptiste said. "Now Governor Cornwallis is offering bounties for the scalps of Mi'kmaq men, women, and children. He has issued a Scalp Proclamation in our own county, a reward of ten guineas for every Indian taken or killed."

The last echo of the drums died in the dark woods. Francis snored, his head resting on Meuse's shoulder. He smelled of sweat but slept like a little boy up past his bedtime. Tomorrow, Francis would leave for Grand-Pré. Meuse shivered, fearing what his cousin might find when he joined the beleaguered Acadians. Would they chase him from the land?

Success in hunting did not make his cousin a man. Now, more than ever, the tribe needed *smáknisks*, men like Meuse's father, like Meuse aspired to be.

This, he thought, was his gift. Bravery was in his blood. The courage to stand up to the White Man. Let his uncles congratulate his exhausted cousin one more time. Next time, it would be Meuse they honored.

Meuse studied the brightly burning coals, all that remained of the smoldering fire. When he looked up, Gehne was looking at him, a sweet smile of compassion on his wrinkled face.

"It has been a long day, my son," he said with a dramatic yawn. "Why don't you walk your brother to the wigwam? He needs sleep before he sets out on his travels. We all need our strength to survive these troubled times."

CHAPTER FOUR

The Move to Nova Scotia

Westborough, Massachusetts, April 1760

Almost as soon as Mother reconciled herself to the move, the Nova Scotia newspapers reported that Indians in Annapolis had fired on the colonists.

Of course, I was the last to know. But I chose a chair in the parlor's corner where I could practice invisibility by never looking up from my needlework. As the menfolk spoke into the evening, I garnered enough information to concern me.

Nat relayed reports he had heard in the governor's office. Bands of Indians, assisted by a few remaining Acadians, had threatened the forts at Windsor, Lunenburg, and Sackville. The governor had advised families to postpone emigration from New England until more peaceful conditions prevailed.

In alarm, I stabbed my finger with my embroidery needle. "Drat," I said, sucking the drop of blood that instantly appeared.

My mother looked up in alarm. "Lucy, why don't you put some water on the stove for tea?" Turning away from me, she addressed my brothers. "Boys, little pitchers have big ears."

But I had seen the worry in her eyes, the slight tremble in the hand resting on her swelling stomach. When Father arrived home, she confronted him at the front door, not bothering to check whether I was listening.

"Nathaniel, are you prepared to put your family's life in danger?"

"Never, my love," Father said, not a wrinkle on his brow. "I've discussed the matter with my parents. We're prepared to postpone the family's journey until the territory is secure. But I will need to travel as planned to protect the property we have claimed."

Father took off his jacket and pulled off his boots. His posture was that of a soldier, straight-backed and determined.

"But how is this any different from you leaving us behind to fight with the British?" Mother asked, shaking out his coat and hanging it on a hook next to the door. "You promised your days as a soldier were over. Now I fear you are putting our entire family in danger."

"And that they are. The British will quell this uprising. By the time you arrive with the children, all will be well. God grants us fortitude for a reason. Once we have settled into our new home, the remaining malcontents will disappear."

Father was resolute. Mother clenched her fists, but she didn't try to change his mind. I watched them, as I had dozens of times since he had returned from the war. Father was so sure of himself, and Mother was eclipsed by his self-assurance and pride. Did he even see her? Clumsy with pregnancy, overcome by waves of nausea, she stirred the soup. That morning she had complained to me she no longer knew whether the vegetables she planted in her kitchen garden were hers to harvest. At what point did they belong to her nephews?

I watched my parents, wondering if this was how marriage worked. A wife diminished in her husband's presence, overwhelmed by his size and certitude. If that was the case, I had no interest in the institution.

Unlike my mother, I did not hold my tongue.

"Why didn't you tell him we're afraid of being alone?" I asked her as she tucked me in. "Tell him we don't want to be abandoned again. That we need his protection here in Massachusetts as much as we will in the colony up north."

"Sweetheart," my mother said, "we won't be alone. I'll stay here with you until it's safe to travel." She reached out to hug me. "I would never abandon you or this new child. Trust your father's judgment. He has only your well-being in mind."

As if to prove her right, Father arrived home the following afternoon puffed up with pride and with my favorite aunt, Caroline, in the back of his buggy. She carried a satchel containing everything she owned.

"Caroline has kindly agreed to stay with you while I am away," Father said.

"What you need is some raspberry tea." Caroline filled the kettle with water. "It strengthens the uterine muscles and ensures a speedy delivery."

Aunt Caroline, my mother's younger sister, was a midwife. She knew things, like raspberry tea and the best herbs for treating a bellyache. I felt better the moment she crossed the threshold. Mother's face relaxed as she sipped her tea, and Aunt Caroline gave me several of the peppermints she carried in her pocket. I forgot how mad I had been at my father.

He quickly retired to the parlor, chased away by the women's talk. Caroline told us she had given up her room in Boston. She would stay with us until it was safe for the family to make the journey to Nova Scotia.

With Aunt Caroline settled into our home, the sun shone more often. She didn't complain when I followed her around the house. Watching her steady hand and envying her cheery disposition, I decided I might be a midwife when I grew up. Under Aunt Caroline's ministrations, Mother regained her strength.

Father proceeded with his preparations for departure. Eight months after returning home, he kissed us goodbye and left for Boston. From there, he would sail to Nova Scotia on the Charming Molly with most of our belongings, leaving us behind with Caroline and a half-empty house. With him, he took one of our horses, two oxen, five cows, six calves, and five swine. He left behind the house he built with his own hands, the rest of the livestock, and our life in Massachusetts.

With him gone, the house was quiet. Mother completed the packing.

With less and less to do, she paced the oak floors. From my spinning wheel in the parlor, I listened to her footsteps, a sound as familiar as the pounding of my heart.

"I know the timber of every board in this house," she told Aunt Caroline as she swept the floor.

"As you will one day know the creaks and crannies of your new home," Caroline said. An independent woman, she wasn't one to get attached, not to things. Aunt Caroline soon announced she would travel with us and reestablish her midwifery practice in the northern colony. Hearing the news, Grandmother and Grandfather Hardy packed their bags and moved in with us. Any day now, we would receive a message from Father telling us the Indian threat had been handled, and it was safe for us to travel.

"Your father is a generous man," Grandfather Hardy said. "He excels at everything he sets his mind to: farming, soldiering, spreading the word of God. You are lucky to be his daughter. You have nothing to fear."

"Now there will be fields enough for all my grandchildren," Grandmother Hardy said. She directed this comment at my mother, who was sitting on a kitchen chair with her swollen feet resting on a stool. She no longer tended her kitchen garden, having allowed my cousins to take over its care. We saw them every day now, pacing the fields, staking the property lines, waving excited arms at the prospect of their good luck.

"But Father," she said, more at ease to speak her mind with her father than her departed husband. "I can't help thinking that these fields were meant to be my sons' inheritance."

I wondered how he would respond. Wasn't that supposed to be the way? A father passed on his land to his sons. But before he answered, William and Nat jumped in, assuring her that the land they would inherit in the new colony would satisfy them and feed their future families. When Mother stepped out of the room, they confided in Aunt Caroline. They had other aspirations and hoped farming would be a task they could delegate to others in their new home.

As the weeks passed, Mother spent more and more time in her chambers. Aunt Caroline urged me to be patient. It was only natural that my mother missed my father. As her time came nearer, she longed to be at his side. I heard the two women talking through the chamber door and wondered how Mother, her body distorted and her ankles swollen, would fare at sea. With each day, her discomfort became more obvious. Caroline darted in and out of her chamber, her brow furrowed.

And then one night at the dinner table, Grandfather announced he had received the news we had all been waiting for.

"We leave next week on the last trip of the Charming Molly," he said.

"The sooner, the better." Mother's face was pallid, but her smile radiated relief. "Now, our new lives can begin."

"Yea!" I shouted. "I'm ready to bake that apple pie."

Any day now, we would travel and join other New Englanders to be Planters in a new land. Annapolis would be our home.

•••

Marblehead, Massachusetts, July 1760

Our crates preceded us, carried by oxcart to the port. The furniture was disassembled, the clothes packed, the kitchenware sorted by size and usefulness. Caroline and I were the first up the gangplank, followed by Grandfather and Grandmother Hardy. Taking in the terrifying view of the roiling sea, I squeezed Caroline's hand harder than I should have. Behind us, William and Nat walked on either side of Mother, grasping her elbows as she walked shakily up the creaky ramp. Besides the forty-eight passengers and their crates full of tools, building materials, and household goods, several dozen livestock followed us up the gangplank, to be stowed below deck.

We were supposed to sail from Marblehead at noon. As soon as we located our cabin, a violent wind came in from the northeast. Flotsam from the harbor knocked against the boat. The sky was gray and foreboding.

Nat settled Mother on her cot with Caroline and me to keep her company. Following Father's instructions, he went in search of Captain Grow to ensure our papers were in order. In his pocket, he carried fifteen dollars. His solicitor had told him that would be enough to secure adequate stores for the voyage. He also carried a gallon of rum, which would guarantee the captain's undivided attention. The wind blew pellets of hail and frigid rain onto the deck. As soon as Nat returned, we shut the door to the small cabin in which we would sleep during our voyage on the open sea. By then, it was five o'clock, and the captain announced the gales were too strong to proceed. We would not sail until the next morning, when the wind, hopefully, would have died down. The boat had docked for the night.

The boys took it upon themselves to find us some dinner. Caroline remained behind to attend to Mother with my help. Mother never complained, but the baby kicked all the time now, leaving little room for her to breathe. No matter how many postures she tried, she couldn't get comfortable. I asked if I could feel the baby move, but Caroline told me to let Mother be. Soon the boys returned, smelling of fish and bragging that they had located a local fisherman who had agreed to prepare supper for the family.

Mother told us to go out on our own. She was too queasy to venture from the rocking boat and would stay behind with our grandparents. The incessant gale winds made walking almost impossible. I spent most of the trek trying to decide which was a more frightening fate: sailing away on the angry sea or being swept away by a wind that might blow me right off my feet. Still, I was grateful for the meal and slept better for it.

The next morning, the Charming Molly set sail for Annapolis Royal by way of Halifax and Louisbourg.

The nasty storm still battered the New England shore. The winds continued, rolling the ship over waves with abandon as the sight of land slipped further and further away. Soon, I wondered if we had left the world behind. Nothing remained but miles and miles of ocean, rising and falling, waves appearing out of nowhere and then slamming the boat with their fury. The boat pitching from one side to the other until I could no longer recall the feel of solid ground. William told me to watch for whales, but after twenty minutes on deck, I gladly retreated to our cabin.

Mother grew sicker each day. She steadied herself against the ship's walls, and even then, she lost her balance. Her skin took on a green pallor as she held her hand over her mouth, fighting another spasm of nausea. I came to dread the sight of Mother bent over on her cot, a bucket braced between her legs. When she had nothing left in her stomach to vomit, she spat. The smell of the putrid green bile filled the cabin's air.

To escape the reek, I spent most of my time on deck, where at least the air was fresh if redolent of salt and fish. I pestered the captain with questions and asked if I could study his maps. "How many miles away is land?" I asked. When birds flew by, fighting the currents of wind, I asked him where they had come from. When waves slammed the boat, I stuck out my tongue and tasted the spray.

On a rare day when the sun broke through the persistent clouds, Caroline escorted Mother onto the deck for some air. They sat on the damp benches and tipped their heads back, eyes closed, basking in the feeble warmth. I joined them and soon got an earful of our fellow traveler's gossip.

A beaky Puritan woman from Connecticut introduced herself as Cornelia Eaton. Eaton was joining her husband, who had staked a claim in the Annapolis Valley. She bobbed her head as she spoke and looked like a turkey. She wore her gray hair short, barely visible beneath her starched white cap. Her hands were rough, her fingernails cut to the quick.

"It won't be an easy life, I reckon," she said, with what sounded to me like relish. She launched into the rumor of a recent skirmish between Acadians, Indians, and colonists that left New Englanders dead on a bridge. Even when Caroline intervened, saying there was no reason to alarm her fellow travelers, Eaton continued. "The Indians scalp settlers, you know," she said.

The color drained from my mother's face. The ship rocked in the violent wind and threw the women against each other. Eaton's bulk crushed Mother against the wall. Caroline inserted herself beside them. "Give her some air," she pleaded.

"What a man won't do for one thousand acres," the woman muttered. "I just hope Mr. Eaton knows what he is getting us into."

Every day was the same. Mother seemed smaller despite the baby growing inside her. The captain, evidently enjoying his rum, grew used to my presence in the cabin. He taught me how to read the compass and pointed out our progress on his maps, marking each day's location with a determined black dot. I watched the dots cross the roiling sea on a trajectory that seemed interminable. When he told me the ports we passed, I asked him to spell out their names and wrote them down in my journal.

Just when I thought all was lost, William pointed out the low hills of Nova Scotia in the distance. On the tenth day, we docked in Halifax, where dock workers took on ballast to steady the bow. The sun came out as our boat rocked in port. But the respite was short-lived. Too soon, we set sail once more, headed around the peninsula for the Bay of Fundy.

Once again, thunder and lightning filled the sky, and a dreary rain streaked the cabin window. I napped fitfully, rocked by the now familiar roll of the sea. When I woke, a brisk breeze had blown away most of the clouds. The ship approached a dock.

We were in Annapolis, at last. British and Massachusetts Bay Colony flags waved on the pier. The captain bade us farewell, telling us that the Committee for Laying out Lands, the Town Committee, and the Treasurer of the Town had assembled on the wharf to greet us. They were all men of great bluster. Behind them, I spotted Father waving. As we approached him, I saw him eye Mother's enormous belly. He raised his eyes to her pale face and quickly assured us the house and farm were ready for our arrival.

Taking Mother's arm, he steered her toward his cart. I followed but did not climb up until he and Caroline had tucked a warm wool blanket around Mother's legs. Once we were all settled, Father clicked his tongue and headed the horses away from town.

As the cart rattled through the darkness, I clutched my journal and recited to Father the strange names of the harbors and capes from Halifax to the Bay of Fundy. Jebucto, Ketch Harbour, Popnico, Ashmetetogan, Merligash. I knew these names, but I didn't know where we were heading.

"Are we there yet?" I asked.

Father assured me the house was only a few miles ahead. "Nova Scotia is your home now, thank the Lord," he said. Mother fell asleep at his side, peaceful at last. Father pulled the blanket up under her chin, and I did the same with mine. The wool was warm and smelled of Father's pipe tobacco.

A worn dirt path led us to a low mountain where we approached a white farmhouse with smoke rising from the chimney. Cornfields surrounded it and fragrant apple trees.

"The rain will end any day now," Father said. "I've built a fire in the hearth, and the house girl has prepared potato soup. In the daylight, you will see our fields. They extend almost to the top of the mountain."

He had named the family's farm Parker Mountain.

Parker Mountain. I mouthed the words, reassured by their familiarity. My family would live on a mountain that bore our family name. This land was ours. We were together now, in the place God intended us to be.

•••

Parker Mountain, Nova Scotia, September 1760

That first fall, everything was strange. Mother was confined to her bed, and Father was often away from home, meeting with the other Planters. When he came home, he complained about the community's lack of support from the Crown, saying the British were represented by only a handful of soldiers at the fort in Annapolis. Having won their war, they seemed to have lost interest in the colony, leaving the colony's governance in the hand of the new settlers.

There was much work to be done. Every day, before he left the house, Father assigned each of us children a task. One day, I fed the hungry cows hay from our limited stores. The next, I paced the cornfields, counting the rows of dried stubs of the disappointing crop. I picked up the dried husks of corn that had not yet been harvested and put them into my basket. "Next year," Father promised me, "more rows of corn will wave in these fields. The oxen and cows will graze in the open fields until they become plump and bright-eyed."

But these first crops, like everything else in Nova Scotia, were a disappointment, planted too late and watered too seldom. As I filled my basket with their shriveled carcasses, I worried about Mother, confined to her bedchamber. When I pleaded with Caroline, asking to sit at my mother's bedside, she shooed me away, saying the baby hadn't descended into the birth canal, and there were positions they needed to practice in preparation for the upcoming birth. No one unpacked the crates we brought from Massachusetts. Like me, they waited for Mother to recover. Unneeded and unwanted, I paced the maze of dry corn, kicking up dust with every step.

Warily, I avoided the edges of the field, alert for wild animals or Indians. In the underbrush, rodents scurried, disturbing the grass. I scanned the canopy, only to be thwarted by the tangle of trees and a flap of wings. Everywhere, it seemed, danger lurked. At the end of the field, I approached the edge of a hemlock grove, and I saw him. A dark-skinned boy no older than I, holding something in his arms. His eyes, like dark acorns, were unreadable. I clung to my basket, debating whether to sound an alarm.

As if to reassure me, the boy smiled, a quiet boy's smile. Even as my heart pounded, I read curiosity in his expression. Not danger. Despite all the warnings I had received, this stranger did not appear to be a threat. As I moved closer, I saw he carried a leather bag.

"*Gwe'*," he said. A strange word. A greeting? He was as hesitant as I was.

Had he come to steal our harvest? At the end of the row, we met, eye to eye.

Every adult I met in the new colony told me I could not trust the natives. Neighboring women cautioned us children about the lurking dangers. "The Indians think the land belongs to them." In Wolfville, the Baptist pastor preached that the Mi'kmaq had come to Jesus, but only as Catholics, bewitched by the Acadians into observing the Papal fallacy.

As I stood there, deciding what to do, the native boy looked me up and down, as if deciding whether *he* could trust *me*! When I did not turn away, he held up his bag, as if it were some sort of offering. His hair was black, long, thick, and straight.

"Waltes," he said. I could not see what was in the bag.

I looked up at the sun, gauging the time. There were several hours left before Aunt Caroline expected me home to help prepare the evening meal. I held up my basket to show him I was busy. I couldn't tell if he understood. "My father will be home soon," I said.

He shook his head. "Home?" The word sounded strange in his mouth. He shifted from foot to foot.

"Home," I said again, sweeping my arm to indicate the field and the white farmhouse.

"*C'est la maison de Lisette, une fille acadienne*," he said.

I recognized this last word. It is what the British called the French people they had expelled from this land after their war. I followed the boy's outstretched finger. Had he known the family who occupied our farmhouse before us? Was he looking for a friend? I'd often heard the British men in town bemoaning the "collusion" between the Indians and the French. Father had described the two forces fighting side by side in the Battle of Louisbourg.

"Acadienne?" I shook my head no.

"*Non?*" A shadow crossed his face.

"The Acadians are gone. My family lives here now."

Maybe he understood, if not my words, my meaning. Shifting his gaze to the ground, he turned away as if preparing to leave.

To my surprise, I reached out and touched his shoulder. I didn't want him to go. His appearance in our field was the first interesting thing that had happened to me since arriving in this desolate land.

"*Ami?*" I called out to his retreating back, one of the few French words I knew. Clearly, this boy was not a threat. *Is it possible*, I thought, *he was lonely too? That both of us were victims of events not of our choosing?*

Slowly, he pivoted to face me. Again, that shy smile. He held up his bag, his face solemn this time around. Testing. "Waltes," he said. As I watched, he showed me what the bag contained. A bowl made of hardwood burl worn smooth as if he had handled it many times, six dice-shaped cubes made of bone, and a bundle of sticks. One side of each die was smooth, the other marked with a cross. Some sticks looked like miniature arrows; others were unadorned. He crouched down in the dirt and emptied the bag on the ground at my feet.

I set my basket down on the dirt next to him to examine what appeared to be a game of chance. Perhaps I should have known better than to approach him, but at that moment my curiosity was stronger than all the warnings I had received.

Spreading a small leather cloth on the ground, he placed the dice in the bowl, never taking his eyes off mine. He shook the bowl vigorously and then slammed it back to the ground, causing the die to dance. When I jumped in surprise, he burst out laughing. I couldn't take my eyes off his bare feet, the taut musculature of his legs.

"Regardez, mademoiselle." He pointed to a die marked with a cross and raised a finger. Then he picked up a stick and placed it at his side. He puffed up his chest, more relaxed now, putting on a show. He returned the dice to the bowl and lifted it again. This time, I didn't startle when he slammed it down. This time, three of the faces showed the marked cross and three did not.

He held up his hands. I gathered he'd lost. Then he held out the bowl to me. I was tempted to take it, but if I did, our hands would touch.

"Amie?" he asked. Friend?

I scanned the fields, looking for Father. He would be furious if he discovered me talking with the Indian boy. I knew it would not matter if the boy was saved.

"No," I said, shaking my head. "No."

His smile faded, the light in his eyes replaced by an expressionless mask. With downcast eyes, he scooped up the game and put its pieces back in his bag.

When he left the field, his footsteps were as quiet as those of a fawn disappearing into the woods. Soon, his silhouette was indiscernible among the trees. I resumed my chores. By the time Father returned, I had cleared an impressive pile of weeds.

For many days thereafter, I reimagined the boy's eager invitation. The townspeople would have me believe I had been in grave danger talking to a native boy, but no matter how many times I replayed the scene, all I recalled was his hopeful brown eyes and his shy smile. I didn't mention the encounter to my brothers. They were bound to react badly. I considered confiding in Aunt Caroline, but she had her hands full caring for Mother.

So instead, the following Sunday, I asked Miss Polly, my Sunday school teacher, why the children of the Mi'kmaq were not welcomed to join the church if they believed in Jesus.

Miss Polly was an elegant young woman who wore her blond braids tightly coiled about her head. She chose her words carefully, as if she was reading a script from the white wall on the other side of the room. "The natives' customs are different from ours, dear. They are primitive." She placed her hand on my shoulder. She had long fingers and manicured nails and wore a silver ring.

"Have you heard of a game they play? Called something like 'Waltes'?" I asked her.

Miss Polly pursed her lips. She removed her hand from my shoulder and shuddered.

"I have," she said. It felt like a reprimand. "The Indians believe the Waltes bowl allows them to see into the future. If a spiritual man fills the bowl with water and leaves it overnight, in the morning, its wood grain will show the past, present, and future."

"Oh," I said. "I thought it was a game."

"A game, yes. A traditional game the Indians play during their heathen rites," she said. "But, filled with water to expose the grain, they also use the bowl to foretell the future. As I said, they are savages." Her blue eyes dismissed me, a warning laced with a flicker of sternness. "I hear that when the French missionaries visit the Indian camps, the priests instruct them to drill holes in the bottoms of any Waltes bowls they find."

"So, they cannot see into the future?"

"The bowls are the objects of heathen beliefs," Miss Polly snapped. She walked away with a huff.

We never discussed the matter again.

I never mentioned the Indian to Father.

Weeks passed before the boy returned, although I looked for him every time I was in the fields. When he was not in town, Father spent his day cutting back the apple trees, picking off pests, and drowning them in a bucket of soapy water.

One afternoon, I was in the parlor embroidering the white lace curtains that Mother had sewn for the parlor window. Father was installing a rod for the curtains when he saw the figure on the edge of the field. "Do you see that?" he asked.

The boy lingered at the side of the cornfield, clutching his leather bag. I wondered if he was looking for me.

I froze right there on the couch, trying to concentrate on my needle-work. Father retrieved his musket from the front room. His hand was on the trigger by the time he threw open the front door, allowing a brisk breeze to blow into the room. He aimed the musket at the boy.

My heart pounded, but I didn't speak up, thinking no good would come of it.

At the clatter of the door opening, the boy startled. He pivoted quickly and fled into the woods, his bare feet skimming over the pine needles.

"Get off my land!" Father bellowed across the field. His words echoed through the fields long after the boy had disappeared.

From that day forward, Father's musket hung over our hearth with ammunition stored close by.

Perhaps the boy was not a convert, I told myself. I regretted mentioning the matter to my Sunday school teacher and worried for days that she might repeat our conversation to my father.

• • •

"Your mother's time of trial has arrived," Father announced over breakfast. "Help your Aunt Caroline, and by nightfall you will have a younger brother or sister."

He summoned my brothers, who were already in the fields, saying urgent business in town required their attention. "Winter is near," he said as he saddled our nag to the oxcart. "We have much to do before the first snows arrive." With all the menfolk gone, I joined Caroline and sat vigil at Mother's bedside, my aunt's consoling words swallowed by Mother's increasingly frequent cries of pain.

"When will the baby get here?" I asked, cringing each time Mother groaned.

"Whenever he or she is ready," Caroline said. "We must let nature take its course. But while we're waiting, why don't you be a good girl and bring me a pot of boiled water and as much clean linen as you can muster?"

Even downstairs, I could not escape my dear mother's pleas. "Caroline, please, something isn't right. Don't. Oh please, don't. I can't bear it anymore." I hung a pot of water over the hearth and dug through a chest for linens and clean rags. When the pot boiled angrily, I carried it upstairs, walking slowly to avoid spills or burning myself with the sloshing water.

Caroline was on her knees between Mother's legs. With palms flat, she massaged Mother's stomach, easing up only when Mother begged her to stop.

Unable to move, I took in the scene, feeling a chill climb up my spine.

"Sweetie," Caroline cooed. "The baby is curled up on its side. I need to nudge its sweet head toward the birth canal."

I tried to picture the baby, cradled one last time in my mother's belly. If only it would come out. Now.

All afternoon and late into the night, I covered my ears to muffle the sounds of my mother's labor. Father had spoken about the "trying hour of nature's sorrow," and now I saw it play out before me. I watched Caroline's increasingly desperate attempts to turn the baby. I saw my mother's face transformed by the agony.

In one last attempt to position the baby properly, Caroline asked me to help her turn my mother onto her stomach. I steeled myself and avoided my mother's pleading eyes.

"Maggie," Caroline said, "I need you to get on your hands and knees. Remember how we practiced? We've got to get the babe to turn."

But couldn't my aunt see? Mother had neither the strength nor will to follow her instructions.

"I can't," she whimpered. "This baby doesn't want to be born."

"Mama," I said, and then couldn't fathom how to end the sentence. Instead, I clutched her hand as Aunt Caroline massaged her back. At first, Mother's grip was strong, painfully so, but as the hour passed, it slowly went limp. The color drained from her face and her eyes lost focus.

"Enough," Caroline said, when the baby refused to move into place. "Lucy, let's roll your mother over and let her rest."

Caroline instructed me to hold wet rags to Mother's forehead. One after another, she pulled out her arsenal of herbal remedies: southernwood, wormwood, mugwort, and barberry. Each time she said, "Let's give this a try." But as each herb failed to relieve Mother's pain, as the baby refused to budge, Caroline's sweet demeanor faded. She chewed on her lips until they bled, fretting about what to do.

"Lucy, sweetheart," she said at last. "It's time for you to leave me alone with your mother." I left my mother's side, but I refused to leave the room. I had already witnessed too much by then. I stood with one hand on the doorknob as Aunt Caroline gently probed my mother's lady parts, oblivious to my presence. When she pulled out her hand, instead of a baby, I saw a gush of blood.

"Dear Lord," she said, wringing her bloody hands, "do not take this good woman from us."

Blood. So much blood. The bedding, the linen, the towels. All soaked, but still no baby.

"Do something," I screamed at her, choking back tears. But Aunt Caroline, her face drawn and weary, didn't hear me.

The redder the sheets, the whiter my mother's pale skin. With eerie resolve, my mother scrunched up her face and pushed with every bit of strength she had left.

"No, Maggie, don't!" Caroline tried to stop her, but it was too late. In another spurt of blood, a blue leg, smaller than that of a doll, appeared. Caroline pushed it back in, but with the next contraction, it re-emerged. This time there were two legs and behind them a baby, blue and struggling, bathed in blood.

And then there was only blood. More than I ever imagined any woman's body could contain. As Aunt Caroline held the newborn, Mother's moans faded to feeble whimpers. Her hand went cold.

"Don't let her die," I sobbed. "Mama, don't leave me."

But she was already gone.

"She didn't say goodbye," I whispered to Aunt Caroline as an eerie silence filled the room. "I never had time to tell her I loved her."

"Tell your sister," Caroline said, wrapping the baby in a blanket, the hint of an exhausted smile on her face.

The men arrived home long after sundown. Hearing them climb the stairs, Aunt Caroline opened the door to my parents' bedchamber, which we had scrubbed clean. At Aunt Caroline's request, I bundled up the bloody rags and carried them to the shed for burial.

"How is she?" my father asked.

Aunt Caroline held up her hands in a gesture of powerlessness. "Maggie fought admirably, but this birth was too much for her. I did everything I could, but it wasn't enough." Pale and cold, Mother lay on the bed, covered by clean white sheets.

Leaving Father at her side, the family gathered around the oak dining table, the very one Father had put together on our arrival, its boards and wooden legs numbered like a complex puzzle.

When Father came down, he said Mother's death was God's will, and we must keep stiff upper lips, but I held him responsible. I wasn't about to say it, but I blamed him for dragging our family to this godforsaken place. The first chance I had, I would ask Grandpa Hardy to let me live with him in his little house down the lane. Or perhaps I would stow away in another lurching boat headed for home. I would, if I had to.

By morning, the news of my mother's passing had spread.

I pinched my nose every time I opened the front door to admit strangers who had never met my mother, who had never inhaled the sweet powder on her neck and would never know the comfort of her sweet smile.

Upstairs, the baby cried and cried. The infant was miserable, ailing, too small for this world, her life force ebbing. Aunt Caroline told Father he would need a wet nurse if the baby survived, but no one arrived to care for the poor thing. When I asked Caroline when the nurse would arrive, she sighed. "Oh honey, she'll never make it through the night."

This was no time for tears, Father said. "God giveth, and God taketh away."

I disagreed. As far as I could tell, He had taken everything and given nothing in return.

The house was drafty and stunk of strangers. Father expected me to stand at his side with William and Nat, to shake the neighbors' hands as they arrived to pray. Instead, when no one was looking, I climbed the stairs to my mother's chamber. I avoided looking at the baby clothes Mother had folded and stacked on the bureau. But I picked up a blanket and held it to my cheek, remembering those last weeks in Massachusetts when Mother had taught me how to crochet, one tangled knot after another. I swaddled the crying baby, inhaling the soft wool, searching for my mother's scent. My tears fell on the baby's beet-red face, despite my father's admonition that tears would not bring my mother back.

I hated Nova Scotia. I hated every stranger crowding into the drafty house. I hated the gray seas lapping the shores of the Bay of Fundy. I hated the morning fog, damp and cold, and the stony spits that extended like the bony fingers of witches into the port where we had landed, not knowing what awaited us.

Downstairs, Father's voice rose above the murmuring of the crowd:

O God, whose mercies cannot be numbered: Accept our prayers on behalf of thy servant Margaret Parker. Grant her an entrance into the land of light and joy, in the fellowship of thy saints; through Jesus Christ thy Son our Lord, who liveth and reigneth with thee and the Holy Spirit, one God, now and forever. Amen.

Light and joy. Here, there was neither, and never would be.

Even as Father prayed, the last rays of sunshine faded from the window. I closed the lace curtains that Mother had stitched with such care, promising sunshine. The baby whimpered and then went silent. The color drained from her tiny face; red was replaced by an ashen blue. Her empty eyes looked right through me.

She was gone. My mother and this child, they both were gone.

I was alone. Oh, dearest Mother, I cried, I am so alone.

CHAPTER FIVE

Leaving the Winter Camp

Nmejuaqnek, Port Royal, May 1761

Every spring, Meuse and his family traveled to Nmejuaqnek, the place of bountiful fish where two rivers met on the southern coast of the Bay of Fundy. These fishing grounds had been the central gathering place for their tribe for hundreds of summers. At winter's end, the family loaded their belongings into birch-bark canoes. They paddled the twists and turns of the Mersey River. When the river widened into the bay, Meuse, sunburned but exultant, inhaled the salt of the sea, heard waves lapping on the rocky shore. He drank in the warming rays of sunlight like a thirsty man drinking icy creek water. Gazing up at the budding branches on the trees, he rejoiced at the season's renewal, feeling fresh blood surge through his body as his family paddled to the place where the river flowed into the mouth of the bay.

Two long, dark winters had passed since Francis had left the tribe to marry his mademoiselle. In his absence, Meuse had sought out companionship wherever he could, but none of his cousins matched Francis's exuberance. Meuse thought of his cousin often, wondering how he fared with Lisette and the LaFleur family. He dreamed that one day, he might seek out his friend again. In Grand-Pré, the Acadians still worked the dikes. Perhaps Francis and his mademoiselle were somewhere nearby. Meuse could ask him how it felt to live apart from his tribe.

"Patience," Anne said, sensing her son's restlessness. As the family approached their summer camp, she handed him a basket piled high with their belongings.

This would be their second summer in Nmejuaqnek since the British had expelled the Acadians from Port Royal. As the family followed the stream to their summer camp, it surprised Meuse how much the land had been transformed in their absence. Last year, oxcarts abandoned by the French had littered the narrow paths. The bleached bones of abandoned livestock and blackened ruins of Acadian houses and barns were everywhere. Unpicked apples rotted in the orchards. But now, new families had moved into their houses, and their fields flourished. It was as if the French had never been there at all.

Where had his cousin gone? Since Francis left his family behind to marry his mademoiselle, they had received no news of him. Last year, Meuse had asked a Scotsman at the trading post if he knew of the LaFleurs' whereabouts. The man had told him with a shrug that some of the Acadians had traveled north to work on the dikes. Now he wondered if that was where his cousin had landed. There certainly was no sign of him here.

Although Meuse had assumed many of Francis's tribal duties, he had not yet killed a moose. He was fourteen and taller than Francis was when he left. In Kejimkujik, his dearest companion was Mimi, even if she wasn't about to challenge him to a race or teach him how to corner prey. He sat behind her during their annual migration, watching her steady stroke with a longing that grew stronger by the day. His mother smiled at his budding infatuation.

When they reached their summer camp, Anne left them to join the women who had already arrived. Meuse and Mimi pulled the canoe up onto the warm sand of the secluded cove. They combed the beach, gathering willow, birch, and ash branches. They carried armfuls of flexible saplings to the site where the women had made a clearing in the scrubby vegetation. There, Uncle Gehne tied the saplings with dried sinew to form frames for their summer shelters. Meuse stretched animal skins over the sturdy skeletons. This had once been Francis's job, but Meuse worked contentedly at his uncle's side, slowly watching the camp reappear, as it had every year of his life. Gehne approved a knot here, added reinforcement there, before joining the men outside around the stone pit they had made for a fire. Once they had finished the wigwams, the women swept the dirt floors, spread dried seaweed to cushion the sleeping area, and put away their belongings. Outside, the uncles gossiped with tribal members who had preceded them earlier in the spring, arriving for the annual salmon run. As he worked, Meuse listened to their chatter, hoping to hear news of Francis.

A trio of Elders from a neighboring camp rode up. The uncles greeted them: *Kwe', welta'si na' nike' pekisin*. Hello, I'm glad you came. The men replied: *Kwe', wela'lin wet-tluen*. Thank you for saying that. But despite the warm exchange, the news they delivered was not good. Joining the men around the fire, they told venomous stories of destruction. "Over the winter, Father Le Loutre's forces destroyed Mission Sainte-Anne and dumped the ruins into Snides Lake," one said.

"Why would they do that?" Old Joe asked.

"They wanted to prevent the mission from falling into the possession of New Englanders. These new colonists are a fierce bunch, prepared for battle. They carry weapons and are prepared to use them," another said. "They've already wiped out many members of the tribes in the colonies of Massachusetts, Connecticut, and Rhode Island." The speaker said he had traveled widely, trading pelts. The horrors he had seen were unimaginable.

Without Father Le Loutre's support, they said, the tribe no longer had a shield protecting them from the British, who now controlled access to their summer fishing grounds. What the Acadians had once called Port Royal, the English now called Annapolis.

Meuse overheard their words and felt a shiver of apprehension. Where, he wondered, was Francis now that Father Le Loutre had abandoned the French mission?

"We're on our own," the Elders kept saying, "no longer protected by the French." Even English citizens affiliated with the Roman Catholic Church had been disenfranchised under the new British governor. Catholics could no longer vote, hold public office, or practice their religion. The Mi'kmaq, who had been converted by one European power, were now under the jurisdiction of another that despised Catholics.

As the men talked, Mimi entered the wigwam with a pile of animal skins. "Have you heard what the men are saying?" he asked her. "Do you think Francis is in danger?"

"With any luck, Francis is off with his mademoiselle, working on the dikes with his father-in-law," she said.

"They say they have burned the French school in Port Royal to the ground," he whispered. "There's no trace left of the Acadian community that lived here." But when Mimi's eyebrows knit together in concern, he dropped the subject, not wanting to contribute to the panic that was already spreading among the family.

From the corner where she organized her cooking implements, his mother watched them warily. "Meuse, your work here is done. Why don't you go help the older cousins gather wood for this evening's fire?"

He squeezed Mimi's hand and headed out into the sunshine. In the canopy, the birds sang: the woodpeckers tapped out a mating call; the chickadees squawked in union. But the joy Meuse had experienced as they pulled their canoes onto the familiar shore had evaporated. Despite the warmth of the sun, he shivered.

•••

Meuse remained eager for news of his cousin, but soon the talk among the tribe's Elders turned from the plight of the Acadians to the relationship between the local tribes and the new British government.

The respected chief of the smaller tribe had always come to welcome the Mi'kmaq back to the summer hunting grounds. They, in turn, provided a generous feast, and he apprised them of the local gossip and news.

The local chief joined the family at the evening's bonfire. After sharing the men's tobacco, he held up a much-handled, stained piece of paper.

"Look at this," he said.

The men passed the document around the circle, touching the official-looking parchment with its unintelligible language and sweeping signatures, pretending they understood the strange English words. They looked up at the chief for an explanation.

"This is the peace pact the British have offered us," he said. They gasped as he threw the offending document into the fire. "Not worth its weight in kindling," he said with scorn. "The British officials scribble lies on a useless piece of paper, and then they kill Indians in their sleep and sink their bodies to the bottom of the bay along with their canoes."

The chief said he had traveled to Halifax in good faith, hoping that he, like the Maliseet, would return with a treaty that would protect the Mi'kmaq of Port Royal. Instead, the British governor treated him with contempt and derision. He had belittled the tribe's proposals and countered with a document that offered no protection.

On his return to Port Royal, the chief had sought counsel from the French. But Le Loutre, who had shielded the tribe for so long, was fighting for his own survival. The priest refused to see him, saying he had neither the time nor inclination to support the tribe's attempt to secure a treaty. "After all the battles we fought side by side with Le Loutre," the chief said, "the French have excluded us from their peace negotiations." In fact, the French governor had gone one step further. He had undermined the peace initiatives between the Mi'kmaq and the British when he freed two Englishmen who had killed seven members of a Mi'kmaq family for profit.

"Instead of negotiating a treaty, Governor Lawrence issued a proclamation. He promised a reward of thirty pounds for every male Indian scalp or prisoner brought in alive above the age of sixteen years. He offered twenty-five pounds for every Indian woman or child captured or killed. His Majesty's forces will pay these rewards out in the province, including those at the fort in the town we called Port Royal and they now call Annapolis." The chief spit into the fire.

The Elders puffed on their pipes, their long faces solemn.

"We are outcasts in our own land," Old Joe said gloomily, staring into the fire. The others agreed, nodding their heads. A low rumble of disapproval spread around the circle.

Sitting behind his Elders, Meuse shifted. "Certainly, the chief is exaggerating," he whispered to Mimi on his right. Yet both saw Gehne's face, riddled with concern.

The chief roared, "We are lambs ready for slaughter."

Mimi's lower lip trembled. "Meuse," she said, "what are we going to do?"

"They won't get away with this," he said. "We will fight back." Now that Francis had deserted them, choosing instead to woo a wife, he would need to step up and join the men in their resistance. This was more important than killing a moose; this was a battle for survival.

"Don't be a child," Gehne hissed back at him. Unaccustomed to his uncle's disapproval, Meuse retreated into a sullen silence. His uncle's reprimand stung. Sometimes it seemed as if Gehne watched his every move, heard every word he said. Meuse slumped, powerless in his uncle's eyes.

He tugged on Mimi's sleeve, pointing out a path into the woods. The two slipped quietly from the heat of the fire. Under the cover of the pine trees, Meuse confided in the one person he could trust.

"Last summer, I met one of these New Englanders," he told her.

"What? Where?" she asked.

"I was hunting for grouse in the low mountains above our fishing grounds, when I recognized the farmhouse where Lisette used to live. The spring that Francis and I both attended the Acadian mission school, we had visited her family there. I was standing in the exact spot where Francis taught Waltes to Lisette."

"Only my brother would try to teach a French girl our traditions."

"Little did I know then that he was courting her at the same time!"

Discussing her brother, Mimi's face relaxed.

"When I saw the farmhouse last summer, I thought of Francis. How much I've missed him since he left us behind to pursue his mademoiselle! And then I saw a white girl carrying a basket in that same field. *Lisette?* I thought. *Is Francis here?* I ran to the side of the field, elated at my discovery."

"Why didn't you tell me this before?"

"My eyes deceived me. It was not Lisette. She, I realize now, was long gone. But a new girl had moved into that house, a blue-eyed white girl who did not speak French. At the sight of her, I recalled how happy Francis had been teaching Lisette our game. How brave I had thought him to befriend his delicate mademoiselle. In my loneliness, I convinced myself that I, too, would be brave enough to befriend a white girl. I longed, as I always have, to follow in your brother's footsteps."

Mimi placed the back of her hand on his cheek. "We both miss Francis," she said. Encouraged, Meuse continued.

"The next day, I returned to the field and brought a Waltes bowl to show her. How foolish I was, looking for a friend! When I approached the girl, she regarded me with suspicion. Her hesitation made it clear she was afraid of me."

"What were you thinking, approaching one of the New Englanders?" Mimi asked. "You heard the chief tonight. These people are evil."

"They think they can scare us away, but I am not afraid of them," he answered.

"Don't you understand?" Mimi spoke with urgency. "The British chased away the Acadians and replaced them with New Englanders. They," her voice broke, "chased the LaFleur family away with my brother at their side." Her voice rose with a passion Meuse had never heard from her before. "The father of the girl you approached moved his family into a farmhouse on a mountain that, for hundreds of years, provided shelter and generous hunting grounds for our tribe. Lisette may have been Francis's friend, but the girl you saw was an enemy, nothing more."

"It wasn't like that," Meuse whined. He was digging himself in deeper but determined to defend his actions. "The young New Englander was skittish. Who knows what she had been told about our people?"

Mimi appeared to think this over. Several times, she opened her mouth without speaking. Seeing her dismay, Meuse regretted having upset her. Especially since she was right. "But it was not the girl I should never have trusted." He swallowed and then continued his story. "It was her father."

"Her father?"

"When I returned a second time, her father spotted me entering the field. I hated him on sight. Standing in his open doorway like a threatening bear, he defended his property with a firestick." Meuse puffed up, all of his pent-up fury spilling out in a torrent. "I hate him even more now that I've learned what evil his people have brought to our once peaceful countryside."

Mimi looked up at him, fear spreading across her face. Was it the New Englanders she feared or his unleashed anger? He slipped his clenched fists underneath his tunic so she could not see.

"I don't know how, I don't know when, but I will have vengeance on this man!" he proclaimed. "These lands do not belong to him any more than they belong to us. Like my father before me, I will take a stand."

There was nothing more to say. In silence, they walked back toward the firepit. Rage had unsettled Meuse's belly, which gurgled angrily as if he had eaten rotten fish. Perhaps it was unwise to have told Mimi of his resolve, but he refused to let fear defeat him.

That night, Meuse woke from a nightmare in which he was running from the white man's musket. He sat up in the darkness, listening to his uncle's snore, the soft rhythm of Mimi's breath. He inhaled the familiar odor of smoke and sweat.

The Elders' stories had populated his dreams, stealing away any possibility of sleep. Now, his hatred coalesced into the vision of the New Englander's face. His blood boiled at the memory of the musket pointed at his back.

Only a white man would claim a mountain to himself.

Meuse slipped out of the wigwam quietly, his bare feet skimming the dry grass. He rifled through the tribe's supplies, looking for a weapon to take with him. His uncle would not approve, but bows and arrows were no match for the colonists' guns. He slipped a hunting knife into its leather sheath and headed away from the camp as the first rays of sunshine peeked over the horizon. He followed the familiar path toward the low mountain where he and Francis had once hunted for small game. Toward the field where he had once watched Francis play Waltes with Lisette. Where he had asked another girl, an icy New Englander, to befriend him but had instead been chased away by her father's musket. Toward the house perched on top of the hill, which the family from Massachusetts claimed as their own. When he arrived at the dirt road that led to the house, he hid behind a large oak.

He heard a clatter of hooves coming down the cart path toward the road north. Hiding in the shadows, he watched as a family rode by him. The men and women were on horseback, the young children seated in an oxcart. He saw the girl sharing a horse with a young man. When the procession disappeared down the narrow path, he fell in behind them, keeping his distance. He was determined not to let the family out of his sight.

• • •

Grand-Pré, Nova Scotia March 1760

Lisette's father, Pierre LaFleur, his trousers caked with mud after a day's work on the dikes, pulled a wooden chair up to the long table in the back of the Harbour Inn.

"We're nothing more than slave labor," he declared, accepting a stein of beer from the innkeeper. "The British may have confiscated our land and kicked us out of our houses, but they 'allow' us to toil in the tidal bore so that their farms flourish downstream."

Francis had become accustomed to his father-in-law's vehemence. Monsieur LaFleur lacked his own father's patient and benevolent spirit, but he had taken Francis under his wing. Francis sipped his beer, struggling to follow the Acadian's foreign words, spoken so much faster than those of his teachers at the Acadian school. Here, he was the only Mi'kmaw among dozens of Frenchmen, a newcomer dressed to play a part he had not prepared for.

Francis's smock, passed down to him by his new father-in-law, was tight. Unaccustomed to the restrictive clothing of the French, he shifted on his stool, unable to find a comfortable position. His heavy work boots, damp and dirty, felt like stones rooting him into his position at the bar. He, too, smelled of the dikes, where he had joined the work crew maintaining the critical earthworks at LaFleur's insistence.

New restrictions had triggered LaFleur's tirade. "The damn British don't want us traveling by boat or canoe. Local deputies asked us to turn in our firearms at the closest fort. When we complained that these demands were intolerable, the local councilman called us 'audacious and impertinent.' He offered us the 'very fair opportunity' to sign an unqualified oath of loyalty."

Of course, they had refused.

"*Mais Pere LaFleur,*" Francis said, "at least our bellies are full, and we have a roof over our heads at night. That's more than many people have."

"*Peut-être,*" Pierre said. "But I still say it isn't proper. Every time I see a man from Massachusetts coming down the cart path with his wagon piled high with corn, I'm tempted to chase him down and claim what is rightfully mine."

Francis, still basking in the glow of sharing a life with his mademoiselle, found it difficult to muster up anger equal to that of his father-in-law. The man's simmering anger was ever-present, the base note beneath his ethic of hard work and family loyalty. His nightly rages, intensified with each stein of beer, were his only outlet and Francis his favored audience. He had offered Francis shelter when no one else would take him in. The man was simple and loyal and, Francis had to admit, entitled to his anger.

Tonight, a half-dozen of their compatriots from the dike joined them at the saloon. Fellow Acadians who had been excluded from exile because of their skill, lured here by the promise of work and compensation. A hard-working group of men who arrived with ragged families in tow to work land they knew better than any of its current inhabitants.

"The bastards," Francis said. "That foreman had the nerve to tell me to pick up my pace. I'd like to see that laggard dig a ditch in eight hours." As he waved his arms for emphasis, the fabric of his too-tight smock ripped. He looked over at LaFleur to see if the man had noticed.

"Right you are," LaFleur said, patting him on the back. "The New Englanders are even more clueless than the British. If we hadn't worked their fields first, they'd be lucky to reap a cartful of stones."

The men at the counter laughed, and the innkeeper poured more ale.

The idea of joining a band of resistance fighters came from a co-worker named Louis. Francis had gotten to know the short, stocky man with a thick mustache who worked at his side as they shoveled the dirt of the dikes. Louis was prone to dark moods and grandiose pronouncements.

He preferred brandy to beer. "There's those who will fight and those who will sit at this counter and complain all night," he said. He had broached the idea of resistance before, but the other men had discarded it when the last bell rang and they headed home to their wives. Tonight, however, the proposal seemed to gain traction.

"If Broussard can stand up to the bastards, why can't we?" LaFleur agreed with Louis, warming to the idea. The British might control strongholds like Halifax, Port Royal, and Fort Beausejour, but that didn't mean they'd pacified those still living in the region.

"A *Monsieur* Jeanson is looking for volunteers," Louis said, slamming his stein down on the oak bar. "If we want to fight for what's rightfully ours, we ought to heed his call. I hear he's rallied a group of Mi'kmaq like you"—he pointed at Francis with a stained and stubby finger—"and Acadians to chase the yellow-bellied cowards out of Port Royal." He picked at the mud under his thumbnail with the index finger of his opposite hand and flicked the dirt onto the sawdust floor.

Two more rounds and they had agreed to congregate at the bridge on the Rene Forêt River the following night to meet up with Jeanson's forces.

"I'll join you," Francis said. He was a successful hunter. Now he could show these new friends he was also a warrior.

"My boy," Pierre leaned heavily into Francis, "if your people join mine, the bastards don't have a chance." He nearly fell off his stool from the force of a powerful belch, but Francis steadied him. "Why, if we can get the British forces to retreat, I can reclaim my farm in Port Royal and give Lisette and you a proper wedding."

The next day, Francis and a dozen hungover dike workers met up with the band organized by Guillaume Jeanson. As they approached the Rene Forêt River, they passed by orchards of apple and pear trees heavy with unpicked fruit.

"*Mon dieu*," Pierre said. "What has our world come to? So many years of planting, pruning, and picking, and now the products of our labor hang neglected, soon to rot on the ground."

Remembering the words of his Elders around the summer's bonfire, Francis sympathized with their sense of loss. Loss was something his people shared with the men who now surrounded him.

"A detachment of 130 British and colonial men set out this morning along the south shore of the Annapolis River in search of escaped prisoners," Jeanson announced. "At this rate, they will cross the bridge on the Rene Forêt early this afternoon. We'll be there to show them what's what. From there, it's clear sailing until we raise the French flag once more over Port Royal."

The men hooted with glee. Jeanson's confidence was contagious. A contented grin spread across LaFleur's ruddy face, and Francis's heart pounded. Here, at last, was his chance to put his talent as a hunter on display for his new father-in-law.

Marching on foot, the band set out to waylay the English, arriving at the bridge before them and waiting in the undergrowth, prepared to ambush the soldiers. They relaxed on their horses, chatting among themselves, weapons tucked into their belts.

When the British detachment arrived, the Acadians surrounded them before they knew what hit them. A dozen colonists, trapped on the bridge, realized their predicament too late; they could not defend their position. Francis, at the front of the pack, aimed his gun at the captain. The two locked eyes: the colonist's blue, Francis's dark and accusatory. Facing this man who had answered his government's call to collect scalps for a bounty, a wave of fury overcame Francis. He pulled the trigger before the soldier raised his musket. Not since Francis had felled the bull moose had he felt such a surge of power. One by one, the dike workers followed his lead. The colonists fell, some onto the bridge and others into the bloody water below. Those who did not die on the spot fled in disarray.

Pierre slapped his son-in-law on the back. "You put the fear of God in them bastards, *mon fils*," he said. Francis glowed with pride. If he'd had his way, they would have headed to Port Royal then and there and finished the job.

Among the aggrieved Acadians, he felt no regret. He'd responded to violence with violence. No need to treat his prey with respect. Here, no Elders whispered in his ear. He felt his blood coursing through his veins. He would earn the respect of the community he had adopted, protect his new wife and family. There was no call for sympathy for those in his way.

But Jeanson had other ideas. "The campaign to harass and ambush the British has just begun," he cautioned. "For now, lay down your weapons and rejoice in a job well done. The battle is not over." He shook their hands one by one, his grip firm. "But today, we sent a message." At his behest, they abandoned the bodies on the bridge and dispersed before the local deputies arrived.

Francis didn't look back. He shook Jeanson's hand and followed his compatriots down the trail. In the quiet of the woods, he heard his father's voice, embedded as always in his head. "My son," Gehne said, "there is dishonor in leaving the fallen behind." But Francis refused to acknowledge his father's words. He was in their world now, and the rules he would live by had forever changed. His father's advice was of no use to him now. Instead, he relived the battle with his fellow fighters later at the bar. He accepted their accolades, a hero once more.

• • •

Nmejuaqnek, Port Royal, May 1761

Early morning fog blanketed the camp, filling it with the acrid scent of the smoldering bonfire.

For a second night, the fire blazed. Gehne passed the pipe to the visiting chief, but now he, too, had a troubled heart. His second son, the boy he had adopted and proudly watched grow into a man, had disappeared the previous night from their camp and had not returned. "I fear," he told his visitor, "your account of the White Man's treachery may have poisoned the young man's heart. I've already lost one son to the French, now another has headed out into the darkness, seeking revenge against the devils you described."

Beside him, Mimi wrung her hands. Ever since she had relayed Meuse's impassioned proclamation to her father, she had shivered as if swimming in an icy sea. Anne, Meuse's mother, shared her blanket with the girl. Neither spoke.

"The boy," Gehne said, "is a gentle child." He whispered to the chief so the women could not hear. The two men smoked; the blazing fire cast shadows on their worried brows. Around them, the tribe danced in a circle to the beating of drums. Fireflies flitted in the darkness. Gehne could see that even though Mimi and Anne huddled beneath a heavy blanket, the thick wool could not dispel the chill of discovering Meuse's empty bedroll.

Later that night, the tribal dance diverted the tribe's attention from the crackling footsteps of men gathering in the nearby woods to decide their response to the recent attack on the British and colonial forces by a ragtag band of Acadians and Indians. The men crouched in the underbrush and listened as a man who identified himself as Major Rogers informed them that intelligence had reached the Annapolis fort that a hostile group of Indians had set up camp on property belonging to the late Sheriff Taylor. "For too long, Indian assaults have plagued our colonies," Rogers said, "and now our soldiers are endangered. Parker has disappeared—kidnapped, we believe, after his holy baptism—with his wife not far behind him. These are only the most recent atrocities, and they cannot stand." Rogers pointed to Parker's stepson Ezekiel at the other side of the field, his eyes ablaze. "The family is bereft, and I have promised them we will hunt down his abductor and put an end to this madness."

It was time, Rogers said with a sneer, "to rid the area of these rude inhabitants."

His companion, a captain, pointed to the wigwams erected on the open field. "What do you see?" He mocked the Indians, dancing with what he perceived as great frolic.

"I am sure," Major Rogers hissed, "there is not a man here whose heart is not already engaged. I ask only for your purse and arm, if need be, to pursue a cause so just in the sight of God and man, a cause necessary for our self-defense."

The men in attendance responded to his call to action. As the Indians danced, they returned to the local hamlets and relayed his message to the menfolk of the community. Late that night and into the early hours of the next morning, they repeated his words from house to house, saying, "Prepare to meet at sunrise before the Indians wake."

Footsteps woke Gehne from a deep and troubled sleep during which his ancestors had warned him of what was to come. The white men marched boldly into the camp just after daybreak. Alerted by the heavy stomp of their boots, Gehne wiped the sleep from his eyes and moved cautiously toward the flap of his wigwam. By the fragile light of morning, he saw the raiders emerge from the shadows of the tall pine trees. There was no time to wake the others. The attack was as sudden as it was vicious.

A tall, uniformed man strode into the camp first. As Gehne watched, the man killed the visiting chief in his bed with one carefully aimed shot. His next bullet ricocheted off of Joseph and hit the Elder Gabriel, who never woke up. Then bedlam broke loose. Men, women, and children, awakened by the disturbance, fled in disorder, unarmed and unprepared, pursued by the armed company. Gehne was one of the last to go. After a last scan of the camp, he followed his fleeing tribe to Rogers Point, where the raiders had cornered them in the lighthouse's shadow.

On the beach, the soldiers murdered the rest of the family in cold blood. As Gehne emerged from the woods, one shot Anne as she stood on the shore, looking frantically for a place to hide. She collapsed onto the jagged rocks, where the pebbles and sand were stained bright red. A dozen Indians who had grabbed their bows and arrows before fleeing raised their weapons, but none used them. The volley of bullets felled them before they reached the beach. In desperation, Gehne plunged into the frigid water of the bay. Although he was not a strong swimmer, he paddled wildly, parallel to the shore. He fought for his life, inhaling saltwater and choking as he struggled to breathe. His muscles cramped and then went numb. Far away on the shore, he spotted Mimi and a few of the younger children escaping into the long grasses and then disappearing up a creek bed.

When the ricochet of bullets died down, Gehne let the surf carry him, numb and bleeding, back to the rocky shore of a hidden cove where his tribe had often fished. He could hear the distant celebratory hoots of the conquerors. He lay there until they headed back toward the tribe's camp, brandishing fallen branches. *Now they will burn everything they have left behind,* he thought. On the wet sand, he closed his eyes, his body surrendering to the cold.

Was his body among those the white men had counted, calculating their reward? Lost in the fog of hypothermia, he wasn't sure if he was dead or alive, if he belonged among those slaughtered or was one of the few survivors of his tribe. He pictured Mimi, who he had last seen escaping into the woods. He summoned Meuse, who had left days before the massacre, dead set on revenge. Even as his body betrayed him, he called out to the survivors, his words slurred, his tongue thick. *Mimi, my daughter*, he said, *you must stay strong. Meuse, my son, you do not know the damage your family has suffered.* He wrapped his arms around them, encouraging them to live even if he could not, begging them to carry on the tribe's legacy. Overhead, crows circled the battlefield, homing in on the carrion.

CHAPTER SIX

Parker Mountain

Parker Mountain, May 1761

Where was Father? We all wondered who had abducted him. Was he alive or had his abductor murdered him?

All morning, strangers arrived at our front door, offering consolation. The angry voices of the men drowned out the hum of sympathy from long-faced women who carried plates of cookies. Salome had banished me to a corner of the parlor, instructing me to do my chores. How dare she tell me how to behave at such at time? She was not my mother. Now, I had neither mother nor father.

The congregation had returned to Annapolis, hoping to find Father at home. Instead, when Ma Salome approached the dark house, I heard her cry out: "Where has he gone?"

Ma Salome, the widow of the man killed at my father's side in Louisbourg, was the center of the gathering's attention. It hardly seemed fair. Family, neighbors, and congregants from the Wolfville Baptist

Church clustered around her, insisting she eat and drink. Through it all, she sat stone-faced, shaking off their ministrations. I might as well have been a fly on the wall.

Without Father there to unite what passed as a family, Ma Salome ignored me and my brothers, speaking only to her own children. The dining room table was heavy with baked goods, but no one thought to offer me something to eat. I was irrelevant, perhaps problematic, the last thing on anybody's mind.

Outside, the crows were going mad.

I watched it all from the narrow wooden seat of my spinning wheel, turning wool into thread for our winter clothes, my only excuse for remaining in the room. My stomach growled like a restless animal. Nat was indignant, furious at being separated from the clusters of men who discussed revenge even before they had determined who had taken my father. He sidled over to where the officers congregated and joined their ranks, whispering about Indians, kidnapping, massacres, and bounties.

The men were organizing a search party. If Father had not returned by the following morning, they would set out first thing. "I'll go with you," Ezekiel declared, in defiance of Salome's insistence that his place was at her side. "I refuse to be left behind," he said, shaking off his mother's concern. How easily boys transform fear into fury. The memory of his own father, dead, didn't deter him at all.

If only I could muster such anger. But that would not have been ladylike, and, besides, I had no desire to join the search party. I did, however, want to be of use. I couldn't sit idly by while the menfolk plotted their next moves. And I was so hungry. I eyed the plate of cookies on the dining room table. If I took one, Salome would disapprove, saying they were for our guests. But then, I thought, Salome disapproved of almost everything I did: my table manners, my penchant for daydreaming, my love of the Samuel Richardson novel, *Pamela,* that Caroline had left behind. "Such foolish sensibility and suffering," Salome declared when she discovered me reading the book. I defended the story, insisting it portrayed paragons of virtue and correct behavior, but Salome replied, "We have the Bible for that."

Idling at my spinning wheel, I recalled this infuriating exchange, overcome by a swell of longing for my mother. My real mother, whose gentle understanding provided a bridge between me and my father. I clasped my locket and lifted it to my lips, only to realize that Grandmother Hardy, seated among the other women, was watching me with tears in her eyes. Grandfather Hardy handed me a dried apple ring as he headed across the room to a circle of men. "You've already lost your ma, poor thing," he said, "and now this business with your father…" Grandpa and Grandma Hardy never complained about Father's remarriage, but I knew they missed their daughter. No matter how hard Aunt Caroline tried to fill the void, they missed my mother as much as I did.

I glanced over at Salome. Seeing her bony fingers resting on her stomach, I remembered the shock of seeing the telltale bulge of her belly under her wet baptism garb. I recalled watching Father drape his jacket around her shoulders and turning away, only to see the boy crouching behind the blackberry bushes, watching them too. His furtive gaze. A fleeting sense that I had seen him somewhere before. As I spun my thread, still hungry, I remembered the boy's dark eyes. And, at that moment, it came back to me where I had seen the Indian boy before. The day I had been in the field collecting that sad first harvest. Before Aunt Caroline had gone to live with Grandpa and Grandma Hardy. Before Father had announced that he intended to marry Salome and informed us children that we would have a new mother. Before Salome moved into our house.

I could see his face clearly, the Indian boy who had wanted to be my friend. The one who fled from Father's musket as I watched but did not say a thing.

Was this the boy who had abducted my father?

William settled into the armchair at my side. "I can only take so much of this," he confided, as if we were conspirators. Trust William to see through the Baptists' smothering concern. In the room, we were the only people not carried away by our emotions.

"I think I know who abducted Father," I said under my breath, wanting no one else to hear. "Do you think the kidnapper was an Indian?"

"What makes you ask that?"

"I may have seen him here once before."

William looked up with surprise. "But Lucy, any information you have is vital. You must tell the officers what you saw."

Unfortunately, Ezekiel overheard us. "What?" His exclamation carried above the chatter of the crowd. "You saw him?"

I looked out the window, trying to avoid his question. Could I recall the boy's features? I feared I had spoken prematurely. As I gazed into the field, I saw two men on horseback approach the house. They tied up their horses outside our front door. Ezekiel conferred with them briefly before letting them in.

The officers strode into our living room with an air of importance, wearing the Crown's insignia on their jackets. They were older than my brothers, but younger than my father. When the taller man looked in my direction, I recognized him. A distant cousin of Father's from the Scott clan, he had spoken kindly to me on several occasions when the family gathered. I felt a warm blush climbing my neck and blossoming over my cheeks.

The other gentleman introduced himself to Ma Salome as Major Rogers. "Call me Samuel," he said, but his air of authority and erect posture said otherwise. He was clean-shaven, as if he had recently bathed. Captain Scott let the older man take charge and headed in our direction. William spoke first.

"Captain Scott, my sister here thinks she may have seen the perpetrator."

At his words, all eyes fixed on me. I inhaled, telling myself I must be brave.

"I saw a boy hiding behind a blackberry bush during the baptism. Muscular, with dark black hair that hung to his shoulders. He wore a leather breechcloth secured front and back by a strap around his waist." I took pains to describe the attire of the boy with as much detail as I could recall. "I remember wondering what he made of this baptism in the river," I said. "I've been told the Mi'kmaq are Catholics."

Both officers snorted in unison at my observation.

"I wondered what interest he had in my father."

"Why on earth didn't you say anything before now?" Ma Salome snapped. The Baptist women gathered at her side tsked, a chorus for her sharp tongue. Her real daughter, the younger Salome, stroked her mother's hand. All of them looked at me, their eyes accusing.

Why hadn't I said anything? They all asked, but I wasn't about to admit I had forgotten the boy altogether when Father emerged from the water, the fabric of his pants clinging to his long legs. Father's bare feet had fascinated me. It was no business of theirs that a fit of jealousy had swept over me as Father took Ma Salome's hand, beaming as if personally responsible for the woman's salvation. I had resented Salome when he had wrapped a woolen blanket around her, resented the joyful hymn with which the congregation had congratulated him.

Instead, I said, "I thought he looked familiar."

With that, I had their attention again. I told them the boy had watched it all, and I had watched him.

"What?" Major Rogers asked. His finger twitched as if seeking a trigger. I noticed this gesture and thought of the Indian boy, his hopeful face. Was this the same boy I had seen at the baptism? False witness, I knew, was a crime. How many Indians had I seen since arriving in this new land? How could I pretend to compare their features? Wasn't it possible that, as I watched the boy crouching on the side of the river, his presence had triggered the memory of another boy, the one with his game? Amid the congregation's chaos as they remounted their horses, could I really say I recognized him with any certainty?

I looked up at the officers again and said, "I'm not sure."

As the congregation left the beach, I had searched for the boy, scanning the bushes. With the sun lower in the sky, the shadows had lengthened. I couldn't find any trace. He had disappeared as quietly as he arrived.

With that admission, my moment in the limelight ended.

"I don't suppose this is of much use to you," William said, placing a supportive hand on my shoulders. The two officers turned away, murmuring. "Obviously," one said, "a savage is to blame."

A young boy, Indian or not, would have been no match for my father. Why had I said anything at all?

I regretted confiding in William. I should have kept the story to myself. Would my testimony condemn an innocent boy as decisively as the bullet Father aimed at his back? Salome would blame me one way or the other for

Father's disappearance. She would use this moment to further ruin my life.

A wave of despair swept over me. Captain Scott, noticing my crestfallen look, took my hand in his. "Thank you for your help. That was very brave of you." His hair was dirty blond with loose curls. His bushy mustache twitched as he spoke.

"Will you find my father?" I asked him.

"Don't you worry," he said. "We'll have the Indian situation under control soon. We'll find him."

His eyes were a sincere blue. When he crossed the room to speak to Ma Salome, I returned to my spinning wheel, happily chewing on a biscuit I had secreted from the table. When they found my father, I decided, I would bake Scott an apple pie. As a token of my gratitude.

I put all thoughts of the Indian boy out of my mind. It was foolish to think the boy who had asked me to play with him was capable of such a dastardly act. My father's fate was in these men's hands. I hummed to myself, tuning out the tumult that surrounded me.

● ● ●

Salome couldn't help but wonder if Parker was also praying. If he was thinking of her, left on her own once again.

Women, neighbors, and congregants took charge of the vigil, urging her to rest, to "be strong." She had no use for their foolish chatter, took no comfort in their consolation. Each day, they arrived clutching their prayer books. They spoke of Nathaniel's disappearance as a test of faith. Salome joined them in prayer, confessing her sins and asking for His forgiveness, but she preferred to pray alone. To seek the Lord's guidance without their interference.

On her knees among Nathaniel's new flock, she accepted the penance of providing an example of forbearance and humility. This was the duty of a pastor's wife. She bowed to His will. Obeyed His requirement for obedience. The quickening in her womb reminded her there was a new life inside her. If it were God's will, Nathaniel would soon return to his congregation. Or so she struggled to believe.

When at last the day's prayers ended, she waited for the visitors to leave. But Major Rogers asked if he might have a moment of her time. He dismissed the cluster of women who surrounded her with an officious nod of his head before pulling a footstool up to her armchair.

"Did you see him?" he asked.

Salome assumed he was inquiring about her husband's disappearance. The day had been long, and it was difficult to concentrate.

"I saw nothing," she said.

"Try a little harder," he urged. "We know this is a challenging time, but the most insignificant memories might prove useful to us now."

With a sigh, Salome made an effort. She remembered remounting her horse and heading away from the beach, wet and uncomfortable, humbled by the ceremony. As the congregation went up the path, a woman pulled up beside her. The woman was among those who now hovered over her, claiming her kitchen as their own. Another Planter wife and Baptist. Her name was Cornelia Eaton.

The encounter was uncomfortable.

"Dear Maggie," the stranger had said. "I recognized you the minute Nathaniel rode up, you on a pillion behind him."

Taken aback, Salome had not known how to respond. This stranger apparently did not know that poor Maggie was dead in her grave.

"I'm not...," she'd stuttered, not knowing what to say. Cornelia had mistaken her for a dead woman.

She knew she did not resemble Nathaniel's first wife, and yet this woman believed they went way back. Maggie and her, that is. She started right in on how their families had sailed to Nova Scotia together on the Charming Molly. "You must remember me," she said. "I think of you as a sister."

As she recounted this conversation, the men shifted restlessly, wanting to hear only about the kidnapping. Salome tried to remember the last time she had seen her husband.

"Nathaniel disappeared into the crowd of parishioners," she told her interrogators. There, that was all they needed to know. That the Baptists had accepted him as one of their own. Patted him on the back as they rode past her, welcoming him into their community. No need to add that he could have bailed her out, rescuing her from Cornelia and introducing her as his second wife. That he'd left her to fend for herself.

The woman had gone on and on.

"I will never forget how sick you were on the journey. Had anyone asked me, I would have told them you were a poor candidate to make it through the first winter, you with your lacy petticoats and girlish curls."

Salome had suffered the woman's foolishness. Salome, a righteous woman, didn't own a lacy petticoat and her bobbed brown hair was straight and unadorned. She had no desire to hear anything more about Nathaniel's first wife. Enough. She tried to cut the woman off. "I'm not—"

But Eaton spoke right over her. "Look at you now, a prosperous matron not afraid to ride forty miles across the Gaspereaux Valley to receive your baptism by immersion. And expecting another child, I see. How many is that now?"

Then, as now, Salome closed her mouth, irritated by the woman's audacity. Certainly, every member of this new congregation knew her story. These officers, too, undoubtedly understood her circumstances.

Nathaniel had been raising three children on his own when they met. Maggie had borne him four, but only three survived. The poor thing died miscarrying the fifth. Salome had two children by her first husband, Ezekiel Cleveland, bless his soul, who had died during the Siege of Louisbourg, right there at Parker's side. It was to join their two families that Nathaniel and she had wed. The one in her belly would be the sixth child in their conjoined family. There were many answers she could have given to the stranger's unwitting question, but she didn't owe her an explanation.

"Five children at home. Lord willing, this'll be the sixth."

Salome looked over at Eaton gossiping with the church ladies. What a simple woman! Did this intrusive stranger not wonder why the others called her by the name of Salome? Did she not notice that her hair was as straight as sticks? Did she not see then—does she not see now—that she did not resemble the woman who preceded her?

And in a dark corner of her anger, she blamed Parker, the gallant soldier who had married her to fulfill an obligation to a fellow soldier. In agreeing to a loveless marriage, she had become nothing more than a generic wife and mother living in the shadow of a man who now called her his wife. A man who had disappeared into thin air, leaving her in a strange house, responsible for children she did not love. Among strangers who thought they knew her when they did not know her at all.

Was it only weeks before that she had confided in Nathaniel she might be with child? That they had exalted at this confirmation of the family they had committed to join, to raise in righteousness?

She steadied herself, closed her eyes, and inhaled deeply, resolved to face whatever challenges the Lord placed before her, no matter how hard, how distasteful.

To her relief, at that moment, Ezekiel intervened. After he pointed out his mother's exhaustion, the officer said they had no further questions. Ezekiel offered to escort them out to their waiting horses. Salome watched her son leave, knowing that despite her opposition, he was determined to join the search party for his missing stepfather.

Would this day never end?

"God, give me strength," she prayed, steeling herself to face the well-meaning women who soon surrounded her once more.

CHAPTER SEVEN

In the Wigwam

Kejimkujik, June 1761

Night and day, his captive prayed. Avoiding Meuse's prying eyes, he chanted the same words over and over: "Our Father, who art in heaven…" Each prayer ended with "amen." Meuse didn't need to understand the foreign words to know what the man was saying. Parker was asking for something, and his pleas were not directed at his captor. The man bowed his head even though he could not tent his bound hands in prayer. With each amen, his anger seemed to diminish. His pursed lips relaxed. He spoke only to his god, his singsong voice low and intimate. His eyes were closed, blind to his surroundings.

Meuse, too, tried to pray. He chanted the catechism he had learned from Father Le Loutre. When this did not comfort him, he offered gifts to the Great Spirit as his Elders had taught him, hoping to disperse the negative energy filling the dark and malodorous wigwam. As the sun set and then rose again, it became harder and harder to ignore the stink of the man's unclean body. Even tobacco smoke no longer covered the smell.

Leaves rustled in the uninhabited woods outside the wigwam's flap. The incessant whisper of Parker praying spooked Meuse. The distant howl of coyotes echoed through his troubled dreams. Each night, the sky, which had been lit by the full moon the night they arrived, became a little darker. By the end of the first week, its light had been diminished by half.

Meuse began to look forward to daybreak, when he could leave the wigwam behind to catch fish in the nearby stream. The winter's snows were long gone. Where once a mighty river roared on its way to the sea, now a lazy stream meandered over gleaming rocks covered with moss. The salmon had disappeared. The sun was high in the sky when Meuse spotted a brook trout as it trolled the stream's bottom. How different the tribe's winter camp looked now that summer had blossomed! A thick green canopy sheltered him from the blazing sun. Squirrels and chipmunks chittered in the long grasses, but the absence of his family populated the forest only with ghosts and memories where once his mother had greeted him with a bright and loving smile.

At first, Meuse snared only enough fish to feed himself. But one morning, waking to the angry growl of the Baptist's belly, he heard his Grandfather speaking as clearly as the chickadees singing in the nearby trees. The old man said, "The blackberry bushes are heavy with ripe berries. Who are you to deny any man the earth's bounty?" Another day passed, and his captive continued to pray night after night. He gave Parker a bowl to use for his waste, telling himself it was simply a matter of ridding the wigwam of the stink that sickened them both. Twice a day, he emptied the basin into the hole where he buried his own feces. Then, watching Parker lick his chapped lips until they appeared shredded and bloody, he offered him a sip of water, followed by a cup of tea on a cool night. His grandfather's words reminded him that his Elders would judge his reputation as an honorable man by his treatment of his enemy.

He had never considered what he would do after taking his captive. The reports of British scalpings and the bounties offered for Indian heads had emboldened him, but he had little experience to guide him. Yes, *smáknisks* like his father had killed the enemy in battle. He recalled his

Elders' stories, their delighted cackle as they recounted the Mi'kmaq attack on the sawmills near the South Blockhouse where they had killed three British. The familiar tall tales of revenge and bravery. When his resolve flagged, he summoned up the picture of Parker pointing his firestick. But this angry vision was soon replaced by the everyday reality of the power-less man cowering in the darkness of the wigwam, the downcast eyes, the continual prayers ending with the familiar *amen*. The vindication he had hoped to experience from his act of vengeance faded.

Cruelty did not come easily to him. He missed his grandmother and grandfather and the smell of warm bannocks roasting over an open fire. A fatherless boy raised by his tribe, he had never been alone before. He missed Francis and the competition of their games. He missed his Elders and their stories of the past and future. Their wisdom and humor. No wonder his grandfather had spoken to him through the chickadee's song. The wigwam had become a prison that held them both, captive and captor. Each day, he left for the woods, singing a mournful song, oblivious to the daybreak choir in the canopy. He missed his mother's steady hand, the softness of her gaze. As he fished, he longed for the wisdom of his uncle's patient lessons.

Not only did he fear his prisoner's death, but he lamented himself as a dead man.

By now, the chief, chosen by his peers from the other six tribal dis-tricts as Grand Chief, would undoubtedly have called a meeting to dis-cuss the tribe's response to the missing white man. Meuse knew his fate rested in their hands.

Lessons he had learned from the Elders came back to him. "Custom," they had told him, "requires that if a warrior takes a woman or child as a prisoner, they must be adopted into the community or set free. A man should be turned over to do chores normally done by women and chil-dren." Now he had become all these things: a prisoner doing women's work, a captive, a captor.

Worse yet, he knew that to preserve honor, a warrior often chose death, both for the prisoner and the executioner. His father had been revered, but he had also died.

What had he been thinking? The tribe had congratulated Francis when he killed the bull moose. The Elders had danced and feasted to celebrate his bravery. But Meuse was alone in the woods with a man whose spirit was as strong as his own. A religious man. A father and a husband to a woman ripe with child.

Meuse woke when the sky was still dark. The reassurance of that first night's smudging had evaporated. Now when he looked into Parker's eyes, he saw his own desperation. He was haunted not by the Christian god Father Le Loutre exalted, not by the *amen* that he understood, but by the stories his Elders told over many a fire: legends of the first sight of the white men arriving in a big canoe; of Glooscap, the master, lying prone on his back, head to the rising Sun, feet to the setting of the Sun, left hand to the South and right hand to the North. His captive's god might have been a father to them all, and Saint Ann the grandmother of Jesus Christ, but the Great Chief was coexistent with all Creation, and Nogami, the Grandmother, owed her existence to the dew on the rock. None of these stories excused his actions. Nor did they offer him guidance on how to move forward.

What had he done? As Parker prayed, Meuse looked to the heavens for guidance but found no answers.

One morning, a skinny mutt, left behind in the flurry of his family's annual retreat, joined him at the fishing hole. His fur was black and matted, but his baleful eyes were wet with sympathy. Meuse watched as the dog lapped the fresh water. Noting the extruding bones of the dog's rib cage, Meuse caught an extra fish that day for his new companion.

"Here, boy," he whispered to the wary animal, offering him tiny tidbits from his catch.

The dog licked his extended hand and followed him back to the wigwam. That night, the matted mutt slept outside the flap of the shelter, breathing in the fresh air, his stomach full and his loyalty established. Meuse too slept at last, his dreams full of animals who came to his rescue, keeping him warm and forgiving him his human frailty. A red fox with his grandfather's face told him he would arrive soon to show him the way home. A fluffy skunk with his mother's kind eyes advised him to be patient. He woke to the mutt pawing the dirt outside the wigwam, trying to find a way in. He knew that further trials awaited him, but at least now he was not alone.

•••

The dog outside yipped, chasing a rabbit in his dreams. The Indian boy sighed at the sharp sound and curled into a ball. How young he seemed as he slept. How foolish Parker felt to be beholden to him.

Once again, he could not sleep. Perhaps because he was faint with hunger despite the meager meals the boy now spooned into his mouth. Perhaps because, as the result of darkness and immobility, his body no longer obeyed him. Like a petulant child, it insisted on being heard. It whined and whimpered like an infant fussing for its mother. It was restless, stiff, and ornery.

They were on his mind tonight, the women he had left behind.

Salome, who he had last heard calling from a trail on the side of the Gaspereaux River. Sometimes he thought he heard her voice in the distance, but then he thought, *That sweet song I hear is Maggie, my first love.* A song as sweet as the summer breeze that rippled the curtain of animal skin. A trill, brave and tender. In it, he heard the woman who had followed him to Nova Scotia, who had trusted him and never questioned his judgment. Maggie, the mother of the children who resembled him. Lucy, who had yet to forgive him for letting her mother die. Salome, proud and strong, tough enough to survive in this hard land.

Maggie had been a delicate plant whose bloom was short-lived but took his breath away. The vision of Maggie sustained him now, comforting him in his despair. It was for Maggie he prayed, and to whom he would joyfully return if this sad saga ended in his demise.

He reassured himself: Salome would never be alone. Soon after she arrived in Annapolis with the parents of her first husband, Ezekiel Cleveland, he had reached out to her, fulfilling his promise to the soldier who had died at his side during the battle of Louisbourg. The Clevelands had claimed a house over the ridge. The widow Salome had moved in with them, allowing her stern mother to take charge of Ezekiel Jr. and young Salome.

Maggie and Parker lived not far away from the Cleveland family, having staked their claim on Parker Mountain, a beautiful piece of prop-erty on the valley side of the ridge. Even in the dark shadows of his wig-wam prison, he could picture it: the fertile farmland stretching down the side of the low mountain, plowed and planted all the way to the bay, where mudflats were thick with mussels. On the other side of the mountain, the property quickly descended to the Bay of Fundy, a ready source of summer seafood. Lush and rugged, if still untamed. Dark woods where Indians lurked. Rocky beaches with rosy-hued sunsets and morning fog that lifted to reveal sunshine dancing on the water.

When they first arrived in Nova Scotia, Maggie had loved to watch the sun set. She had insisted on walking over the mountaintop every evening, Lucy holding her hand. The boys frolicked by their side. With each climb up the mountain, Maggie and Nathaniel had made plans for their future. Until she took to bed at the end of her pregnancy, she accompanied him to church every Sunday and gave thanks for their good fortune. Even when bedridden, she insisted she was not afraid. Lucy hovered at her side, her pink brow as wrinkled as an old lady, but Maggie laughed off the girl's concern, crocheting blankets for the new baby as the days grew shorter and shorter.

He realized now, he had never told her how much he loved her.

He had seen men die in battle. He had crossed stormy seas and faced down Indians on his land, but when Maggie died, he had thought he could not go on. Fortunately, Caroline took the children in hand while he grieved for his sweet wife, burying her in Nictaux in a plot big enough for the whole family. During those dark nights, he prayed as he had never prayed before, seeking redemption for his thoughtlessness. Several pews behind him, Salome sat stoically, silent in her grief. When spring arrived, the time for grieving had passed. He picked up his trowel and insisted his sons join him in planting the year's crops. They plowed and seeded the corn, beans, and squash. When Caroline announced she would be moving into her parents' house, Parker reached out to Salome, telling her of his promise to Ezekiel. Now it was Salome or her mother who called the children to dinner. Not only his own, her two children too. Parker's stepchildren jumped with fear when their stern grandmother summoned them. They had inherited her cold black eyes and imperious manner and sat at his table like distrustful invaders invited to a feast.

Now, there were eleven at the nightly gathering. Salome never flinched when he mentioned Maggie, but neither did she offer sympathy. When she spoke of her own departed husband, it was with respect but never passion. Salome's parents, who had insisted that their widowed daughter joined them when they emigrated to Nova Scotia, approved of the match and happily stepped in to fill the void created by Caroline's departure. By the end of that first year, Nathaniel and Salome joined the two households on Parker Mountain. Soon another child was on the way, and the house was filled with children's voices and the aroma of baked goods and roasting chicken. All that remained of the dark winter of despair was Parker's habit of prayer. Salome, sensing his need, joined him in seeking a parish whose devotion equaled his. All week long, he planted and worked the soil with his fellow colonists to establish a thriving community. On Sundays, the brood settled into a pew behind him. They traveled from church to church, giving thanks to God for all he had provided.

From its beginning, Salome bore her pregnancy effortlessly. Their family flourished. When they discovered the Baptist Church in Wolfville, Parker felt his life was complete, every physical, psychological, and spiritual need fulfilled. Was it so long ago that he had been baptized with Salome at his side? It seemed like another life, that sunny morning when the minister held his head under the water at the ocean's edge and announced he had been born again in His name.

Now he lay on the dirt floor of the wigwam, recalling that moment. The cold water, the crisp breeze, the goose pimples. The hallelujahs of the crowd on the beach. Was Maggie watching, even then? If he joined her now, would she forgive him? Forgive him his confidence, his pride? Forgive his fickle nature? He never meant to desert her.

Watching the young Indian sleeping like a tot, he again resorted to prayer. Whatever my crime, he prayed, forgive me. Loosen my shackles; let me return to my family. And if that is not your plan, let me lay in the Nictaux cemetery beside my beloved Maggie.

The dog whimpered, this time a sad and lonely yelp. The boy stirred and woke up. Parker turned his head away.

For seven nights, they had been locked in a battle he did not understand. Tonight, he turned away. He did not want his captor to see his tears. The sight of such weakness would only empower him.

•••

By the second week in the wigwam, Meuse had settled into a routine that soothed him.

First thing in the morning, he urinated on the trunk of a nearby hemlock and then disposed of Parker's waste in a hole far enough from their camp that the smell did not follow him. Then, as the chickadees and blue jays serenaded the forest, he headed to the stream for fresh water, accompanied by the mutt, whom he now called by the Mi'kmaq word for friend, *Oqoti*. With an enthusiastic stretch, the dog lowered his snout to the ground while raising his haunches high and lapping at the lazy stream. Meuse did the same, cupping his hands and swallowing the ice-cold water. When sated, he filled a tightly woven basket with water for Parker. On the way back to the wigwam, he collected ripe berries. Each day there were more, and the responsibility of caring for his captive seemed less onerous.

On his return, Meuse threw open the wigwam flap to let in the crisp morning air. The summer sun was strong, and a beam of light illuminated the gloomy interior of the shelter. Waking, Parker blinked. Meuse held the basket of fresh water up to his captive's mouth, and the man drank, leaning forward to shift his weight off his inflamed wrists. His wrists were raw, white only where the ties held his hands together, angry red where the blood could not flow. Parker, who at first flinched with pain as he shifted to move his arms, now held out his hands like dead things. He could not move his fingers. They hung there, useless and without sensation.

Meuse pulled his knife out of its leather sheath. He cut the rope that tied Parker's wrists. In silence, Parker rubbed his hands together. He shifted his bound ankles, eyeing the tethers that limited his mobility.

Meuse chewed thoughtfully on his berries. When only a few remained, he offered Parker a small fistful. Parker shook his head, holding up his swollen hands once more, his fingers useless, numb, and bloodless. He opened and closed his fingers, wincing each time he tried to bend them. When the digits began to pink up, and his face no longer contorted with pain, Meuse again offered him the fistful of berries. This time, Parker answered. "Thank you."

With his hands free, he steepled his fingers and chanted: "Our Father…"

Meuse had become accustomed to—had even taken comfort from—these words that Parker had recited over and over the past week, day and night. In the deep darkness of despair and the hopeful glimmers of early morning light, Meuse recognized the rhythm from the prayer he had learned in the French mission. Silently, he moved his lips in concert with his captive, reassured by their predictability. Because he knew the prayer in French, the English words were no longer gibberish. He knew what Parker was saying when he recited, "Forgive us our trespasses as we forgive those…"

When Parker arrived at *amen*, Meuse once again offered him the fistful of berries. "Eat," he said. This time, the man accepted. He sighed when the sweetness of the ripe berries burst on his tongue. The juice from the berries stained his white lips red, a startling contrast to his pasty skin. Bruised blue circles beneath his eyes betrayed his exhaustion. His face resembled the masks worn by the Elders during their sacred circles. Masks representing revered ancestors who returned to this earth to share precious words of wisdom. Like the voices of these spirits, Parker's presence at that moment seemed unworldly.

"Forgive us our trespasses." On this eighth day of Parker's captivity, the two men recited these words together.

Overcome by the sentiment, Meuse loosened the remaining ties on the man's ankles. He first checked to be sure that the ropes still restricted his captive's movement and prevented his escape. Then he whistled for Oqoti. The dog's tail slapped the wigwam's skins in eager anticipation. Today he would check the traps. If he was lucky, there would be meat for their evening meal.

CHAPTER EIGHT

The Vigil

Parker Mountain

The Baptists were not without their merits. They fed our family well. The creaminess of their biscuits was second only to the sweetness of their pies.

I had taken to hiding out in the keeping room whenever I could. The thick walls made the warm room the only place in the house where the Baptists' prayers could not reach me. I nibbled at a slice of the pumpkin pie I had put aside for William for lunch. I planned to tell him I was considering asking Caroline if I could go live with her at Grandpa Hardy's house. At least until Father returned. But before William came in from the fields, I heard the familiar *tap tap* on the keeping room door, followed by Captain Scott's pleasant tenor. I brushed the crumbs from my apron.

The Baptists were praying in the parlor, as they had every day since Father's disappearance. Ma Salome spent hours on her knees, her narrow lips pursed in dogged propriety. Salome Jr. knelt beside her, a devoted acolyte, adjusting her cushions and offering fresh tea on the hour.

But Captain Scott was not a praying man. During his daily check-ins, we had ample opportunity to chat while the Baptists prayed. Today, he asked me why I called Salome by her Christian name.

I gave him an earful.

"When Grandfather and I visited the clockmaker, he said Father had remarried well. To 'old stock from New England' and 'tolerably pure.'" I imitated the old man's vernacular, which I'd found quite amusing. "He said the people here in Annapolis are near about one-half applesauce and the other half molasses, except to the east where there is a cross of the Scotch." Scott laughed, which pleased me no end.

"I am supposed to call Salome 'Mother,' but I've settled on 'Ma Salome' for now. Being a widow, the clockmaker says she found herself an applesauce man. That's where my father came into the picture. He was the apple for her sauce. A widower with three children and a household to run, ripe for the picking."

Scott belly-laughed at my description of my father's recent marriage. He seemed a steady sort, lacking the self-importance of so many of the men in this neck of the woods, even if he wore a uniform.

"Pa buried my real ma in the Nictaux cemetery. He left my brothers and me at home, motherless, under the charge of a stern nursemaid who arrived too late to care for the baby, who died the morning of Ma's funeral." I told him the nursemaid offered no solace, instead instructing me to box up the baby's things and spare Pa the heartache.

Knowing I had probably gone on too long, I stopped there. Just in time, because the Baptists stopped praying, ready for lunch. I offered him the piece of pie I had set aside for William, hoping he did not notice the corner I had nibbled off.

What I had wanted to say was this: *At least I am alive, as I hope and pray my Father is.*

Molly, the baby that died, would have been my actual sister, not step. I thought about that sometimes, that I should have had my actual flesh and blood in the bed beside me. Instead, I shared a room with Salome Jr., with her eyes as cold as flint and a haughtiness that she shared with her full-blooded brother, Ezekiel. If Salome's new baby turned out to be a girl, she, too, would share our bedchamber. But she wouldn't be my actual sister, "step" being a qualifier I took seriously. To do so otherwise would be to call Salome my mother, and that I refused to do.

Brother-wise, I told him, I have two real ones, nearly men now and ornery as hell. And then there is Ezekiel, who arrived with the Salomes and wants nothing to do with any of us.

Scott said he knew Ezekiel and thought he was a perfectly good young man.

"When my father announced his intention to remarry, he told us, '*five children at the dinner table and, God willing, many more to come.*' In my father's eyes, we are all the same."

At that, I stopped. Father was not here, and Salome ruled the roost in his absence. Better I not complain about Salome Jr., who never left her mother's side. But certainly, he could see it for himself. When Major Rogers, a graying self-important chunk of a man, begged his pardon and asked for Salome's attention, Salome Jr. clung to her mother's skirts, refusing to let the major push her aside. Even in his presence, she was her mother's spy.

Captain Scott finished his pie. "Mighty good," he said.

"Well," I answered, "the Baptists are good for something." He chuckled and tapped my chin with his knuckle. When William arrived for lunch, I told him all the pie had already been eaten.

I might have been mistaken, but I was almost certain Captain Scott winked at me before shutting the door as he left. Only our cobbled-together family remained, on our own for dinner. Salome warmed some stew on the hearth and instructed me to set the table. The boys discussed the latest updates from the search party as we girls waited on them, happy to have things somewhat returned to normal.

Ever since the Baptists asked Father to be their minister, Salome had prayed endlessly before every meal, listing all the things we have to be thankful for: the corn growing in the field, the fat cow in the yard, the Lord's blessing on our growing family. I would have thought she could skip all that now, given how much we had not to be grateful for—Father's disappearance, the trail cold as winter snow—but no such luck. As our stomachs growled, Salome went on and on. The steaming platters of food grew colder and colder.

When Salome finally said *amen*, William echoed, "Thank you, Lord," by which I was sure he meant *Thank the Lord we can eat now*, not *Thank you Lord for the food on our table*. William had grown six inches since we arrived in Nova Scotia, and he was hungry as a coyote in winter, even in this time of distress. When I ladled the stew into serving dishes in the kitchen, he hung over me like a predator, sampling each dish. "Consider me the taster," he said, "willing to sacrifice my life for your safety." I regretted having given away his pie.

William once told me that as soon as he was eighteen, he intended to slam the door behind him and pursue a life of meditation and scholarship. I hoped the baby would be more like my brother than his mother. But given my luck, he would be colicky, born with a sour look on his face, and fuss all day long.

Even when exercising Christian restraint, a family of seven can empty a heaping bowl in the twinkling of an eye. I had my hands full running in and out of the kitchen, refilling serving bowls. All the while, Ma Salome sat at the opposite end of the table monitoring us all. 'Old stock,' the clockmaker called her. In my book, the woman was a snow queen. When she enchanted my father, she sentenced me to a lifetime of servitude.

But today, maybe for once, that was a good thing. I was so busy doing my stepmother's bidding that for a moment I forgot my dear father was gone and who knows where. But just in case, before I crawled into bed, I asked the dear Lord for his forgiveness.

• • •

Nathaniel, Salome woke up thinking, *where have you gone?*

Another morning alone. She woke in Parker's house, surrounded by his children, and he was not here to make her feel at home. She thanked God that her precious Sally—whom Lucy insisted on calling Salome Jr.—was there at her side, a loyal and faithful helper to help her dress and survive another day. She had already lost one husband to the war between Britain and France. Now, she faced the possibility that she might lose another to the conflict between the colonists and the local Indians.

After the first wave of nausea receded, she pulled herself out of bed. Her breasts were swollen and sore. Sally helped her into her dress. Downstairs, the children quarreled as they waited for their breakfast. She could hear Lucy's grating voice above the others, lording her familiarity with the house. "We never eat raisins," she said.

Her new stepdaughter was a handful, insisting the porridge be made the way her mother had always made it.

Another wave of nausea swept over her as she descended the stairs with Sally leading the way. In the days since Nathaniel's disappearance, the baby had made its presence known. A shifting here, a gentle poke there, a discomfort not unlike gas pains. She rubbed a knot out of her belly.

The midwife, Caroline, assured her the baby was healthy, kicking, and growing as expected. Caroline had not complained when Salome took her place in Parker's household after their hasty marriage and had agreed to monitor her pregnancy. She had moved in with her parents, who were still mourning Maggie's loss. Salome knew that Caroline, as one of the few midwives in the valley, had skills that were highly in demand. But Salome, knowing that Maggie had died in her sister's care, also found her reassurances far from comforting.

She preferred the daily visit from Major Rogers and Captain Scott, who spoke with confidence and authority. They stopped by every morning after breakfast to update her on the progress of their search.

"Have you put on the teakettle?" she asked Sally once she had taken charge of the cook stove.

"Lucy did it," Sally said, glaring at her stepsister.

"Well then, perhaps you can set out some biscuits. The officers will be here any minute now." She put an apron on over her long, brown house dress.

By mid-morning, Major Rogers had settled on a chair, balancing his cup of tea on his knee. He assured her they had the Indian situation under control, describing the recent early morning raid on a suspect band of Indians squatting on private property close to Parker Mountain. "We have dispersed the natives. They will not bother us again."

"But my husband… Has there been any progress in locating him?"

"We believe a local Indian abducted your husband. By negotiating treaties with the weakened tribe, we will be in a powerful position to secure your husband's release." For just this purpose, he told her, a half-dozen heathen children were being detained in the jail in Annapolis.

He did not speak down to her, which she appreciated. Not all men credited her with the intelligence to understand their worldly dealings, although she had been fortunate enough to have married two who took pride in her ability to read and write. She had been a worthy partner to both. Major Rogers continued, explaining the current approach to securing British supremacy. To achieve this goal, Governor Lawrence had announced the aim of reducing the Indian population. Already, he had banned native fishing activities, freeing the local waters for commercial fishing and denying the Indians a ready source of food and commerce. The provincial government continued to relocate the remaining Acadians, eliminating their support of a resurgence by the French. These actions would, he told her, ready Nova Scotia once and for all for the influx of settlers arriving from the American colonies and other Christian communities.

Salome found little solace in Rogers's proposal, which did not bring her husband back. When she did not reply, Captain Scott reported that the search party had found no trace of her husband and had extended its search further up into the Annapolis Valley. They had found no items of his clothing. Nor, God forbid, his scalp or lifeless body. He delivered this enthusiastically, as if it were good news, but he seemed to direct his comments at Lucy, who had settled at her spinning wheel but had not begun spinning. The girl gasped at Scott's ill-chosen words, and he quickly assured her that any day now he was certain they would locate her father.

Salome suspected her stepdaughter had a crush on Scott, as she had been unusually attentive to her appearance, brushing her hair and cleaning her face until it shone. Although the captain was ten years her senior, at least in his presence she was less rebellious in her actions, more refined. Salome would have hated for the officers to witness one of her stepdaughter's willful tantrums. Sally complained constantly about her stepsister, and Salome often had to bribe her daughter to take a carriage ride with

Lucy. Sally said that while William and Nat delighted in their sister's spunk, Lucy's outspoken declarations embarrassed her, especially in front of members of Parker's future congregation. Caroline and Lucy shared a streak of independence, which continued to annoy Salome. When the pompous minister from Wolfville asked Caroline if Grandfather Hardy had accepted God's will after Maggie's tragic death, she had complained in Salome's presence that the Baptists treated "man as a machine to be worked on." Lucy agreed, saying no religion could reconcile her to the tragedy of losing her dear mother.

But Salome doubted the gallant captain believed his own words. And she flinched at the audacity of the man to say such things in front of her daughter. Despair and negativity would poison the child, as well as the one she carried.

In Salome's opinion, Lucy could benefit from some hard work. But without Nathaniel's support, she didn't have the time or the will to take up the task. At least the religious community surrounded her during this bleak time, and, God willing, their righteousness would wear off on the willful child.

"Girls," she said, reaching out a hand to Sally, who hovered at the side of the men, prepared to clear the plates. "You mustn't allow such thoughts to preoccupy you." Then she asked the children to kneel beside her and join her in a prayer for guidance from the Lord.

"Let the governor's actions succeed," she prayed.

Sally prayed for her mother's health and happiness.

Lucy prayed that her father's captors treated him kindly.

"Now off with you," Salome said. "The day's chores need to be done."

When the girls left her side, she added a private prayer of her own. *I have made so many sacrifices. Please, Lord,* she said, *let this be the last.*

Just then, Mrs. Eaton knocked on the front door with a gaggle of Baptists behind her. Since Nathaniel's baptism, they had claimed him as their pastor and spoke of his disappearance as a test of their faith. Salome stood, adjusted her apron, and steeled herself for the onslaught. As they opened their prayer books, she wondered whether they would have any use for her if Parker never returned.

God is looking down on us, she thought. *He took Nathaniel from me; He is judging my commitment, my trust in His everlasting love.* On her knees among Nathaniel's new flock, she resigned herself to the responsibility of providing an example of obedience and humility. Of resignation to His will. The quickening in her womb reminded her, even now, that there was a new life inside her. If it were God's will, Nathaniel would soon return to his congregation.

• • •

Today, when Captain Scott arrived, he looked right past the praying Baptists and caught my eye. I couldn't have been more thrilled.

"I have some news for you, Lucy," he said.

Three weeks had now passed since Father disappeared, and even the Baptists were giving up hope. "The Lord's will be done," they said when they departed in the afternoon. Major Rogers and Ezekiel were as tight as thieves, bossing all the men around, assigning them to daily search parties that continued to return empty-handed. Ma Salome remained stoic through it all, having mastered the role of the grieving widow. Too easily, I thought. Sometimes I felt as if Captain Scott and I were the only ones who hadn't given up hope.

Caroline hardly ever visited anymore; she was always busy helping Grandma Hardy or birthing another baby. If the British had not yet recruited enough Planters, it seems the New Englanders were busy reproducing fast enough that they would finish the job themselves. As usual, I asked Captain Scott to join me in the keeping room for a fresh piece of pie. The donations of food had slowed down, but I had taken it upon myself to spot freshly baked goods when they arrived and squirrel them away in a cabinet in the keeping room, where we could enjoy them away from Salome's appraising eye.

Captain Scott accepted my invitation and followed me into the keeping room. Major Rogers and Ezekiel cornered William and Nat to share urgent news from Governor Belcher, the man who had replaced Governor Lawrence when the provincial government moved to Halifax. Rogers rolled off the new governor's title (President of His Majesty's Council and Commander in Chief of the Province) with such relish that I was certain he thought just by saying it he gained importance. Today, Rogers's expression was dramatic and dark, the long hairs of his eyebrows shading his dark eyes like errant storm clouds. The news he delivered was obviously not to his liking.

Captain Scott, in contrast, seemed undisturbed.

I cut him a large slice of pie. Scott smacked his lips in anticipation. "Did you bake this yourself?"

I was tempted to lie but behaved myself.

"No, it was a gift from a neighbor," I admitted. "But I set it aside for you." I blushed, knowing the admission was brazen, but Scott accepted it with a grateful nod.

"Mighty tasty," he said.

And then he relayed the latest news. In June, Governor Belcher held a "Burying the Hatchet Ceremony" at his farm in Halifax.

"Hatchet?" I asked, wondering what the forest implement had to do with my father's disappearance.

"A peace-making ceremony," he said, "between the government and the Indian chiefs." The governor promised the chiefs English protection and liberty, and the chiefs agreed to fidelity and obedience to King George in exchange.

"Did they really bury a hatchet?"

"They actually did."

"So, if the Indians abducted my father..."

"Which we are certain they did."

"Does this mean he will come home now?" I hadn't felt so hopeful in days.

Scott took another bite of his pie. He had to wipe his mouth with a napkin before proceeding.

"Unfortunately, the local Indians are no longer in the area, so we do not know where he might be." He looked up as if deciding how much to tell me. "The Port Royal Indians fled after the skirmish we had the day after your father disappeared."

So much for hope.

The skirmish, he said. A bit of an understatement, if you ask me. Captain Scott's evasion disappointed me. Even as the Baptists prayed for Father's safe return, Major Rogers boasted of their raid on the Indian camp. William said they had divvied up the day's bounty as if conducting an awards assembly. Major Rogers touted the success of the raid, saying it guaranteed the end of the annual migration of Indians to their traditional summer fishing grounds near Annapolis.

"But if a local Indian abducted my father," I said to Scott, "certainly the search parties would have uncovered some clues in the camp the tribe left behind."

Scott sighed. "Even though our raid was successful, we believe some of the Indians escaped. The natives know this island better than any of us. Lord knows where the abductor is hiding."

Our raid, he had said, if not with pride, then with matter-of-fact objectivity. I was taken aback. He was, of course, only second in command, but he admitted he had been there at Major Rogers's side. The significance of his role was only now dawning on me. The men had not only chased the Indians away, but they had also massacred them as they fled. Not only the men of the tribe, but the women and children who slept at their sides. The bounty they bragged about was blood money.

I remembered Father's words when he had returned to Massachusetts from the battle at Louisbourg. "That day was the last I will ever wear a soldier's uniform." I could see him still, how he had held my mother close to him, promising he would never go to war again.

Despite the boyish hue of Scott's complexion and his charming smile, this man, who flirted with me so effortlessly, spoke of murder without batting an eye. Apparently, unlike my father, watching others die hadn't bothered him at all.

I didn't offer him another piece of pie. I had trouble swallowing my own.

"But now that this treaty is signed, won't the Indians return?"

Scott licked the last of the crumbs off the delicate plate. "Not likely," he said. "Besides, the government in Halifax is already considering rescinding the treaty in its entirety. They feel it encourages the pretensions of these Indians to claim land within the province. This, of course, remains unacceptable."

"But if the Indians don't return, how will you know where to find them?" I asked, giving up all hope that Scott was the key to Father's rescue. "How will you know where to look for my father?"

Instead of answering, Scott studied his napkin. Once he had thoroughly wiped his mouth, he handed me the dirty linen and excused himself to rejoin the others.

I rinsed off the plate with a sinking feeling in my stomach. Captain Scott seemed nice enough—he was certainly the best of them—but these men and their treaties were not to be trusted. They boasted one moment of the slaughter of an entire village, and then they buried the hatchet only to dig it right back up again.

CHAPTER NINE

Kejimkujik

Oqoti guarded the wigwam with diligence. If any animal passed while cruising the night—bear, deer, or moose—the mutt barked until the predator turned heel, never ceding his post. The quarreling crows kept their distance, perching in the highest branches of the pine trees before starting their daily wrangling. The mutt was a loyal companion and happily accepted whatever scraps Meuse could spare, although they were few, and he remained skinny and hungry. Meuse could see that even Parker had grown fond of the dog, almost smiling when the mutt's twitching muzzle slipped under the wigwam's flap, his brown eyes beseeching them to let him in from the wet and cold.

With each day that passed, Parker's countenance changed. He no longer regarded Meuse with unbridled suspicion. When Meuse offered him food, he ate. When Meuse exchanged the bowl in which he pissed and shat, he thanked him. When his clothes reeked, he accepted Meuse's offer of a leather breechcloth, which he now wore as if it were his own. Still, Meuse took great care to secure his captive whenever he left the tent. Parker continued to pray morning and night, but now, when Meuse returned from his foraging, the white man waited for him before getting on his knees. He had mastered the maneuver despite the difficulties presented by his shackled ankles. He'd roll to one side and bend his knees before pushing to the other side to rise. When he was upright, they recited the Lord's prayer in unison. Where at first Meuse had only formed the English words with his lips, now he vocalized the soft vowels and strange diphthongs. He whispered the lines under his breath, thinking *if only Francis could see me now.* Parker's closed eyes didn't acknowledge his participation, but after they finished and he had rolled to his side to sleep, he no longer turned away from Meuse in the darkness of his corner. The presence of Oqoti, the sentry at the door, was an added safeguard. If the man were to try to escape, Oqoti would alert Meuse at once.

But tonight, Oqoti was restless at his post. He howled when a clap of thunder woke Meuse just as he was drifting off to sleep, thinking of Francis and wondering whether his cousin was with his mademoiselle. When torrential rain followed the thunder, the dog once again poked his head into the wigwam. This time, alarm filled his eyes.

"Come inside, Oqoti," Meuse said. The rain pummeled the animal skins stretched over their heads. Drops of water dripped from Oqoti's snout.

But the dog ignored him and continued to whine with short, emphatic yips.

"What's wrong?" Meuse asked. Parker, too, was awake now, curled in a fetal position in his corner.

Oqoti extracted his head from the wigwam but barked louder. *It was unlikely that any predatory animal would hunt on such a night,* Meuse thought. But the dog's insistence alarmed him.

Unless, of course, they were seeking shelter from the storm.

When the dog would neither quiet nor join them in the shelter, Meuse rose from his bed, his heart pounding. The *rat-a-tat* of the rain made it impossible to listen for danger. As the claps of thunder continued, a strong wind began to lash at the shelter.

The tent was dark. The rain had extinguished the fire Meuse had built that night, eliminating the only source of light. Dark thunderheads obscured both the moon and the stars.

The dog's barking turned into angry snarls. Meuse could almost hear the animal's bared teeth. He sensed a warning, realizing that the skinny mutt would be no match for a frantic bear rooting for food. Crouching near the flap of the wigwam, Meuse listened for the sounds of struggle, dreading the high yip of a dog being attacked by a stronger predator.

The wind continued to whip. Twigs and branches pummeled the wigwam, whistling with a fury that only nature could muster and against which any man was helpless and humbled. When the dog stopped barking, Meuse feared the worse. Just as he was about to succumb to hopelessness and despair, a strong gust blew open the flap. A bolt of lightning lit the sky. Its light revealed a large man standing outside.

"Francis!" Surely, Meuse was hallucinating. His cousin stood in front of him in the pouring rain.

Oqoti had settled on his haunches beside Francis, who held the flap of the wigwam open while rested a reassuring hand on the dog's wet fur, calming the animal with the same bravado he had displayed during many a tribal hunt.

Certainly, this was a vision, Meuse thought. *A message from the Elders.* He looked over at Parker expecting…what? The man had turned into a skeleton? An Elder's mask? Glooscap himself? Certainly, a time of reckoning was upon them.

But Parker returned his gaze. He also saw the intruder. *Who is this?* his open eyes asked. His expression was wary. Curious, perhaps, but not unduly alarmed.

Francis stooped to enter the wigwam. Oqoti followed him in and sidled up to Meuse, rubbing his legs. The smell of wet fur filled the air. Francis was about to hug Meuse when he spotted Parker curled up in the corner.

"Who is that?" he asked.

Meuse, disoriented, followed his gaze. Nothing was real. Was this Francis who spoke or a wily spirit?

Oqoti wagged his tail, delighted at the new arrival.

"You're the one who abducted the white man they call 'Parker'?" Francis asked. Disbelief furrowed his brow.

The dog licked Meuse's face.

Parker sat up, duplicating the clumsy movement he used to get to his knees, but this time he attempted to sit up on his heels. Francis watched in amazement as the man struggled.

"The entire valley is teeming with search parties," Francis said. "Bands of men set out from Port Royal every morning determined to find him. To find you."

Seeing Francis in front of him, Meuse remembered the sense of loss he had felt when his friend abandoned him for his mademoiselle.

"Are you living with the Acadians now?" Meuse asked, slowly accepting that Francis was real. Why was he here?

Francis held up his hand, displaying a wedding band. But his expression remained solemn.

"I am," he said. "I've joined Lisette's family in Grand-Pré."

Meuse studied Francis's face. There was a weariness there that belied his good news. Why had Francis appeared now, emerging from the storm like a prophet? Was he here to warn of the search party's imminent arrival? Only Francis could have guessed Meuse's whereabouts, but what purpose would it have served for him to lead them here? What had caused him to leave his mademoiselle behind? There was something more Francis was not saying.

"What is it, my friend?" Meuse asked. "What brings you here?"

Francis's eyes darted around the wigwam as if looking for something he could not find. As if the sight of Meuse and his hostage were the last of his worries.

"The British have expelled the Acadians," he said. "The LaFleurs have lost their home. Many of the men working the dikes were imprisoned and then loaded onto boats headed for foreign lands."

"The devils," Meuse said, glancing over at Parker, aware of the enemy in their midst.

"But that's not the worst of it," Francis said. "When I heard that Lisette's family had been arrested and taken into custody, I left my post on the dikes in pursuit of my wife. I went to the local trading post and traded my horse for a seaworthy canoe. There, I overheard news of a raid on Port Royal. Horrified by the news, I headed at once for our tribe's summer camp, but found only death and destruction. Concerned for my father's safety, I rode here, hoping some members of our tribe had escaped before the raid."

Francis stopped speaking. Tears welled in his eyes.

When he began again, Meuse could barely hear him. "But obviously, they are not here."

Meuse stopped breathing, waiting for his cousin to finish.

"They're gone," Francis said at last. "Meuse, our family. Your mother, our Elders, Mimi. They're all gone."

#

As the thunder slowly faded into the distance, Meuse and Francis stood in the door of the wigwam. Francis lowered his head to hide his tears. When he had collected himself, he continued his tale. He described the bloody carnage he had discovered on returning to their camp in Port Royal the week after the raid. The only spark of life he found was a black smear where the bonfire had once burned. The wigwams had been leveled. There were rusty stains on the flattened grass where bodies had fallen among the wreckage.

Meuse was paralyzed by the gravity of his cousin's news. At their feet, Oqoti stood guard, their only protection from the forces of evil that Francis described. When Francis finished, they did not speak. They might have stood there forever if Parker, as if in response to the waves of grief filling the wigwam, had not begun to pray.

"He does that," Meuse said. "Prays."

Francis snorted. "I wonder if his countrymen prayed before they fired muskets at our Elders."

They both looked at Parker, whose lips moved with silent entreaties, his eyes half-closed.

"No one was left," Francis said, "but ghosts. No bodies to bury. The white men scalped their victims and carted the bodies off to bury in shallow graves."

"Uncle Gehne?" Meuse asked.

"Gone."

Meuse pictured his uncle's impish grin. His gentle guidance. His kind brown eyes. He tried to remember if he had thanked Gehne for all he had given him.

"Mimi?" Meuse asked, his voice breaking. Let her be alive, he thought.

"Gone."

Was it only weeks ago that he and Mimi had set up camp in Port Royal? Exchanged confidences under the canopy of trees as they looked into each other eyes? He had never told Mimi he loved her because she had always been there at his side. She knew him as no one else knew him. The night of the bonfire, when he had declared his need for vengeance, she had been the only one he had trusted with his confidence. He had promised to protect her.

Sweet Mimi, whose spirit name was Sunlight Dancing on Water. Whose favorite colors were red, orange, yellow, and white. Whose spirit walkers were a mother and child. Meuse had always assumed that once he killed his bull moose, Mimi would be the woman he would marry.

"I heard the rangers might be holding a few children at the fort."

"But you heard nothing about my mother?"

Francis looked at him before speaking softly. "She was not there."

In the fire of Francis's gaze, Meuse saw his mother dying on the sand. He saw blood spilled. His only flesh and blood, all that remained of his birth family, extinguished by the white men. In his cousin's eyes, he saw a vision of his mother, prostrate on the beach as waves broke over her, returning to the earth where she would join his father. Slowly, the magnitude of his loss overcame him. He would never again kiss her goodnight. Never sit at her side as she taught him how to skin a grouse. She would never care for him when he was ill nor dance with him in celebration. She was gone from this world forever. This was what Francis had meant when he said, "They are all gone."

Meuse had become accustomed to his solitary vigil in the wigwam, but he had never imagined that he would not eventually return to the bosom of his family. Even if in death, he had assumed they would greet him back into the community as a hero who had stood up to the enemy. Now that community no longer existed, wiped out by the white men. Francis survived because, lovesick, he had joined the Acadian families in Grand-Pré. Meuse survived because, at the time of the raid, he had already abducted Parker. He calculated the timing in his head. By the time he had arrived in the Kejimkujik woods with Parker in his canoe, the tribe's summer camp had come under attack. The white men had murdered his mother. His fury at the white men's evil Scalp Proclamation, his desire for vengeance, had saved him, while everyone he loved and who loved him had died.

There were no words to describe his horror. There were no prayers that would make it right. The enormity of his loss was unbearable. His first instinct was to join the spirits of his family on the other side. They had left him behind, and he would follow them. He would take his own life, as the white men had taken his father and now his mother. He pulled his knife out of its sheath on his belt and held it up before him like a mirror. In the afterlife, he could comfort his mother, see his father once more.

But Francis, seeing his gesture, restrained him.

Francis, who had time to absorb the tragedy, had come to another conclusion. "We are the survivors," he said. "I came to Kejimkujik because our family's spirits still inhabit this earth. I came to speak with them, but, in doing so, I found you here. This is a message from the Elders. Our meeting today is our destiny."

Meuse looked at his cousin, the knife still clutched in his hand. He remained mute, not understanding his cousin's intent.

"We are the survivors," Francis repeated. His eyes blazed. "Don't you see. The future of our family is in our hands now."

The Elders, Gehne among them, had taught Meuse and Francis that they were responsible for the next seven generations. That the earth depended on them. The animals depended on them. Their tribe depended on them. The decisions they made now would determine the fate of all the generations that came after them.

Meuse mulled this over. They no longer had a choice, his cousin insisted. They were men now, entrusted with the future by the heinous acts of the invaders. As Meuse returned his knife to its sheath, he realized the fever he had seen in Francis's eyes was not anger, it was determination.

•••

Francis took Meuse by the arm and steered him out of the wigwam. The rain had settled into a gentle mist. In the dark, they sat on a fallen log. They did not sleep but took comfort in each other's presence. When the first pink of dawn began to light the sky, Francis told his story.

Their tribe was not the only family Francis had lost. The LaFleurs, too, had suffered under the new British government. As Meuse struggled to absorb his unbearable loss, Francis described the events that had sparked the flames of his anger long before the ashes of the raid had fanned it to a blazing wildfire.

"One Sunday in the late fall, I accompanied the LaFleurs to the Church of Saint-Jean-Baptiste in Grand-Pré, where Abbe Daudin was holding mass. A company of soldiers came to the door of the church and read a proclamation. They instructed the congregants to appoint deputies to represent them and deliver their arms to the fort at once. Monsieur LaFleur was chosen as one of the deputies. After they had delivered the arms as commanded, they were instructed to appear before the Governor's Council in Halifax."

As he spoke in a quiet monotone, Francis dug a hole in the grass with his muddy boot, causing a worm to wriggle away into the loam.

"When LaFleur returned, he told us that the Governor's Council had accused the men of treachery and asked them to take an oath of fidelity to the Crown. Of course, the deputies refused. Without even the pretense of judicial process, the Council stripped them then and there of their estates and liberties."

"And your new home?" Meuse asked.

"No longer our home. As we packed up our belongings, Abbe Daudin promised the deputies he would put up a fight, but his promises were in vain." Francis looked down at his hands, still strong and powerful, but when he opened them, he held nothing but air. He shrugged his shoulders and sighed.

Soon after the men had returned, Governor Lawrence ordered the arrest of all parish priests at Grand-Pré and Port Royal. Abbe Daudin fled into the woods, and several days later, he surrendered.

"With no one to defend us, the English ordered all the Acadians in the Annapolis Valley out of the country. In town after town, they summoned the men to meetings where they were taken hostage and held until they surrendered their families. Monsieur LaFleur hid in the woods. He attempted to flee, but armed patrols seized him, as they did anyone found on the roads or at the boat landings."

"And your Lisette? Where was she while all this took place?"

"While I worked on the dikes, they imprisoned the entire LaFleur family, along with the others from Grand-Pré, in the fort in Port Royal."

Francis spent the night in a makeshift shelter in a cove where they had often fished. "I did this to remain near my beloved, but I could not save her." He choked back tears now, a fierce sorrow overtaking him. He clenched his hands into fists at the memory of his helplessness. "I could not reveal myself. I waited in the darkness, yearning for an opportunity to fight back."

"All gone," Francis had said to Meuse when describing the brutal massacre of their tribe. But for him, the loss was even greater. In a matter of days, he had lost two families.

Meuse reached for his cousin's hand and covered his clenched fist with his smaller, more delicate hand. Francis looked up as if summoned back from somewhere far away. He relaxed his fingers and entwined them with Meuse's.

"What could you do?" Meuse asked.

"I couldn't sit idly by." Francis pulled his hand away. An echo of his former bravado surfaced in response to Meuse's gentle sympathy.

In Grand-Pré, he located the work crew that had worked under the supervision of Lisette's uncle. The story they told was a familiar one.

"Man after man described the French inhabitants leaving unwillingly, the women in distress, carrying their children in their arms and pulling decrepit parents in carts behind them. At dawn, they had watched the military officers load the Acadians onto seven vessels escorted by a man of war ship bound for North Carolina.

On the third day, he met a man who had been a friend of Lisette's father. At the sight of Francis, disheveled and downcast, he asked the younger man to sit down beside him.

"LeFleur is a good man," he said. "The only bloke with the knack of positioning hollowed-out trees into drainage ditches so they channel tidal waters out to the sea. Without his knack for repairs, these dikes will be vulnerable to every storm and tidal surge." He chewed on a toothpick. "I heard the officers marched the entire family up the gangplank of the British ship Pembrook."

The man stopped talking. Looking around to be sure none of his fellow workers were watching, he hissed in Francis's ear, his breath rank with garlic and tobacco: "I also heard the Acadians on board the Pembrook rebelled. During the night, a fortuitous wind blew the ship away from its escort. The passengers seized control of the vessel. After killing the crew, they escaped, every one, sailing up the Saint John River. *Mon fils*, a local Maliseet who knows of my friendship with LaFleur told me his tribe has offered to protect the family. The LeFleurs are on their way up north now to a refugee camp on Beaubears Island in the Miramichi River."

Francis spoke more quickly now. He raised his hands to his face as he relived the hope inspired by the man's tale.

"The very next day, before I could head up the Saint John River and find my beloved Lisette, I overheard the news of the raid on Port Royal."

He turned to Meuse. "I could not leave then, knowing my family had died with no one left to mourn them. I would have to wait to find my beloved."

Meuse listened, his eyes wide. Here, at last, was the reason Francis had returned to the family's winter camp. To grieve, to honor the dead. This, they would now do together, no longer benefiting from Uncle Gehne's loving gaze. "But then I found you," Francis said. "You are all the family I have left."

Meuse nodded. "We will honor our dead," he said, "but then, you must go look for Lisette. She is the woman you have chosen. Besides, the French have always come to our aid in the past. Like the Acadians, we are refugees now, too. To survive, we need all the help we can get."

They talked most of the morning and into the afternoon. By then, the storm had passed. Brisk winds blew away the clouds. They huddled outside the wigwam under a bright, blue sky.

"Now," Francis said, "we must pray for our fathers."

At the mention of prayer, Meuse remembered they were not alone. Inside the wigwam, his captive waited for him. "But what about Parker?" he asked. "What are we going to do about him?"

•••

There were two of them now. Parker realized he had missed his chance. He was no match for the two braves, not to mention their loyal dog. Any chance of escape was over. He should have moved faster when Meuse untied his wrists. He should have taken advantage of the boy's innocence to convince him to untie his ankles. He'd had three weeks to wiggle his way free while the boy was out hunting, and instead, he had waited for his compatriots to come to his rescue; he had foolishly trusted in God and the Crown.

The Indian who had arrived in the middle of a thunderstorm didn't blink or seem at all surprised when he first saw Meuse's captive. In fact, he seemed impressed by Parker's presence. In an excited spurt of unintelligible language, he appeared to congratulate his friend, and Meuse had blushed with pride. Any sign of compassion Parker discerned in his captor disappeared at once. As the two boys talked, Parker watched their faces, fearful that the older boy lacked Meuse's passivity, the boyish sweetness he could not disguise. At any moment, the newcomer might suggest they finish the job. For the first time in days, Parker felt he was in danger.

But soon the animated chatter slowed, and the boys spoke in quiet, serious tones. The newcomer appeared to deliver bad news because Meuse's eyes opened wide, and he reached for his knife. Fortunately, his friend restrained him. The young men turned their backs on Parker and walked out of the wigwam, where he could see only their silhouettes lit by the faint hint of the sun rising behind the clouds. He heard sobs and saw Meuse crumple to the ground as if his legs would no longer support him. His friend knelt beside him, and the two silhouettes rocked as one, their arms intertwined. Then there was only the sound of raindrops still falling from the trees. The two boys remained outside. Parker tried to determine his fate by watching the dog who stood guard at the doorway and never took his eyes off him, ready to sound an alarm at any unexpected movement.

When Meuse returned to the wigwam in the early afternoon, his expression had hardened. The other Indian clenched his fists. Meuse once again tied Parker's hands behind his back, this time pulling the sinew tight, unconcerned when Parker winced from the pain. He tightened the ties around Parker's ankles, looking up to the visitor as if seeking approval for his cruelty. Despite the residue of tears on his cheeks, Meuse's face was unreadable. He did not look at Parker; every movement he performed was for an audience of one.

By now, Parker was certain that the only weapon in the wigwam was the butcher-style knife that Meuse wore in a sheath on his belt. Parker knew the boy was adept with the weapon. He had watched him skin a duck with one sweep of its sharp carbon blade, the hardwood handle steady in his grip.

Before the newcomer's arrival, Parker had begun to hope that he and Meuse had reached a tenuous detente, each sensitive to the other's pain, but now a shiver of fear overtook him. In any culture, he knew gangs of boys could be brutal. If only he knew what news the second boy had delivered. Instead, he waited. He watched. He listened for any French words he might understand among the guttural spurts of their conversation. Were they talking about him? About revenge? Had the boy warned Meuse that a search party was nearby, or was their business of another kind, plans for a raid or another attempt by the French to challenge the Crown's sovereignty?

Did they speak of his family? Were they deciding his fate?

Or, concerned only with themselves, would they desert him, leave him tied up and helpless God knows where, with no chance of escape? Worse, would they use Meuse's knife to scalp him and deliver his bloody scalp to their tribe as a bargaining chip?

Parker's hair was thick and wavy. It had always been a source of pride, a sin of vanity. He felt his scalp prickle as if responding to his terror, the site of his vulnerability.

Parker had played many roles: he had been a dutiful son, a hard-working farmer, a soldier, a faithful husband to two women, and the father to a half-dozen children who depended on him. In this new colony, he had pictured himself as a spiritual leader to a population in need of guidance. Through it all, he had trusted in God and worked hard to provide for his family and his community. Never before had he felt so utterly helpless.

Had Salome forsaken him? Would William, Nat, and Lucy return to Massachusetts as orphans? Would the new baby arrive, never to know its father? His sons, he thought, were no older than the boys who held his fate in his hands.

He was dirty now, half-dressed in an Indian's oily hand-me-downs. He was hungry. He needed to piss and to do so would be one final humiliation. He saw absolutely no way out. With the arrival of the second Indian, all his patient efforts to calm his captor, to coax a shred of humanity from the savage, all his prayers, had come to naught.

Even the bedraggled dog had turned on him.

"Oh Lord," he prayed, but it served no purpose. He was far from home. His God could not hear him.

• • •

Delaps Cove, July 1761

After the raid, Gehne hid out among the reeds in Delaps Cove for two weeks. He built a shelter from driftwood and subsisted on crabs and seaweed.

"I am the only one left," he told the jays who watched him from the overhanging branches.

He huddled in the shadows on the edge of the beach like another piece of flotsam tossed up by the lapping waves. Every time a wandering deer's hoof broke a dry branch, the crack made him jump. When the wind fluttered the green needles of the pine's canopy, he heard white men coming once again. Afraid to build a fire that might give him away, he shivered. He shivered from the cold. He shivered from fear. He shivered from utter desolation.

"I'm the only one left," he whispered to the wind, watching a fleet of commercial fishing boats offshore.

When he closed his eyes, he saw Meuse's mother, Anne, collapse on the beach. He saw the sand turn red from her blood.

"Meuse, my boy," he cried. "I could not protect her."

On the third day of the third week, the Elders joined him. Peregrine Thomas and Old Joe handed him his pipe and watched as he lit it in silence. After he had inhaled deeply, he passed it to them. They clustered around him, trying to keep him warm.

"We knew outsiders would come," Old Joe said. He repeated the oft-told story:

Many years ago, a Mi'kmaq girl dreamed that a small island floated toward the land. On the island were bare trees and men—one dressed in garments of white rabbit skins. She told her dream to the wise men, but they could not explain the meaning. The next day at dawn, the Mi'kmaq saw a small island near the shore, just as the girl had dreamed. There were trees on the island and bears climbing among their bare branches. The people seized their bows and arrows to shoot the bears. To their amazement, the bears were men. Some of them lowered into the water a strange canoe, into which they jumped and paddled ashore. The man dressed in a white robe came toward them, making signs of peace and goodwill. Raising his hand, he pointed toward the heavens. Gehne knew the story because Father Le Loutre had often used it to demonstrate how his Catholic beliefs were compatible with the traditional stories that had been passed down from one generation of Mi'kmaq to the next. He compared the man in the white robe to Jesus.

Peace and goodwill. For most of his life, Gehne had believed him.

But Father Le Loutre was gone, and the man in the white robe had come ashore with a musket.

Peregrine Thomas nodded. The bears were men. But these bears did not hide in the shadows, willing to share their territory with its current residents. Their meat did not provide fat that would nurture a hungry man through a long, cold winter. These bears were hunters, and the Mi'kmaq their prey.

Sometimes the Elders shimmered in the early morning sun. When the fog lifted, they appeared transparent, and Gehne would wave his hand through the air to make them appear and disappear.

They were the only company he could trust. When fishing boats came too close to shore, he hid behind boulders or followed a narrow path to the waterfall, where he hid behind a curtain of water. He thought of his daughter, Mimi, who he had left behind as he swam frantically through the waves to escape the volley of bullets. Mimi who had never challenged him. Who he had trusted to carry on his tribe's traditions. He thought of his son, Francis, who he had not seen since he had left their winter camp with the Acadians. Francis who had killed a moose and dreamed of marrying a French girl named for a flower. He thought of Meuse, the son he had taken in as his own.

Seven generations, he told the porcupine watching him from the underbrush. What we do now will determine the fate of the next seven generations. The porcupine only waddled away, unconcerned with his dilemma.

The Elders perched on the rocks at the side of the waterfall and tossed small pebbles at him. They laughed when he squirmed, amused at the game.

He had run away. What other choice did he have?

They listened as he tried to defend his actions. The squirrels responded with chittering, the crows with aggravated squawks. An eagle flew high in the sky so it could watch everything: Gehne hiding behind the waterfall, the Elders perched on the rocks. The eagle spread his wings to fly higher, catching a willing draft, to watch the fishing boats empty the bay of the tribe's sustenance. He circled with a tilt of his majestic wings and saw the fort where officers marched prisoners up the gangplanks of boats. He saw the mudflats of the Annapolis Basin and flew down to pluck a tiny crab from the mud.

A blue heron stood on one leg, asleep. He had seen it all.

Gehne waited to die, afraid to survive. The only one still alive.

"But are you?" the Elders asked. "Our time has come, but we hear your stomach growling. When you sleep, we hear you calling out for your children."

"Do they respond?" he asked. To hear their answer better, he came out from under the waterfall. The mud of the creek bottom oozed between his toes. Tiny animals made their home in the cracked skin on the bottom of his feet. He lay out on a large rock, and the sun warmed him. In the trees, chickadees and nuthatches began to sing.

He thought of Mimi. He pictured her long, black braid swinging behind her back like a horse's tail. He saw her as a fancy shawl dancer with white feathers in her hair, dressed in her favorite colors, red and orange swirling around her as the fringes of her shawl waved beside her like reeds blowing in the wind.

They were all gone. But the animals kept him company. They were all gone, but the earth was still here to nurture him.

"And you," the Elders said, "must protect this earth against those who do not honor it."

He was mad, he knew that. Mad from the pain. Mad from all he had lost. But not alone. Hiding in the cove, so much he had loved surrounded him.

He hadn't died with the others. He had run away, and now he had to figure out how to survive.

"We're with you every step of the way," the Elders assured him.

On the twenty-first night, he heard Mimi calling him. Her girlish voice was soft, coming from a great distance, muffled but distinctive. *Aluasa'si,* she said. *I fade in and out.* In the last orange glow of sunset, he saw her beckoning.

"You see?" Old Joe said, laughing as he disappeared into the darkness.

Gehne looked up to the heavens. There, he saw the eagle circling by the light of the moon, waiting to show him the way.

CHAPTER TEN

Lucy's Grand Idea

Parker Mountain, July 1761

I knocked on Ma Salome's chamber door, but she didn't answer.

William had offered me a ride into town, but without my stepmother's permission, I wasn't allowed to leave the house.

I heard rustling behind the door. "Ma Salome, are you there?"

When my stepmother opened the door, her hand rested on the door-knob. "What is it, girl? Don't you have chores to attend to?"

For a moment, the door joined us, each with a hand on either side of the knob. It was as close as we had ever stood. Then I let go, and Salome nearly lost her balance.

"Out with it," she said.

My mouth flew open when I saw her widow's weeds spread out on the bed.

"He's not dead, you know." Why had Salome kept her mourning garb? Certainly, she hadn't expected Father to die when she moved her things into his bedchamber. Beside the long, shiny black dress, she had laid out a smaller version, which, I realized with horror, Salome Jr. had probably worn to her father's funeral. Now it was precisely my size. A shiver of foreboding climbed up my spine.

"Don't use that tone of voice with me, young lady." Even though her words lacked their normal sting, I smarted at the reprimand. Clearly distracted, Salome turned away from me and smoothed the black fabric of the two dresses. With a sigh, she sat down and patted a spot on the bedcover beside her. She smelled of cedar chips and dust. I couldn't refuse her gesture, although the thought of sitting next to her made my skin crawl.

"Lucy, every day that passes makes it less likely they will find your father," Salome began. Her tone was unexpectedly apologetic. "As women, it is our job to carry on. The Lord giveth and He taketh away." As if to demonstrate her point, she straightened her back and lifted her chin.

"Well, either way, you won't get me to wear that hateful dress," I said. "And it's too soon to say that He has taken my father. If you really love my father, you know he is brave and has survived worse. You would pray for his return, not dress for his funeral."

"Caroline should never have lent you her epistolary novels." Salome's condescending and patronizing smile infuriated me. What did she know about the divine *Clarissa*, whose quest of virtue was constantly thwarted by her meddling family?

I wasn't about to let her lecture me, so I stood up and headed for the door, having forgotten why I had knocked in the first place. But before stomping out, I said, "William says there will probably be a hostage exchange." I was stretching my brother's words. What he actually had said was, "Our only hope is that they will free him in exchange for a jailed Indian."

William and I were the only ones in the family not fueled by righteous anger or comforted by the Baptists' prayers. William and Ezekiel argued endlessly about the recent treaty signed in Halifax. Not a word of their quibbling would bring my father back. William said the Indians were here first and had a right to the land. That without access to their fishing grounds, they would starve. Ezekiel said the natives were lousy farmers, and besides, when France gave Britain title to the land, the tribes lost any claim to the territory.

British officers were holding a half-dozen Indian children in the brig at the Annapolis fort, Ezekiel said. William answered that he hoped that as soon as the search parties found where their father was being held, they'd agree to a trade.

My father as wampum. Didn't they see the coldness in that?

"The British are dead set on eliminating the local tribes." William said. "It's unholy. They distribute blankets infected with smallpox knowing the natives will fall ill."

Ezekiel laughed. "Yeah, I heard Lord Jeffrey Amherst did the same thing in Massachusetts."

Ezekiel might as well be a loyalist. Caroline said that when the colonists in Massachusetts launched the revolution against the British, he would be on the losing side. She added that if she weren't caring for a dozen pregnant Planter ladies, she'd board the next boat back to Boston so that she could support the rebel's cause.

I was sick of politics.

Still, Ma Salome's words stuck with me. "It's women's work to carry on." Now that I had discovered Captain Scott, who I had once been sweet on, was a murderer and a hypocrite, I realized that neither the officers nor the Baptists were likely to bring my father home. William had taken to calling the self-important officers "God's Army," always in a tone that made it clear they were anything but. In Massachusetts, he had kept his opinions to himself, but now that he had grown up and looked adults in the eye, he wasn't afraid to speak his mind. So, after thinking things through, I had decided to "carry on" in my own way.

Instead of going into town with William, I asked him to accompany me on a walk through the fields. The dry cornstalks hid the view of the house. On the far side of the pasture, I told him the truth about my encounter with the Indian boy.

"He wasn't a warrior," I said. "It was obvious he was looking for a friend." I described the bowl he had carried and told him about Miss Polly's claim that the Indians believed the Waltes bowl could reveal the future. "He seemed lonely."

William listened, kicking dirt as he had as a boy rooting out insects from the soil. He was as tall as Father now but more slender, and he often thought long and hard before he spoke.

"He seemed lonely," I repeated. "I wish I spoke more French so I could have understood him better. I think he was looking for a friend."

"The Annapolis Valley was a tribal fishing ground for his people for hundreds of years," William said. "Now most of them are gone." We strolled around the field until we reached the opening where the boy had disappeared into the woods.

"Do you remember," I asked, "when Father spotted an Indian in our field?"

He stopped and thought this over.

"I do." He looked off into the woods as if expecting to see the intruder. "Wait. Are you saying that was him?"

I nodded. "Father pointed the musket at his back and chased him away, yelling at him to get off our land."

"*Our* land," William scoffed. The sarcasm in his voice strengthened my resolve.

"Do you think," I asked, "the children being held in the brig in the fort are from the same tribe as he was?"

William didn't answer, but he turned toward me, ready to hear me out.

"Because, if so, they could tell us where he might have taken Father. Especially if by doing so, they are given their freedom."

William mulled this over. "The raid was a bloody horror. Most likely their parents are dead," he said.

"Ma Salome said the same thing about Father." I blinked back the tears welling in my eyes. "I refuse to believe that's true."

William pulled me in for a hug. My tears left a wet stain on the familiar shoulder of his jacket. I'd been so intent on shutting out unwanted solicitations from overwrought neighbors and Baptist congregants since Father's disappearance that I hadn't confided in anyone during this whole ordeal. But if anyone could understand, it would be William. Or so I thought. His response disappointed me.

"You may be right. But don't you think the proper authorities to handle such an interrogation are Major Rogers and Captain Scott?" he asked. "These matters are best pursued by government officials. It would fall to them to negotiate any hostage exchange."

I choked back my tears, sorry I had let him see me cry. I had counted on him to help me come up with a plan. But I wasn't about to give up so easily, and I wouldn't leave the matter in the hands of men I had come to distrust, so I gave it another try. "During the raid, Rogers and Scott murdered the children's parents. How could the children possibly trust the officers now? I can only imagine the horrors they witnessed."

William nodded, mulling over my words. "The attack was vicious. I agree, these children are the innocent victims of heartless men. I'm proud you see this now," he said. "Even our father, a soldier, would never condone such cruelty." We began walking again. If I didn't return soon to help Ma Salome with supper, someone would notice our absence.

"Maybe," William said, hesitating, "we could enlist Caroline's help. Ask her to volunteer her nursing skills. Those poor children must be suffering."

He picked up the pace. I skipped to catch up with him, relieved that he had come through for me after all.

While Ma Salome prepared the evening meal, Salome Jr. and I set the table. In my hopeful mood, I finally agreed to call my stepsister "Sally" as she had always asked me to do. When I did, Ma Salome nodded with approval. Salome wore her everyday dress and apron, and I did not speak again about seeing her unpacking her widow's weeds. It was my fervent hope that Salome had packed them back up, just as I had my pathetic heddus hairpiece.

•••

Annapolis, July 1761

William waited for me in front of the Sinclair Inn on the main street of the Annapolis seaport. When we had discussed asking Caroline for assistance, William suggested the inn. It wouldn't be too far away from Caroline's mothers-to-be, and we could have a private conversation there without neighbors or others in the family listening in. I figured Salome would faint dead away if she knew we were frequenting a public house. Not that we intended to imbibe. Still, I felt quite grown up walking with William into the inn, the first establishment with a strong drink license in Nova Scotia.

Caroline joined us at a wooden table in the dark dining room, a candle lighting her dear face. At the counter on the other side of the room, a raucous crowd of seamen, laborers, and artisans enjoyed the inn's strong ale. Its malty smell mingled with the light spice of cider and the mellow base of whiskey, tickling my nose more than the cloud of pipe tobacco smoke hanging in the air. The large building was a popular gathering place. I was surprised that William seemed to know it quite well, waving to several of the laborers assembled for a game of ninepins.

"How are you doing, sweetheart?" Caroline greeted me, giving me a hug. She hadn't come by the house for a week, pleading a run of babies being born.

"I'm trying to stay strong," I said.

"We've missed your visits," William said, taking a seat in a high-backed maple chair with golden and brown damask upholstery. I sat at the edge of a high-backed bench, facing the bar.

I wasn't at all surprised that Caroline no longer visited our family on a daily basis. I suspected she had had her fill of Salome and the Baptists, and I certainly didn't blame her for choosing her pregnant patients over the dreary vigil at the Parker homestead. In fact, I envied her and wished I could live with her at Grandpa Hardy's until Father returned. At the thought of Father, I tugged on William's sleeve.

"Ask her," I said. William had agreed to be our spokesman.

"Lucy's hatched a plan," he said, leaving it to me to ask the favor.

"Captain Scott says Father's probably an Indian hostage," I jumped in, "though the search parties haven't seen hide nor hair of him." This unfortunate expression rolled off my tongue before I could take it back. Both William's and Caroline's mouths fell open at my blunt expression.

"I mean, I know he's all right, but no one knows where he's being held."

At that, William came to my rescue.

"Perhaps it wasn't wise, but I told Lucy that the best outcome we can hope for is a hostage exchange negotiated with the local tribe. The Bury the Hatchet Proclamation encourages local governments to put together exchanges to settle their grievances."

"Tell her about the children in the jail," I said.

Caroline had yet to say a word. She kept looking back and forth from William to me as if she was trying to figure out what we had in mind.

William cleared his throat. He harrumphed several times before speaking in a weary, sober tone. "You've heard about the raid on the Indian's camp?"

"Yes," Caroline answered. "The one the day after your father disappeared?"

"Well, perhaps this is fortuitous, although tragic…"

"Tell her!" I had never been more frustrated with my brother.

"After the raid, they escorted a half-dozen Indian children to the brig at the fort." William spoke softly now so no one else could hear. The fort was just around the corner from the inn, and it was possible that among the men imbibing at the bar there were members of the voluntary band who had killed the parents of the children he was referencing.

"The barbarity," Caroline said. Lucy made a note of that word, "barbarity." It seemed so apt.

"We were wondering if you might take a look at the children," William said.

Caroline wrinkled her brow, not understanding. "William, I'm a midwife, not a doctor. I'm sure the Royal Forces would frown on any overture on my part."

"But those poor children," I said. "They saw their parents murdered."

Caroline's expression softened. It wasn't her way to refuse to offer solace where she was able.

William was all business now. "Introduce yourself as a nurse. Offer to provide care for the children. I doubt the officers have much experience with little ones. These children voluntarily surrendered."

"And why, may I ask, are you concerned with their well-being? Don't you have heartache enough at home?" Caroline asked.

I thought William would never come to the point. He hemmed and hawed and looked to the bar for rescue, but still I figured the plan would go over better coming from him. When I couldn't take his silence anymore,

I kicked him under the table.

"We think the children might know where Father's abductor might have taken him," he said. "They are from the same tribe and would be familiar with the tribe's seasonal camps. And Lucy"—he looked at me—"pointed out that they would not share that information with the officers since these same men killed their parents."

Since William was blaming everything on me, I decided to speak up. "And if the governor agrees to a hostage exchange, the children could go home in a swap for Father." In my excitement, I could hardly breathe. "We could save them, and best of all, we could rescue Father!"

Fortunately, the din of the inn's patrons offered cover. A few flushed faces turned away from the bar, looking for the source of my exclamation. Caroline held a finger to her mouth, warning me to shush, which I did but not before issuing one final plea. "Please?"

William held his hands up in the air, absolving himself of any responsibility. Then Caroline put her chin in her hands and appeared to think the matter through.

"If…" Caroline said. "If they would allow me to enter the jail. If the governor would agree to a swap. If the children could direct us to the tribal camps. If we could find where he is being held. If"—at this, she looked away—"If he is still alive."

She took my hand. "Darling, there are so many things we do not know."

"But what do we have to lose?" I asked. "What are we supposed to do? Nothing?"

That decided her.

William said, "I'll ask Ezekiel to speak to Major Rogers and see if the governor would be open to a hostage exchange."

Caroline replied, "Let me know what he says. If the governor agrees and will give me access to the children, I'll do what I can."

Before we left, I kissed them both on the mouth and then blushed red with embarrassment. In an inn with a strong drink license, emotional displays must not have been uncommon because none of the customers blinked an eye at my unseemly display of emotion. *My effusive gesture*, I thought with glee, *would have horrified Salome.* Of course, Salome would never have set foot in such an unruly establishment.

•••

Ezekiel and William went at it all morning, arguing about politics and plotting the best way to go about finding Nathaniel. Salome wearied of William's whiny voice, preferring her son's authoritative tone and pragmatic suggestions. William seemed intent on convincing him of a course of action that Ezekiel dismissed as a pipe dream. Lucy, in her usual snit, stomped around the house, neglecting her chores. Salome couldn't make head nor tail of her stepdaughter: one moment the girl walked around with a gray cloud over her head, the next she begged to go out dancing as if she hadn't a care in the world. How Nathaniel fathered such a flighty girl, she couldn't fathom. Without a proper mother, he had allowed his daughter to dispense with any sense of propriety. Should Nathaniel never return, Salome feared she would have to resort to strict disciplinary measures to straighten the willful girl out. In the meantime, she hoped her behavior didn't rub off on Sally, who had inherited her father's unflagging dignity and calm disposition.

Breakfast had not agreed with her. Her morning tea and toast stewed right on top of the baby, turning her stomach sourer by the moment. Her lower back ached. The persistent jab of the infant's elbow made any attempt to get comfortable futile. She shifted and sighed, unable to find a tolerable position. Thank the Lord, the Baptists had moved their prayer circle to the New Light Church, where Minister Moulton had agreed to house the new congregation until her husband's return. Cornelia Eaton, still convinced she was Salome's closest friend, encouraged her to join the others in prayer. But Salome hardly thought it appropriate to support Moulton, who, by all reports, had moved to Nova Scotia only to escape bankruptcy in Massachusetts, a consequence of a failed mercantile career.

Cornelia, who still called her Maggie, had taken it upon herself to coordinate the Baptists' comings and goings. Salome intended to have a serious talk with Ezekiel as soon as her confinement was over. In his stepfather's absence, he would be a worthy leader for the new congregation despite his youth. For the time being, however, he was under the thrall of Major Rogers and fancied himself a crucial member of the ongoing search for Nathaniel.

"Treaty or no," she overheard him saying, "they are the enemy, and we will treat them accordingly."

"But they are children," William said.

She rolled onto her side and tried to prop herself up. As she swung her feet to the side of the bed (oh, how her ankles had swollen), her water broke. Alarmed, she called out for Sally, but her daughter was in the kitchen washing the breakfast dishes and didn't hear her. She had no choice but to summon Lucy instead.

"Yes, Ma Salome?" Opening the chamber door, Lucy took one look at the wet bedding and turned as white as a sheet.

"Sweetheart," she said. "Give me a hand."

The foolish girl just stood there with her mouth wide open, leaving the door ajar. Any of the boys might have witnessed Salome's unseemly distress.

"Are you having the baby now?" Lucy asked. She looked as if she was about to swoon as she clung to the doorknob.

Salome, sitting in the puddle, sighed. The girl was as useless as a button without a buttonhole, and the baby was well on its way.

"I don't know where Caroline is…" Lucy stuttered.

"Forget Caroline. Go fetch Sally, some towels, and a bucket of boiling water."

When Ezekiel was born, Salome's mother, a stoic woman who believed in decorum, had attended. Sally arrived on her own, without outside assistance. Childbirth came easily to Salome; each baby made their way into the world without creating a fuss. The last thing she needed now was a wide-eyed child exposing the gentlemen of the household to the messiness of a woman's woes.

"Go!" she said, thinking *I'd rather do this alone than with this girl fluttering at my side.*

By the time Sally arrived with clean towels draped over her arm and a pot of water, the baby's head was crowning. Sally shut the door and propped her mother up to put the towels in place, just in time for the first gush of amniotic fluid and blood.

A half-dozen pushes, and the baby arrived, a healthy, red-faced boy screaming at the top of his lungs. Sally caught the baby and handed her mother a fresh towel. Wrapping little Henry in a blue blanket, she rocked him until her mother indicated she was ready to take him from her. Salome had named him Henry after a charismatic member of their new congregation.

"Is it going to die?" Lucy asked from the doorway. She had yet to cross the threshold.

Useless. Hysterical, Salome thought.

Sally offered to bury the afterbirth in the kitchen garden.

"Be sure you dig deep enough so that the crows don't come after it," Salome said, taking the baby from her daughter. He latched onto her breast enthusiastically, and she waved the girls away.

"Go tell the others they have a baby brother," she said.

"Half-brother," Lucy corrected, having found her tongue at last.

Salome supposed Minister Moulton would have to baptize the baby. When Nathaniel asked her to marry him, they had both agreed they wanted a large family. Looking at the baby sucking contentedly at her bosom, she wondered if this would be the first of many or her only real tie to the Parker family. At least she had delivered, joining the two families in blood as well as matrimony. Henry was their first child together, the only one born in Nova Scotia.

•••

Annapolis, July 1761

"How long can it take?" I had been waiting for Ezekiel to re-enter the house for what felt like hours. I lingered at my spinning wheel with my eyes glued to the front door, hoping he would finish his business before Ma Salome summoned me to help with the new baby.

"Lucy, stop fidgeting," William said. "The longer they are out there, the more likely it is that they will come to a satisfactory conclusion." He made a show of reading the newspaper, but I suspected he was as antsy as I was. "Ezekiel is only doing this because he figures there is something in it for him."

That morning, Ezekiel had agreed to present William's proposal to Major Rogers. But first he had let William beg awhile, enjoying William's earnest floundering as he made his case.

"The captives are the military's concern," he said, "not ours."

"But Father's only chance now is a hostage exchange," William insisted. "And for that to happen, we need to find him first."

I listened to their discussion as I toasted the morning bread over the fire. Ezekiel had pondered, seeming to enjoy William's discomfort. After their conversation, William told me Ezekiel had already decided to present our plan because he figured he could take all the credit. He was desperate to catch Major Rogers's eye and prove his worth to his superiors. All William had to say was, "Who knows what opportunities might open up for you if we could pull off an exchange?" He might even garner the governor's attention.

And so, when the officers arrived for their daily visit, Ezekiel purloined two cigars from my father's humidor and invited the major to join him on the front porch.

"You'll enjoy the view," he said. "From the mountain, you can see the entire Annapolis Basin."

The major accepted his offer. "Your stepfather is a lucky man to have been granted such a lovely property."

"The Annapolis seafood rivals any we had in Massachusetts," Ezekiel said. "Now that we no longer have to compete with the Indians, the fishing industry promises to surpass even the plentiful agriculture in the valley."

"The commercial dories have already doubled their catch," Rogers bragged, taking his time choosing a cigar. "Before we chased them away, the Indians shared our catch, but now it is under our control."

Ezekiel snorted. "The natives are like animals, half-civilized and wild." My skin crawled as they closed the door. These were the men we had entrusted with my plan?

I spun some more yarn, imagining the conversation that was taking place outside the door. I knew Ezekiel would never credit William with the idea he was about to propose (and certainly not me). He would claim it for his own. "Whoever kidnapped Parker undoubtedly fled to familiar ground. If he was a Mi'kmaq—as we assume—he most likely returned to another of their camps."

"Maybe," Rogers might reply. "But Indians are everywhere on the peninsula. Short of rallying the entire Christian population, I wouldn't have a clue where to look."

At that, Ezekiel would blow a blue plume of smoke into the air. "The hostages we are holding at the fort might know where the local Indians make their winter camp."

Fortunately, as I fabricated their conversation without any real knowledge of what they were saying, a thunderstorm blew in, and they were forced to return inside, their cigars smoldering and stinky. They stood in the doorway and removed their dripping jackets without acknowledging our presence. William buried his head in his newspaper, and I pushed my pedal vigorously to show my industry.

They continued their conversation in the parlor. Now I could hear them.

"Good luck getting the prisoners to talk," Rogers said. "They are a motley crew, sickly and illiterate, barely holding on. Even if they spoke English, they would have no reason to help us. I don't know about you, but I'd like to see them gone. They are a drain on our limited resources. We would have been better off had they died with the others."

"Agreed," my stepbrother said, and I eased up on the pedal, trying to catch his every word. "But perhaps there is an opportunity here to exploit them to our advantage." Ezekiel was in his glory, speaking as an equal with the decorated officer. Now that they had vanquished the Indians, the local government would soon assume authority over the new community. It was obvious to me that Ezekiel figured he, the son of a war hero and stepson of a revered Planter and soon-to-be-Baptist minister, would be a prime candidate for a position in the government.

"The governor is encouraging hostage exchanges as a symbol of reconciliation," he said. "Now that we have solved our Indian problem, this might offer the perfect opportunity to curry his favor."

"Yes?" Rogers said. His curiosity had been piqued.

"I know a young woman, a nurse and midwife, willing to interrogate the

Indians being held in the jail. Under the pretense of treating their illnesses, she might gather information on the migration patterns of their parents."

Rogers snorted. "And I assume this young lady is a friend of yours?"

"A relative, nothing more. No longer young. A working woman, plain and too old to be of interest but educated with a working French vocabulary."

I bit my tongue. Hearing Caroline described this way made my blood boil. But now was not the time to give Ezekiel a piece of my mind. There would be plenty of time for that after Father was home.

"And if she could provide us with this information?"

"Not only might we find Parker, but we could facilitate an exchange of hostages, ridding ourselves of the children filling our jail cells while heeding the governor's call. And you would be given the credit for Parker's recovery."

"Clever," Rogers said. "Unlikely to succeed, but perhaps worth a try."

Ezekiel relit his cigar. I could see his mental gears clicking. I hoped then that the major might offer him an appointment in his regiment or give him a position at the fort, because I wanted him out of the house. The idea of living under the same roof as this ruthless, plotting man sickened me. That he was now a part of my family made me feel dirty, sullied by his raw ambition and lack of compassion. But then I heard the words I had been waiting all day to hear.

"I'll make it work, sir," he said to the major. He stubbed out his cigar. The two men shook hands.

William and my eyes met. Our plan was proceeding! With any luck, Father would be home soon.

• • •

As soon as Caroline took off her coat, I pounced on her.

"Did the Indian children eat the food we sent?" I asked. I was dying to hear how her visit to the jail had gone.

"Let her be," William said. He had accompanied Caroline back from Annapolis and now helped her settle in front of the fire. "Our aunt had a hard day." Caroline set her bag at her feet. She stared into the fire as if we weren't there. I put a cup of steaming tea on the table beside her.

Salome poked her head in from the keeping room and invited Caroline to join the family for supper—a generous offer, since there was no love lost between the two women. William hovered over Caroline like a protective dog, his forehead pleated with concern.

"It was my idea. I deserve to know what happened," I whispered to him. "Did she tell you if the children told her where Father might be?"

Even in her stupor, Caroline overheard my question. She looked up, as if unsure where she had landed. "Dear Lucy," she said, "I'll tell you everything. But first, I need a moment to collect my thoughts."

Salome entered the room with baby Henry in her arms. When Salome turned her back, Caroline winked at me, somewhat revived at last. William had sworn us to secrecy about our meeting at the Sinclair Inn, but this acknowledgment made me hopeful that all had gone well. As much as I wanted my aunt to myself, I agreed to wait to hear her story until after supper. Salome said she needed to put baby Henry to bed then and give us some time to ourselves. Sally volunteered to wash the dishes. I thanked her, warming to the usefulness of our new friendship.

While Sally washed the dishes, I boiled a pot of water for tea.

When Sally was done, she headed upstairs to help Salome with the baby, leaving William and me to sit with Caroline. Ezekiel was out for the evening, probably plotting with the very officers Caroline had visited in the afternoon.

The household settled down for the night, Caroline curled up in an armchair, burrowing into the wool blanket William gave her to cover her lap.

After a long sip of tea, she shut her eyes. I prayed she would not fall asleep and was relieved when she sighed, rubbed her eyes, and then began to recount her visit to the jail.

"After you dropped me off, William, I followed Major Rogers up the stone steps to the fort's administration building." She described the intimidating fortress, a stalwart earthwork with bastions at the corners of the walls, imposing and impenetrable. From the top of the stairs, there was a view of both the Annapolis River and the Basin. "It towers over the town like a protective parent," she said.

"But when we entered the officer's quarters, it was quiet, as if there was no one there." William chose that moment to interrupt and tell me that Halifax was the capital of the province now, the fort no longer the seat of the government. Instead, it was primarily used to house the Acadians and Indians the British had rounded up for expulsion. I wished he wouldn't interrupt Caroline's story. I was eager to hear about the captive children.

"Captain Scott was the only one there, sitting alone behind the reception desk," Caroline clasped her fingers as she talked, "whiling away the time by drawing stick figures on a pad of paper." She lowered her voice and imitated the officers' conversation. "'Scott,' Major Rogers said, 'would you be so kind as to escort Miss Hardy downstairs to the jail cells? She's a…,' he paused, looking me over as if trying to determine my worth, 'a nurse?'"

"I told him I was a midwife," Caroline said. "But that I cared for many children in my line of work. Scott refused to acknowledge me until he had finished his drawing."

"The cad," I said.

"The cad," Caroline agreed, taking another sip of her tea. My patience was wearing thin. When she began again, she spoke with more urgency.

"'It's a fool's mission,' Rogers told Scott, pushing me aside. 'A woman has no place in the strenuous work of local governance, but I was given no choice. Ezekiel Parker requested the visit.' He explained he hadn't had the heart to turn down the poor boy's request. The kidnapped Parker was his stepfather and a revered man in the community."

"Scott took his time," Caroline continued, "but eventually he set down his pencil."

"'Lucy's aunt, am I correct?' he asked, opening the heavy door leading downstairs to the jail cells."

At the mention of my name, my heart skipped. Captain Scott remembered me. No matter how despicable his nature, this pleased me.

Caroline said she glared back at him and headed down the stairs, determined not to show her fear. In the darkness, she saw nothing but was overcome by the stink of urine and sickness. Scott walked four steps behind her, pinching his nose in disgust.

Two long flights down, Caroline arrived at a damp, dark, and airless corridor lined with jail cells. Rats scurried into the corners as she approached. She clutched her medical bag. She had removed most of her midwifery necessities, replacing the forceps with rolled bandages and an assortment of elixirs she had purchased from the local apothecary. Over her shoulder, she carried a sack of fresh fruit and several jars of tea. "The young prisoners," she told us, "had been in the jail for the nearly three weeks since the raid. I expected them to eye the food hungrily, but instead they looked up at me with suspicion."

"They're a sorry bunch," Scott told her as they approached a small cell at the end of the corridor where three Indian children crouched barefoot on the dirt floor. A boy, so small she had trouble determining his age, recoiled at the sight of the uniformed officer. The oldest, an adolescent girl, placed a protective arm around the boy, comforting him in their native language with soothing syllables that neither Scott nor Caroline understood. A shivering young toddler sneezed with her mouth open. Scott turned away, trying to avoid the putrid spray. The little one's face, caked with snot, was flushed and red with fever.

"I'll leave you to it," Scott said. "But I doubt you'll get much out of these three. They probably won't last as long as it would take to arrange a hostage swap. Knock on the door when you're done, and I'll come and fetch you."

Caroline paused. I could see she was reliving the dreadful encounter as she spoke. She smoothed the blanket over her lap.

"When the heavy door at the top of the stairs slammed shut, it cut most of the light to the cells."

I tried to imagine Caroline left behind in the darkness by Captain Scott. I was ashamed to have once fallen for this dreadful man's superficial charm. But I would confess my sins another day. For now, I was engrossed by her story.

"Poor things! Abandoned in a claustrophobic cell, dependent on men who neither spoke their language nor wished them well, who begrudged every trip down to the basement to check on what they called, in my presence, 'chattel.'"

"*Avez-vous faim?*" I asked, digging through my bag. I pulled out an apple and sliced it as the children watched, their eyes wide. The young boy grabbed the fruit right out of my hand as I opened the jar of tea with the other. *"Parlez vous français?"*

Nothing. Caroline assumed they spoke French. Most of the local Indians did. "But if they did not, I realized, mine was surely a fool's errand." Moving slowly, trying not to startle them, she pressed her palm to the sick tot's hot, clammy forehead.

"Pauvre fille," she said. In her inadequate schoolgirl French, she had trouble conveying her sympathy. *"Je m'appelle Caroline."* It was all she could do to comfort the children. *"Je suis une amie."*

At last, the older girl looked up. *"Je m'appelle Mimi,"* she said, pointing to her chest before reaching for a piece of apple. She broke the fruit into two pieces and gave them to the younger children. The young boy, maybe four, maybe five, was the first to eat. Tentatively, he took a small bite, closing his eyes. Then another. Then another.

"Mimi," Caroline repeated. She offered the jar of tea, and the girl drank. Obviously, these children were not being fed. If she could accomplish nothing else, she would demand Rogers and Scott provide adequate nourishment to the children until their fate had been determined. A fate that, she now realized, she held in her hands.

"I'm here to help," she said, or hoped she said, in her faltering French.

"Ce n'est pas possible," Mimi said. *"Morte. Toute notre famille est morte."* Caroline described the tracks of salty tears that streaked the girl's cheeks. Her eyes were expressionless, as if she too had had her life taken from her.

Caroline stopped then, looking up at William, tears sprung to her eyes. In her work as a midwife, Caroline often delivered bad news. But never, she told us, had she felt so responsible. She could tell a grieving mother that the death of her stillborn child was God's will, but these children had witnessed their parents murdered in front of their eyes. They knew who was to blame.

I handed Caroline a handkerchief, my favorite, embroidered by my own dear mother, her sister. She gazed off into the distance, lost now in her memories.

"Voulez vous rentrer chez soi?" Caroline wasn't speaking to us. She was

addressing the girl. Would you like to go home? She spoke softly, trying to reassure the poor thing, to show she meant her no harm. To distinguish herself from the cruel men who held the children hostage.

Caroline twisted the handkerchief, worrying her hands.

"The girl asked for another slice of the apple, the white pulp bright against her skin, the red of the skin the color of blood. Skin and bones, her long braid tangled and dirty. And all I could think was, *why would this girl trust me?* I wished I could offer something more, but I was unwilling to make promises I could not keep. How could I expect this child to trust me when I did not trust the men who had sent me as an emissary?

Still, Caroline said, she had to try. "Tell me," she continued to speak French to the girl. "when your family leaves their summer fishing camp," she avoided the past tense, the grammar easier that way, "where do they go? What other place do you call home?"

Mimi's forehead wrinkled in concentration. A good sign. At least she was trying to understand.

"*En l'hiver*," Caroline tried another approach, "*Où habitez vous?*"

The girl swayed. Afraid she was about to pass out, Caroline put an arm around her for support. She lifted the bottle of tea to the girl's lips, urged her to sip.

Mimi swallowed the lukewarm liquid and whispered under her breath: "Kejimkujik."

Caroline did not understand.

"Where?"

"*Le lac. En l'hiver.*"

The girl said her tribe returned to Lake Kejimkujik in the winter. Now Caroline understood. For a slice of apple and a sip of tea, the girl told her what the men wanted to know. She entrusted Caroline with her hope, believing Caroline was there to help. Caroline poured another cupful of tea for the ailing children and wrapped the youngest in a blanket.

"Keep them warm," she told Mimi.

A few biscuits and a stick of jerky. That was all she had offered.

"Kejimkujik," she said to Mimi. "Soon, you'll go home to Kejimkujik." If this was true, she didn't know. There may have been no survivors of her tribe who could take the children in. But the girl's face lit up, and she reached out trembling arms to clasp Caroline, who held her longer than was wise given the illness that surrounded her.

"I'll hold these bastards to their word," she told us now, her story almost done, her face lit as if with fever. I hugged her, more grateful than I could possibly show. Dear, sweet Caroline. With her help, we might soon find my father. But the picture she painted of those poor children will haunt me for my entire life.

"We must make sure these children go home," I said, taking my aunt's hand in my own.

"It's not that easy," Caroline said. The dark circles under her eyes grew darker by the hour. She had not slept since planning her visit to the jail. "When Scott finally responded to my pounding on the wooden door, I told him what the girl had said."

"Kejimkujik," he said. "That makes sense. But the lake covers a lot of ground." He immediately sent a messenger to summon Major Rogers. By the time I took my leave, Rogers had returned to the administration building, but he didn't appear at all pleased to learn a hapless woman had pried this vital information out of the incarcerated girl.

"I told him that the children need to be cared for," Caroline continued. "That I would return every day until he determined whether your father was being held in Kejimkujik. They needed food, better blankets, and a doctor's attention. I even offered the Baptists' assistance in their care."

That pleased me no end. I would like to see Cornelia Eaton descend those dark stairs carrying her prayer book. Let her bake pies for the poor children.

"At the mention of the Baptists, Rogers snorted, not liking it one bit. But I had him there. Once the Baptists became involved, the entire community would know the condition of the children they had locked away to die.

"Whatever you say," he said. "Scott here will take care of you." Scott rolled his eyes but took out his pencil to make a list of the supplies she required.

Caroline could see that, like Ezekiel, Rogers was eager to show his political acumen. "The sooner we locate Parker, the sooner we can send a note to the governor proposing our plan for a hostage swap," Rogers said to Scott. "If the search party locates Parker, we can wash our hands of all this foolishness." With a dismissive wave of his hand, Rogers headed off to summon the troops.

"And now, my dear niece, I must do the same."

No matter how much I pleaded, I could not convince Caroline to spend the night. I offered my own bed, but she said the day had been long, and she was exhausted. William agreed to take her home to Grandpa Hardy's house. He fetched her coat and wrapped it around her as if protecting a piece of fine china and then went outside to prepare the horse and cart. While he did so, I sat with Caroline, pretending she was my mother, and everything was right in the world.

CHAPTER ELEVEN

Uncle Gehne and the Ancestors
Teach Meuse a Lesson

Kejimkujik, July 1761

Francis slept for two days after his arrival in Kejimkujik. On the third day, he awoke, stretched with a renewed man's vigor, and demanded to know what was next.

"What is your plan?" Francis asked Meuse, tilting his head toward Parker.

The plan, Meuse thought. He wished he knew.

He stroked Oqoti's head, searching for an answer. The dog stretched out on the dirt floor. His limbs twitched involuntarily, his muscles unable to contain his pleasure. Meuse scratched behind his ears.

Meuse looked to his friend for guidance. "Parker's a spiritual man," Meuse said. "A *sagamore*. I abducted him during a ceremonial rite. I wanted to send a message to his people, let them know that if they were born again, it should be with humility."

"In his absence," Francis said, "those same people murdered our family."

They studied the man asleep, or feigning sleep, on the floor.

"We should kill him," Francis said. Francis, who had killed a moose without hesitation, had been celebrated by his tribe as a hunter. "What weapon should we use?" he asked.

"Maybe. But I can't help but wonder if this man is a killer," Meuse said, "or would he have stopped them?" He knew this man now; he could see the possibility. His hand rested on the sheath holding his knife.

"No one can stop them," Francis said. "The British gave these families from Massachusetts land that wasn't theirs to give. The settlers believe they are entitled to their properties, and they want us gone at all costs. We are nothing to them but unwanted intruders."

"So, what do we do?" Meuse knew what Francis wanted to hear. What was one more death when there had been so many already?

Only the dog seemed content with his fate.

"I came here to pray for the dead," Francis said. "I came to honor our Elders. If this man is a spiritual man, as you say he is, let him pray before we slay him. Maybe his God will forgive him for his family's sins."

Meuse considered his cousin's words. When it had been just him and Parker in the dark, there had been an intimacy that united them. Their isolation had made it easy to be vulnerable. There had been the solitude, the darkness, their very dependence on each other. Parker had responded to his acts of kindness with a servile humility. Meuse had been moved by his captive's devotion to his God and had, at times, aspired to the same. But now that Francis was here, that intimacy had evaporated like morning fog, and he could see the man clearly. He saw a man still seething with anger. A proud man who had struggled to release himself from the bonds that held him. A smelly man wearing clothing that reeked of urine. A member of a hostile community, any of whose members would kill him without remorse. They had killed his mother, his uncle, and the girl he loved, along with the Elders who might have guided him now that he was lost.

"I've had enough of prayers," Meuse said. "Let's kill him." He handed Francis the knife. Meuse hoped that Francis, the celebrated warrior, would rise to the occasion. What did he have to lose?

Francis regarded the prisoner. "No," he said. "This is your kill. I left home searching for love, and you opted for vengeance. This man's soul is in your hands, not mine." He regarded his friend with curiosity. "But whatever you decide, I'll be at your side."

What would their Elders say? Francis waited for Meuse to act. Meuse shuffled his feet, uncomfortable under his friend's clear-eyed scrutiny. If they were the only ones left, the future of their tribe, of the next seven generations, rested in his hands. What should he do with this captive, at once the enemy and also his responsibility?

There would be no nobility in Parker's death. It would serve no purpose. It wouldn't feed his tribe. His bones would not produce a broth that could sustain a man when all food sources had withered. Unlike the bull moose, his skin could not be used to warm a family in the winter or shelter them from the snow. His scalp had no value placed on it. The earth would not benefit from his death.

"He stinks," Francis said, holding his nose.

"Maybe we should leave him to fend for himself in the forest. Let the animals decide his fate," Meuse said. "Let his God be his judge."

Parker's eyes blinked open and then shut. If he understood their discussion, he gave no sign.

"Let's leave him and go find your mademoiselle. My rowing skills will come in handy on the journey."

Francis considered his offer, but then shook his head. "I'd appreciate your help, but you can't just walk away from what you have done," he said.

Meuse examined the knife in his hand.

For generations, the tribe had buried their ancestors in Kejimkujik, in the fertile earth of their winter camp. Meuse's own father was interred not far from here. What would his Elders say if he were to take this man's life, leave his body to rot, and sully their tribal resting place?

Meuse waited for their advice. He fingered the knife, listening for their voices in the wind. Then he slipped it back into the sheath. He knew what their answer would be. The knife's purpose was to provide sustenance; it was not an implement of murder or weapon for revenge.

"If the decision is mine, I cannot harm this man. When I abducted him, his life became my responsibility."

Francis snorted with disdain, but Meuse's resolve was strong. Through mime and mimicry, he instructed Parker to take off his clothes. He gave him a wet rag and watched him wipe off the excrement that had caked between his legs. Francis held his nose, wrinkling his face with displeasure. When at last Parker was clean, they left him, naked and tied up once more, under Oqoti's willing custody and went to the river to wash his clothes.

For the first time in his life, Meuse took the lead, aware of Francis walking behind him. His cousin had not questioned his decision. Instead, he accepted it with a frustrated flip of his wrist. Meuse held his head high, emboldened by the conviction that his Elders would approve of his actions.

As they scrubbed the garments in the stream, a shadow passed over the water. They looked up and saw an eagle circling over their heads. When it dived, as if to catch a fish, they followed its descent to the shoreline only feet upstream. That's where they spotted Gehne, knee-deep in the tepid water, in the middle of an animated conversation with the recently murdered Elders.

"Old Joe," he said when he saw the dirty clothes floating in the stream, "are these stained garments yours? You must have had one hell of a fright to make such a mess. Oh, right, I remember now. The white men shot you. I suppose that scared the crap out of you." He laughed at his own joke and picked up the tunic, examined it, and began scrubbing it energetically against a rock.

Francis stared at his father in bewilderment. Right there in front of him, talking nonsense. He turned to Meuse. "Did you know he was here? Is this what you meant when you said our ancestors were watching us? That their spirits would decide Parker's fate?"

But Gehne did not look like a spirit. He was as opaque as they were. A wicked grin lit up his face as he teased Old Joe, even though neither of them could see anyone else there.

Gehne held up the soiled tunic to check if he had erased the stains.

"My nephew has a tunic just like this," he told his invisible friend. "A sweet boy who inhabits the earth still. Where was he the day the white men came?"

Meuse, a nephew only in name, saw before him the kind man who had taken him and his mother in when his father died. Who had promised to take the place of his father. Could the spirit of Gehne talk to his father now that they both had passed? He considered asking the vision for guidance but was afraid of frightening the specter away. Instead, he watched as Gehne placed the tunic on a rock to dry and then proceeded to piss in the stream, a long, steady, yellow arc.

He had never thought spirits would be as obsessed as Gehne seemed to be with bodily functions.

As Meuse puzzled this out, Francis waded slowly toward his father. Like a hunter stalking a doe, he made no noise, but with each step he took, a ripple spread slowly across the surface of the placid water. As he neared his father, the disturbance tickled his father's thigh, and Gehne turned toward him, instinctively checking to see if he was in danger.

"Francis, is that you?" Gehne asked. He did not appear surprised to see the two boys standing in the river. He opened his arms, greeting his son with a wide smile. Tears flowed from his weary eyes.

"Father?" Francis asked. "Is that really you? Are you alive?"

"I have no idea," Gehne answered, pinching the skin on his arm. "Well, I am standing right in front of you, one way or the other," he chuckled.

Father and son embraced. Just as Meuse wondered if they would ever let go, his uncle turned to him.

"Meuse, is your mother nearby?" He peered off into the woods, sniffing for a fire. "I've brought some friends home with me. Tell your mother to prepare a feast. We've been on a long, arduous journey."

But his mother was dead, Meuse knew this. But then, so was Gehne.

"Come here and give your uncle a hug."

Gehne's lips were cold but wet.

"Now go find the women and tell them we have company. I'm famished and will happily accept a cup of tea and some bannock to hold me over until Anne prepares a suitable feast for our many guests."

While they spoke, Parker's clothes had dried in the bright sunshine. Meuse scooped them up and headed up the path toward their camp. Gehne and Francis followed. Parker's fate was now the least of Meuse's concerns.

• • •

"*Pjila'si,*" the old man said. He sucked the marrow from the squirrel bones, gesturing with greasy fingers.

"My father, Gehne, welcomes you to our camp." Francis spoke in broken French as he handed Parker a piece of squirrel meat. Salmon sizzled on the fire next to a pot of boiling fiddleheads.

There were four of them now and a steady stream of chatter. Oqoti's tail wagged as he cruised from man to man, sniffing their feet for news of their travels. Meuse and Francis had spent the day fishing, foraging, and trapping, putting together the generous feast that Gehne had requested on his return. While they were away, Gehne, who spoke neither English nor French, kept the Baptist man company. He led Parker to the stream, where they swam and lay on the rocks to dry. Now, dressed in the same garments he had worn to his baptism, Parker sat, unbound, outside the wigwam in front of the blazing fire that held the mosquitoes at bay. Soon the time would come for him to find his way home, but for now he gathered his strength in the company of men he was beginning to trust.

Before they ate, Meuse turned to Parker. Tenting his hands, he mimicked prayer, raising an eyebrow to invite Parker to say grace. Parker nodded, understanding the gesture. All four men bowed their heads and said the Lord's Prayer, Parker in English, Meuse and Francis in French. Gehne wordlessly moved his lips in meaningless syllables as he smiled beatifically. There was more than enough food, enough for those present and for the spirits who protected them. Every time Parker emptied his plate, Meuse offered more. When they could eat no more, Oqoti stretched out beside them and gobbled down the scraps that remained. The dog quickly fell into a deep sleep in which he ran and yipped and sighed with pleasure. This made the men giggle.

When the summer sun approached the horizon and the sky blushed rose, Gehne took out his pipe. He cleaned out each piece with deliberation: first the stone bowl, then the wooden stem wrapped in animal skin and decorated with beads and feathers. Once cleaned, he held up each, first in one direction, then another. Seven times in all. The ritual reminded

Parker of the prayers he recited to prepare for communion. Parker could tell the young men had heard the old man's stories before. They listened with respectful attention, but their eyes glazed over. In their sated state, their contentment did not differ from the dog's. The familiar words, their full bellies, they were willing participants in the ritual.

In broken French, Francis explained that while Gehne claimed the pipe was a gift from the Elders during his journey, the boys knew that the prized possession never left his hands. The pouch on his belt was as much a part of his attire as the wrinkled black hat that perched on his head. With their encouragement, Parker examined the pipe carefully, admiring its craftsmanship. Something had changed since the older man arrived. Parker felt safer now. A tentative benevolence had replaced the boys' skittish threat. Maybe it was the fresh air, the refreshing swim, or the glow of the setting sun, but tonight in their company, he didn't think of escape.

Gehne filled the pipe with tobacco and sweet-smelling grass. He puffed and then handed it to Parker. Parker, too, inhaled deeply. Although he could not identify the herbs, a wave of contentment followed each puff. He passed the pipe along and watched Francis smoke. For the first time, he admired the young man's strength and nobility. His ready smile and the loyalty he had demonstrated in his friendship to Meuse. Meuse was the last to take the pipe. His eyes softened with every inhale. His body, wiry and tense, finally relaxed. Such a tender-hearted boy, really, still a child.

As darkness settled in, a cool breeze stirred the trees. In the distance, small animals scurried in the leaf litter. The forest came alive.

"Forgive us our trespasses as we forgive those..." Parker thought he heard an echo of the Christian prayer in the breeze that passed through the pines.

Gehne laughed. He regaled the younger men with more stories Parker could not understand. Parker strained to hear the voices whispering in the wind. In a treetop, a raccoon chittered. It wanted to descend, but the gathering blocked its way.

"Forgive me." This time he heard Meuse's voice, an adolescent timber that occasionally cracked and dipped into manhood. But the words were in English. Free of accent, effortless, no halting intonation. A casual apology uttered with the breeziness Parker's son once used after dropping his napkin on the dining room floor.

Francis sidled over to him. In his poor French, he attempted to explain the ritual he had just witnessed. The pipe, the sacred path. After fasting and sacrifice, he said, a time for prayer and humility.

Fasting and sacrifice. In the past few weeks, Parker had experienced these and little more. And hadn't it been a sacred path he had also been pursuing when he was kidnapped the very day of his baptism? Humility was the only aspect of Francis's explanation he did not understand.

Hadn't they humiliated him enough?

The strangeness continued. The clicking in the trees. The clip clop of horses approaching. But if strangers approached, wouldn't Oqoti stir from his slumber? This must be a dream, nothing more.

The older man Parker now knew as Gehne never stopped talking. Sometimes to the younger men, sometimes to Parker, who could not understand a word he said, sometimes to no one at all. All evening, he smoked and chatted convivially, laughing until a river of tears ran down his face. Francis, whose French was only a little better than Parker's, was the only one among them who attempted to interpret his father's words. Now he said that his father kept the company of his Elders, who had rescued him following the *l'incursion*.

This last word, among the drone of pidgin Indian and French words, caught Parker's attention. This he understood.

"Incursion?" he asked.

Francis's expression froze. His relaxed joviality disappeared with the inquiry.

"*L'incursion de votre peuple*," Francis said. "The *abbatage*."

Abbatage. Parker knew that word. Slaughter.

The tittering in the treetops stopped. Meuse stopped humming. Oqoti opened his eyes, sensing danger. Gehne turned his flighty attention to Parker.

"*Je ne comprends pas*. What incursion?" Parker held up his hands. Oqoti growled softly. An owl hooted above their heads.

As Francis described the raid on his family's camp, Gehne fixed his dark eyes on him. Parker swore he knew nothing, placing his hands over his heart. *"Je ne savais pas,"* Parker said, struggling to recall the few words he had learned in French. This was the first he had heard of the raid. *"C'est horrible."*

Why had the old man laughed at his words? Why had he heard other voices gasp in horror when he knew they were the only souls here?

"Lord, forgive us all," Parker said.

There was nothing more he could say. In the awkward silence, Francis fetched a drum from its hiding place behind the camp. By the light of the fire, he pounded a steady rhythm, an insistent lament that echoed through the dark woods. Like a heartbeat, an unspoken common language they all understood. After a while, Gehne and Meuse rose and danced around the fire. Their shuffling steps conveyed grief so deep Parker could hardly bear it. They chanted in time to the drum, a rhythmic song in their strange language, punctuated by grunts and hoots. They were four, but Parker would later swear he heard a resonant bass, the high lilt of a child, a woman keening, a pigeon warbling, a croak unlike that of a frog or man. A chorus soon echoed by the howls of wolves and coyotes lurking in the dark woods. Late into the night, Francis drummed, the Indians sang and danced, and Parker tried to understand.

When the fire faded, Francis set down his drum and stared into the dying embers. Gehne reached out to Meuse and held the weeping young man in a vigorous bear hug. Parker gazed into the darkness. In the shadows, he thought he saw a black bear standing erect, pounding its chest. Or was it a man in a white robe, his hand raised as if blessing them all?

CHAPTER TWELVE

The Rescue

Ezekiel pulled his horse up front, right behind Major Rogers and Captain Scott. William rode in the rear. Because this was a rescue party for his father, the officers expected him to be on board. Salome had asked both her son and older stepson to join the search effort. William only hoped that his presence might counteract the violent impulses of the other men. There had been so much carnage already. The governor had approved— he took every opportunity to remind the other members of the party— an act of reconciliation.

Major Rogers, overhearing his words, sneered. *In name only*, he said. *In name only*. "You're as jumpy as a rabbit, my boy." Rogers laughed off William's trepidation. "A few more hours and we'll find our man."

Major Rogers led the rescue party along the narrow path bordering the River Mersey, until recently known by the Acadians as the *Riviere Rossignol*. The annual migrations of the Mi'kmaq had etched a narrow dirt path along the shore. The leafy canopy over their heads was mid-summer thick, so they rode in the shade, protected from the blazing sun. Behind Rogers, Scott rode, second in command and a willing audience for Rogers, who bragged that the governor had personally congratulated him on his political acumen in setting up the exchange. He repeated the governor's praise but never acknowledged Ezekiel's contribution.

Regarding Parker, Rogers reminded them that any exchange required the pastor's safe return. "If an outrage is committed by any of the Indians, the Tribe or Tribes they belong to shall cause satisfaction and restitution to be made to the parties injured," he quoted the recent resolution.

My father, William thought, *is not the only party injured here.*

Referring to the jailed children, Rogers quoted the line and verse of the agreement. "The opinion of the Board is, that as those in prison are not worthy to be kept as hostages, and where they have already been a great expense to his Majesty, they should be released in exchange for the American hostage to show the Indian's sincerity of friendship, and that it may persuade them to support His Majesty's interests."

"Not worthy." "A great expense." William smarted at the words that Rogers read with a contemptuous smile, but he clamped his mouth shut. *Let them free my father first*, he thought, *and then I will see that they fulfill their obligation.*

His stepbrother, Ezekiel, always one step behind the lead officers, had dedicated more hours to the search party than any of the men on the expedition. William knew he resented the major's refusal to acknowledge his help in getting the governor's approval, but he still entertained hopes of being offered a position in the new government. Captain Scott, another born follower, complained only that they might not have the clout to punish the kidnapper properly once they had located him in this dismal forest.

Ezekiel rode in line, followed by a Scotsman who had been hired as a guide. A Mr. Campbell—a local hunter—who was familiar with the terrain. He was a rough and wily man, dressed in leather and smelling of tobacco. When Rogers introduced him, he cautioned his men to watch their tongues around the guide, a second-generation Scot whose loyalty was only to himself. As they rode, Campbell pointed out the landmarks that guided the Indians on their journey. Of course, he said, most of the natives preferred to travel by canoe.

Now the men not only had to watch for the danger lurking in the woods, but they had to patrol the river, looking for natives around every bend.

William was alert to the possibility that the men were headed into a trap. Acres of forest surrounded Lake Kejimkujik, woods where the Mi'kmaq had made their winter camp for decades, centuries, maybe millennia. The Indians knew every turn of this trail and could conceal themselves in thick underbrush. Although the soldiers carried muskets, they proceeded cautiously, alert to danger. The Indians were known to lay traps for bears, large enough to swallow a man. They hunted moose and large game. Even now, Rogers might lead them into hostile territory, where they would not be able to defend themselves.

Following a path worn down by the annual migration of the Mi'kmaq, they started out from the end of Eleven Mile Lake east of Annapolis and followed the river southward. The Mersey, Campbell told them, crossed the entire peninsula, flowing first through Lake Kejimkujik, then Lake Rossignol, before it emptied into the Atlantic Ocean. The path along its shore was riddled with roots, so he instructed them to guide their horses with care. Campbell warned that, despite the urgency of their mission, speed here was the real enemy. Their journey required caution.

Undaunted by the danger, Rogers was in his glory, visibly puffed up by the governor's mandate. He never questioned whether the expedition would be successful. Despite Campbell's rough edges, he was a reliable guide and a man of good humor. As they climbed the rocky trail, he pointed out what he called "picture rocks," rude drawings etched with a hard tool on the flat surfaces of the rock. As they neared the lake, he told them the Mi'kmaq called this territory the Fairy Lake.

Rogers laughed. As if the expedition, which he viewed as one of revenge, was a fairy story. But William understood. The thick woods were redolent with bird calls and twinkled with the flashing eyes of small mammals. Even at midday, the sun barely filtered through the lush canopy. Many small streams rushed into the river, where fish leaped with flashes of silver, propelled by strong currents carrying them to the sea. Here, nature dominated. They were the intruders, diminished by the grandeur of the pines over their heads, barbarians among the fairies.

They stopped only once, to drink fresh water from the stream. Besides fresh clothing for Parker, Salome had packed a wool blanket and provisions for the men: jerky, cheese, and loaves of hearty bread. Before the final push, they tied up their horses, sat along the edge of the river, and ate. They were ravenous. A passerby might have thought the scene a picnic rather than a search party rooting out a criminal. The men took turns relieving themselves on the wide trunk of a mature maple tree. Rogers, pacing back and forth, refused to sit down. Instead, he lectured his troops. "Discipline prepares you for any battle. Hunger sharpens the senses." Despite the youth and inexperience of his men, he was determined to follow up his successful raid with a skillful extraction. "Soon, we will ride home with the abductor in chains and accept accolades from our grateful constituents. Ezekiel, my friend, we will invite your mother Salome and your siblings to join us in celebration. William, we will return your father to his flock where he belongs. Peace will be restored. Victorious in our mission, we'll return to the fort in Annapolis and dispense with the last of the Acadians."

His voice boomed through the forest. His restless energy ruined their appetites.

"Carry on, men," he said. "We have important work to do here."

Reluctantly, the men remounted their steeds and followed Campbell up the path toward the Mi'kmaq winter hunting grounds. They were quieter now. William's heart pounded with anticipation, or was it dread? Was that smear in the bright blue sky a wisp of smoke? Was that chirp a bird singing or the distant sound of voices talking? Their hands rested on their muskets as the horses trotted steadily toward the lake they now saw shimmering through the trees.

• • •

Parker Mountain, Nova Scotia, July 1761

Ma Salome latched onto the possibility of Father's return as the justification for an "all hands on deck," top-to-bottom cleaning of the house. Under her supervision, Sally and I were made to haul every blanket outside and beat them for all they were worth. I swept every floor and scrubbed the floorboards. We boiled the curtains in a pot on the hearth. Then we polished the windowpanes with vinegar and dried each with a rag until the last streak disappeared. With William gone, I had lost my last ally in resisting my stepmother's discipline. Sally and I cleaned from sunrise to midday. As soon as Ezekiel and William had headed out to join the search party, Salome had assigned us our tasks. A sterner despot than even Major Rogers, she didn't allow us a moment's rest.

In the frenzy, I hardly had a moment to reflect on the possibility that within days my father might return home. Not that anyone remembered his rescue was all my idea and Caroline's doing. Caroline now spent most of her time at the fort with the wee ones. When she stopped for supplies, she warned me not to get carried away, not until they found my father alive. But for once, I was siding with Salome. Just the idea that Father might soon return filled me with the urge to clean things up. I was aching to sing hallelujah with the Baptists. Scrubbing the windows, I rejoiced every time a ray of sunlight burst into this once-dreary house. Outside, the apple trees were heavy with fruit. I threw open the windows and inhaled the sweet perfume that filled the room. Baby Henry chortled at my side, his chubby legs kicking with delight. Hard as it was to admit, I had become fond of the little babe.

Father would be home soon. Caroline had not yet told the poor Indian children they might soon be freed. She didn't want to give them false hope. But that morning, when she'd stopped by to collect a load of old clothes—castoffs that we children no longer needed—even she had been cautiously optimistic. No one was sure when or where the children would go, their parents being slaughtered and all. The eldest, Caroline said, had taken over caring for the little ones, nursing the toddler back to health under Caroline's tutelage. The hope was that Father, having spent these weeks in captivity, might provide some guidance as to their placement. William had taken on the responsibility of seeing this process through. Before he left with the search party, he'd told me he didn't trust Rogers and Scott at all. If he were not there, he said, he doubted they would free the children. He feared they would scoop Father up, even if it meant slaying his captor.

The Baptists were all atwitter at the prospect of their pastor returning to his flock. Salome said Father would need some rest and time for recovery, but they ignored her and were busy planning a Service of Thanksgiving. Mrs. Eaton passed around a sign-up sheet at Sunday services to be sure everyone contributed their fair share to the supper afterward.

Putting the cart before the horse, Caroline said. After Caroline left with the children's clothes, Salome packed up a parcel of Father's clothing that she wanted to freshen up before his return. Lord knows, she said, what shape he will be in. I was taken aback by the thought of my proud father in rags. Whenever such thoughts overcame me, I tried to picture the Indian boy. *A boy who played games so earnestly could not be a killer*, I assured myself. I didn't believe he would harm my father.

Before he left, William accused me of being a hopeless romantic. "Better that than a cynic," I'd replied. William reminded me I had poorly misjudged Captain Scott when he first came to our house, serving him pie in the parlor. Now that I realized how vile and cruel that man could be, William took the opportunity to remind me that things are seldom what they seem.

He held up Salome as an example. One would have thought, he said, that in our father's absence, Salome's unhappy lot would be anxiety and tears. "Remember when Salome and Father first wed?" he asked. "She preached the precepts of the gospel."

I understood what he meant. I remember her lecturing me: "Wives submit to husbands as unto the Lord." As if to highlight my unpleasant demeanor by contrast, she had cultivated a cheerful and happy submissiveness. How I disliked her for that!

But now I questioned the cheerful and happy part. When he was present, Ma Salome let Father take the lead. But left on her own, I noticed a new side of my stepmother. When it was necessary, Salome displayed strength and a steely competence. She made childbirth look easy. And while she curried favor with the Baptists, she had no trouble getting them to move their services elsewhere. These traits were beginning to endear Salome to me.

William said Father would have his hands full when he returned. "Bravo," I replied. "There is nothing wrong with a woman standing up for herself."

"In her proper station," William said. Even my dear brother thought a woman must follow the lead of her husband.

Be that as it may, today my proper station was elbow-deep in a bucket of soapy water. I wasn't complaining. William had joined the search party, and at any moment the men might discover my father deep in the Indian woods and free him to return to his family. When he returned, my father would be surprised at what he found. In his absence, I had learned a few things from his new wife. What had once been a household divided was beginning to function as a family, one united and prepared to welcome him home.

• • •

Kejimkujik, July 1761

Ezekiel spotted the smoke first, wisps like ghosts rising from a fire abandoned in the middle of the day. Rogers signaled a halt. The men checked their weapons, tamped down their powder, and reloaded the shot. They hemmed and they hawed, itchy for action.

"Ready?" Rogers asked. We nodded and followed him stealthily down the dirt path. There, we encountered a camp and quickly concluded it had recently been occupied. A dying fire smoldered a short distance from a roughly hewn wigwam.

"Ezekiel," Rogers whispered. "Check inside." Ezekiel dismounted. "Approach cautiously."

Rogers aimed his musket at the animal skin that served as a flap for the primitive shelter. *How like Rogers*, William thought, *to assign this task to another*. Ezekiel, like every young foot soldier, did not question his commander's order. Instead, in slow motion, he tiptoed to the wigwam. Holding his breath, he peeled open the flap.

"No one here," he shouted back.

After inspecting the inside of the wigwam, he reported signs of occupation: animal skins laid as beds, cooking instruments, and discarded clothing.

Not far away, a dog barked.

Rogers snapped to attention. He waved the men toward the sound. They trotted behind him along the narrow path. The dog's yapping intensified as the glint of water appeared through the trees. Rogers signaled them to stop just as a mottled mongrel charged them, teeth bared. Rogers aimed his gun and shot. With a furious yowl, the dog twirled in the air. He seemed dead set on returning to his master but collapsed halfway down the path to the stream, no longer able to stand. Rogers kicked the whimpering animal aside and pointed toward the water. "This way," he hissed. William winced.

"Oqoti!" A young Indian, eyes wide in alarm, ran recklessly toward them. They pulled on their reins as he cried out in his native language. The search party had found what they were looking for. Captain Scott and Ezekiel raised their weapons, ready to fire at Rogers's command. But Rogers reloaded his musket, relishing the drama of the confrontation. The boy fell to his knees besides his dog's limp body. Sobbing, he looked up at the men, right into the barrels of Ezekiel's musket.

"Oqoti!" he cried again.

All weapons were aimed in his direction.

William held his breath, dreading the inevitable shot. But before the men discharged their guns, Parker appeared. His father! Breathing heavily, he ran toward them, up the path from the stream. Resting a hand on the Indian boy's shoulder, he shouted at the officers, "Don't shoot!"

"Pa!" William cried out, elated at the sight of his father. Parker, dressed in western clothes, appeared pale and gaunt but alive. Behind him, a second Indian appeared.

"Arrest them," Rogers ordered. Scott leaped from his horse, still pointing his musket at the kneeling boy. Ezekiel aimed his gun at the other Indian, who raised his hands in surrender.

Parker ignored Rogers and embraced William. He smelled of the river, fresh grass, and smoke. The disgruntled Scotsman took charge of the horses. Gathering their reins, he led them down the path to the stream and tied them to a tree. From his actions, William discerned he wanted no part of whatever came next.

William clung to his father, relieved to see that, although bedraggled, he appeared unharmed. Neither bound nor scalped. In the company of his captors—if these Indians were indeed his captors—he was allowed to walk free. He did not seem afraid.

"Are you alright?" William asked him.

Parker nodded. "They held me against my will, but they treated me humanely."

Rogers snorted. "Kidnapped during an ambush? Hardly humane, if you ask me. We have been looking for you for weeks now. Point out the responsible party, and we will finish this now."

•••

Meuse, immobilized by fear, stared down the mouth of a musket. Oqoti's lifeless body sprawled at the side of the path. With his hands in the air, Francis faced down the intruders, a soldier prepared for battle.

Out of view of the soldiers, William heard someone muttering under his breath.

"Silence!" Rogers shouted. He cocked his head, listening for sounds in the woods.

Parker replied, "What you hear is a loon. We are the only ones here. There is no need for any more violence."

Rogers redirected his gaze down, toward Meuse. His eyes simmered with hatred. "I give the orders here," he said to Parker under his breath, "thank you very much." His message was clear: this was his rescue. His victory.

Ignoring Rogers's warning, William addressed his father, explaining their presence. "We have been charged with arranging a hostage exchange. The British will free three Mi'kmaq children being held in the fort in Annapolis in return for your surrender."

"*Enfants?*" Francis stepped forward, releasing his upheld arms.

"*En échange des filles captives,*" William translated, hoping he had the French words right.

"Is that true?" Parker asked Rogers. "Where are children being held? Why? Has this anything to do with the raid on the Indian settlement in Port Royal?"

"Ah, yes," Rogers answered, his evident pride in this accomplishment distracting him from the task at hand. "We have eliminated that vexing Indian problem. Once you are rescued, our community will be secure at last."

"And the exchange?" Parker asked.

"Loose ends," Rogers said. "If I had my druthers, we'd settle this right now. But the governor authorized the exchange of some worthless children rounded up after the raid, so I must follow his orders. But that does not mean we cannot arrest the offending parties and punish them as we see fit. These two? Are you certain there aren't more guilty parties here?" With a hopeful look of anticipation, he gazed off into the distance, prepared to expand his search.

"No," Parker said. "Only one."

All eyes riveted on Meuse.

"Him?" Rogers asked.

"He is the one who abducted me," Parker said after a moment. Meuse did not flinch.

"The other people here are the family of the children you are holding hostage," Parker added. "Let them be," Parker said to Ezekiel, who still aimed his gun at the second brave. "If you are to return your hostages, they will need to have a family to return to. In any case, this boy had no part in my abduction."

"Cuff the scrawny one, then," Rogers ordered.

The frown on his face showed his disappointment. But he had an arrest to his credit, and William hoped it would satisfy his bloodlust. A guilty party to march through the streets of Annapolis before a cheering crowd. A sinner to escort up the stairs to the gallows.

Scott rested his weapon against a tree, dissatisfaction written all over his face. He would not get to use his gun that day. He wrenched Meuse's hands behind his back, cuffed him roughly, and then, tired of restraint and unable to resist the urge, shoved the helpless boy against a tree. Meuse fell to his knees.

"Two dogs down," Scott said. "All in a day's work."

Ezekiel joined him, adding a few satisfying kicks of his own. Their work done, they yanked Meuse to his feet and marched him to where the horses were tied to an oak tree near the river's edge.

William told Francis he was free to go, the sooner the better. Dismissed by the officers, Francis beckoned to his father, who emerged hesitantly from behind a tree. William watched as Francis spoke softly to the wispy old man who appeared confused, disoriented by the day's events.

"Mimi?" The old man's eyes opened wide in response to something Francis said. "Is my Mimi alive?" Who he spoke to was not clear, but William looked up, recognizing the name.

"*Oui*," he said. "There is a girl named Mimi among those being held in the brig in Annapolis."

"*Elle est ma soeur*," Francis told William. Pointing to Gehne, he added: "*Il est notre père*."

The old man continued muttering in Mi'kmaq to himself. "This isn't over Pa," William assured his father, turning to watch Rogers lead Meuse away in handcuffs. William draped a protective arm around Parker when he saw his father wince as the officers manhandled their captive. Meuse looked straight ahead, his expression blank, as they tied him to a horse.

As he walked away, William heard Francis curse the men who could kill so coldly. He hustled his father away from the site of carnage, whispering assurances that they would return, once the search party had departed, for the dog whose soul had been sacrificed for their survival and whose body would now become food.

"Come, Father," William said. "It is time for us to go home." They caught up with the other men by the stream. William helped his father up into the saddle and walked beside him as the search party headed back toward the river.

Campbell led the line of men on the ride back to Annapolis. The Scot no longer shared his knowledge or love of the terrain. Silently, they rode late into the night. Each, for reasons of their own, was eager to complete the exhausting journey.

•••

As Meuse had once bound Parker to his horse, now he was tied to the man they called Scott. The captain secured his hands behind his back, causing his shoulder muscles to cramp. His tendons, forced beyond their elasticity, strained every time the horse hoofs hit a rock. His legs were tied to the steed's barrel chest. A thick rope joined the two men as the slender officer goaded the horse impatiently. Each bounce shot stabs of pain up Meuse's backbone. The leather horn of the saddle dug into his belly, causing waves of nausea and rubbing his skin raw. Ahead of them, the man in charge reprimanded his Scottish guide. "No dallying, my man. We have a prisoner to deliver." He grunted every time the Scot slowed to maneuver his way through brambles or stopped to assess the best way to cross a shallow stream. Parker also rode somewhere behind them in the darkness, accompanied by his son, the one he called "William." William was the only one among them who had dared to look Meuse in the eye as they set out on the journey.

Meuse longed to hear Uncle Gehne conversing with his Elders. At first, he listened for voices, but they were silent as the men crossed through the thick forest. If only his father would appear to guide him. But then he remembered Gehne's words: his father was ashamed by what he had brought on himself. His mother had died with more dignity than he soon would. Far from the warrior he had aspired to be, he was a casualty of his own making. A foolish child who played at battle, only to be defeated by unworthy playmates. A hunter's prize of less value than a skinny deer's carcass whose meat had gone bad.

He could not see Parker riding in the darkness behind him, but from time to time he heard him conversing with his son in a soft voice. Meuse closed his eyes, remembering the exaltation on William's face when he had spotted his father alive. The stab of jealousy he'd felt. The sight of the father and son reunited had defeated Meuse as much as the soldier who had thrown him to the ground. When he had responded to Oqoti's agonized death cry, he had expected to see the search party. Sooner or later, he knew they would come for him. Even as he joined Parker in prayer, he had accepted that his days were numbered. What sent him reeling into hopelessness was William's joy at his first sight of his father. Gehne's delighted grin when he learned that his daughter Mimi had survived. Francis walking away with his arm around his father. What had sealed Meuse's despair was the realization that he was once again a fatherless child. And worse, a disgrace to his tribe, the family that nurtured him.

I am not worthy of mercy, he thought. *Let these men do what they will; there is nothing more they can take from me. How foolish I was to think I could stop them.*

The party rode all night. By the time the sun rose over Annapolis, Meuse could no longer feel his legs. The ache in his shoulders had spread to his scalp, which throbbed in time to the horse's gallop. *Let them kill me now*, he thought, though he had enough of his faculties intact not to utter this in any language they would understand.

In single file, they rode up to the officers' barracks at the fort overlooking Annapolis. In the distance, Meuse saw commercial fishing boats heading out to sea.

"I'll take my leave now," William told the officer. "Once I have my father settled, I will return so that we can arrange the official exchange ceremony."

"Take your time," Rogers answered. "My main concern is our prisoner. By day's end, I intend to walk him up the steps of the gallows."

The horses stood restlessly in front of the large stone building. Meuse's eyes met Parker's. Already, the Baptist appeared a different man, standing taller, erect and proud. For the journey, he had changed into the clothes his son had brought. A starched white linen shirt hung loosely on his emaciated frame. His expression was weary, yet authoritative. His hair had been combed.

"Don't touch the boy until you have fulfilled your obligations," Parker said to Rogers. "I am not free until those children are safely home."

Rogers snorted. "Pastor, you were free the moment I set eyes on you."

Parker could not disguise his disgust. "The Indian who kidnapped me behaved more honorably than you have. May God save your soul." Just as it looked as if the two men might come to blows, William inserted himself between them.

"Now, now," he said. "We all need a night's sleep before we complete our mission. Father, if you don't mind waiting a few moments more, I'll go find Caroline. I believe she stayed all night with the children in the jail. Rogers, you need time to update your men and notify the governor of the success of our expedition. Who knows? The governor might choose to be present for the formal exchange since it reflects so well on your governance." William's face revealed no emotion, but his father nodded at his cagey attempt to manipulate the major.

"I need a few days to recover," Parker said. "And I respectfully request that my son William play a part in the return of the hostages."

At that, Ezekiel stepped forward. He was sullen, with dark rings around his eyes, and his uniform was wrinkled from the days of travel. As the major's right-hand man, Ezekiel had spoken little during the long ride home except to echo his mentor's bluster. Now he addressed his stepfather: "Mother is waiting for you. Grant me the pleasure of escorting you home. Let the officers deal with the culprit. Salome and the children are eager to see you."

William added what nobody else had thought to tell Parker. "In your absence, you became a father once more."

"A son?" Parker asked, a delighted smile transforming his weary countenance.

"A son," Ezekiel said. "Only one of many we can now hope, thanks to Major Rogers's heroic efforts."

With that, Ezekiel and Parker rode off, discussing the newborn and his wife's effortless delivery.

Even Rogers had lost his bluster. "Very well," he said. "I'll notify the governor. Men, take the prisoner to a jail cell at once and arrange 24-hour security. If that mousy midwife is about, tell her to prepare the children for a journey."

He rode off as William helped Officer Scott untie Meuse. When his shackles were off, Meuse stumbled, limp and broken. *He's as good as dead,* William thought, as they carried Meuse down the prison stairs. In the dank darkness of the holding cell, their prisoner crumpled to the floor.

CHAPTER THIRTEEN

March to the Gallows

Parker Mountain, July 1761

Ezekiel rode up to the house with fire in his eyes and Father, gray and gaunt, behind him. It was the most glorious sight of my entire life, better even than seeing the wharf in Annapolis after my seasick voyage on the Charming Molly. Sally and I had just put baby Henry to bed, but what with all the cheering and hugging—and many a tear—baby Henry woke right back up, bawling for all he was worth, his face beet-red with angry tears flowing down his chubby cheeks.

"It's your Pa," I cooed, comforting the baby as if he could understand. I held him up so that Father could meet the new member of our family. Sally stood beside me, her eyes on the ground. She shuffled her feet, uncomfortable in his presence. Father hardly knew her, and I could see now that was hard for her.

"A healthy lad," Father said, taking baby Henry from my arms, not at all intimidated by his bloodcurdling screams. "Full of piss and vinegar."

After a thorough investigation (toes counted, private parts examined), he handed Henry to Sally and said, "A fine brother for you all. Where's your Ma?" Sally smiled shyly. All this time, Ma Salome had been busying herself in the kitchen, pouring water for tea and slicing bread and cheese.

We had so many questions for Father and piled them one on top of the other. "How did the Indian ambush you?" I asked.

"Did the Indians have guns or tomahawks?" Nat asked. "Where did they find you?"

"Did they try to scalp you?" Ezekiel asked. "Did you fight back?"

I had more questions than any of the rest. "Did the officers arrest your captor? Did you live in a wigwam? Did braves dance a war dance when you arrived? Did you know a search party was looking for you the whole time?"

"Were you afraid you would die?" Sally asked in her timid voice.

Father just smiled, waiting for a break in the verbal assault. When we had run out of questions, he said, "God was at my side the whole time." It was a most unsatisfactory response.

Ezekiel, as full of himself as ever, informed us that Father was tired, and we might as well all go back to bed and save our questions for the morning. And this was despite the fact—I thought but did not say—Father wasn't even his own flesh and blood. I resisted telling him so only because I did not want to anger Father so soon after he had returned.

Instead, the family gathered around him in the parlor. Ma Salome poured tea and permitted us the rare treat after bedtime.

Father was weary, that much was evident. I couldn't take my eyes off his haggard face. He had lost weight and, it seemed, his air of righteousness. I wondered if his baptism had stuck, what with being kidnapped and all. Tonight, he looked like any common man tired at the end of a day's labor, hardly the benevolent pastor prepared to carry the spiritual burdens of his flock.

"Lucy, my love," he said. "Come here and give your father a hug."

At his invitation, I let go of all the trouble and turmoil of the past few weeks. While the others watched, he held me in his arms. I laid my head on his bony shoulder, the heat of a blush rising from my neck to my face.

"I knew you would come home," I whispered into his ear.

"Enough, Lucy," Ma Salome said. Reluctantly, I stepped aside. I watched as Salome welcomed Father with a timid peck on the cheek.

When the grandfather clock struck ten, Salome shooed us children up to bed. But late into the night, through the chamber wall, I heard Father and Ma Salome talking. Although I could not distinguish their words, the rise and fall of their voices was as lovely a song as any lullaby my own dear Ma sang when I was a babe.

By the time I woke the next morning, William had returned from the fort. We learned a formal hostage exchange was to take place there that afternoon in front of the governor and a tribal chief named Chief Bâtard. With the local Indians all dead or in hiding, the governor had summoned a chief with whom he had negotiated a recent treaty. For the ceremony, Father was ordered to report to the fort to be officially freed, despite his protest that he'd prefer to recuperate at home. The whole affair was to be kind of our own "Burying the Hatchet" ceremony. Father said the ceremony was political hogwash, and apart from his freedom and mercy being shown to the little ones, it served no earthly purpose.

William, who had guarded the prisoner all night at the fort, was uncharacteristically quiet. Ezekiel asked Ma Salome to press his dress uniform, as he was certain to be on the dais, perhaps at the governor's side. William, who had not slept a wink, did not share his enthusiasm. Instead, before I had a chance to corner him, he asked to speak to Father in private. I was angling for a description of the kidnapper, still wondering if he was the Waltes boy, but I had no choice but to wait until William concluded his business with Father. In my eagerness, I staked out a post outside the parlor door. I would flag down William at the first opportunity.

Their discussion was interminable. At first quiet, William's voice became increasingly more agitated as the conversation went on. I overheard Major Rogers's name repeated often and Captain Scott's, but despite a valiant effort, I could not figure out the cause of William's concern. Then I heard William exclaim: "He's dead set on marching the poor lad to the gallows!"

The Indian, I thought.

"As if there hasn't been carnage enough," Father replied.

They continued to speak for nearly an hour. Ezekiel passed by, carrying his pressed uniform and rolling his eyes. Ma Salome spotted me at my post and reminded me there were dishes that needed cleaning and a baby that wanted changing. "Yes, ma'am," I said, but even then, I refused to budge.

Finally, William emerged, leaving Father behind to rest in his armchair.

"Lucy," William asked me, "how long have you been standing there?" His harsh tone startled me. My own dear brother, as dismissive as the rest of them! Had he forgotten that I had come up with the plan for freeing Father from captivity?

"I need to speak with you," I said, sullen and hurt. Didn't William always find time for me, even when the others dismissed me so callously? A rogue tear escaped my eye.

He sighed. "Sorry, Lucy. I didn't mean to snap at you. I have my hands full."

But I wasn't about to let him off so easily. "Was it him?" I asked. The question exploded from my lips. I couldn't have held it back any longer even if I had tried.

"Him?"

"The Indian boy, the one I saw. Was it he who kidnapped Father?"

William shook his head. "Lucy, you needn't concern yourself with this sordid matter."

"William, how can you say that? The rescue was my plan. Mine and Caroline's! I suppose you didn't mention that to Father. You and Ezekiel took all the credit." I wanted to hurt him. I was that angry. "You, Major Rogers, and Captain Scott think you're the heroes, but that's not fair." I could feel the heat rising in my face and resisted a strong urge to stomp my foot. "I saw him first," I said.

Salome emerged from the kitchen, wiping her hands on her apron.

"Lucy," she said, "whatever has gotten into you? Your brother is exhausted. Let him be."

It took every ounce of forbearance I could muster not to burst into tears.

Fortunately, William came to my defense. "We're all a little emotional today. My little sister most of all." He put an arm around me. I melted at his tender touch, forgiving him instantly.

"Lucy, you have chores to do," Salome said. I glimpsed Sally spying on us from the kitchen.

"Just give us a minute," William said.

Salome, with one last glance over her shoulder, returned to the kitchen, tut-tutting the whole way. William turned to me and said, "His name is Meuse."

"The Indian boy?"

"Yes."

"Can I see him?"

William did not answer.

"Are they going to hang him?"

William opened his hands, a gesture of helplessness I understood. Inside the parlor, I heard Father praying. With the door half-open, his words were clear: "Have mercy on his soul."

"Lucy," William said. "Father's home. I'll be sure he knows you deserve some credit for his rescue. But this is a nasty business, and you're best off keeping your nose out of it."

My own brother! Didn't he know me at all?

This time, I held my tongue. I loved William, but I refused to let him dismiss me that easily. William hadn't slept in two days, and I didn't mean to add to his exhaustion. But I was wide awake, and I'd heard enough to know Meuse's fate rested in my family's hands.

●●●

Annapolis, July 1761

Using a rag and a bucket of soapy water, Caroline bathed the children and, with Mimi's help, dressed them in the hand-me-down clothes Salome had packed in brown paper. The older girl had a steady hand, a gentle touch the children trusted. She was a natural caretaker who knew when to help and when to step back.

"You will travel on horseback," Caroline comforted the girl, relying on an Acadian woman awaiting deportation in an adjacent cell to translate her words. "Your brother is waiting for your return."

Before William had headed home, he had updated Caroline on the situation. "Monitor the children," he said. "I'll be back as soon as I can. We cannot trust Rogers and Scott with the prisoners." William said the older girl's father, a survivor of the raid, was a hard case himself, crazy from the shock. Hopefully, the children's return would snap him out of it. There was a brother too, so maybe the family had a chance.

In William's absence, Captain Scott insisted on standing guard whenever Caroline visited the children. He turned his back while she scrubbed their bony backs and dumped buckets of soapy water over their greasy hair, but he turned around just as she handed Mimi a clean set of underclothes. Caroline tried to shield the girl from his leering assessment. Caroline, like Lucy, had developed an intense dislike of the officer, whom she found supercilious and not very smart. She had watched with horror as he had shoved the boy William called Meuse into the smallest, darkest cell, where puddles of putrid water pooled on the dirt floor. In the unlit corners of the ceiling, spiders guarded enormous webs where dozens of flies had already perished. The man was too aware of his own good looks and strutted through the fort's hallways as if modeling the posture of a dashing soldier. All she saw was a brute who treated the boy like a bag of garbage he had been asked to dump.

When a rat ran across the boy's cell, he laughed and said "dinner?"

The children witnessed it all from where they huddled in their cell. The indifference. The heartless cruelty. When Caroline suggested the boy be given a blanket (the basement lacked both heat and insulation), Scott replied, "Why bother? He's as good as dead already." In his presence, Caroline resorted to womanly wiles that she usually eschewed. Batting her eyes, she convinced him that if the prisoner didn't make it through the night, Major Rogers would be denied his march to the gallows. Begrudgingly, he located a burlap bag, which he threw into Meuse's cell, barely missing the largest puddle. When Meuse pulled it over his shivering body, his teeth chattered so hard neither of them could tell what language he used to thank them.

Encouraged by her attention, Scott flirted whenever he became bored. Twice, she asked him to keep his hands to himself. He chuckled each time as if pleased to have elicited a response.

A sad state of affairs. Caroline resolved not to leave the children's side. Even though she had a half-dozen ladies about to go into labor, she was afraid that if she left the fort, the children might perish before they were returned to their families.

By night's end, Caroline had decided to accompany William when he escorted the children home to their tribe. As much as the pregnant ladies of Annapolis needed her, these children had touched her heart. She wouldn't abandon them now.

• • •

William returned to the fort late in the afternoon, somewhat improved by a short nap and carrying a satchel of provisions Salome had prepared for the hostages. Before descending into the malodorous basement, he shared a warm bun with Caroline, who came up from the basement to sit with him on a bench in the administrative office. Rogers and Scott ignored them, as they were engrossed in frenetic preparations for the governor's arrival. Under their command, two young second lieutenants scrubbed and polished the floors. Rumors of the exchange had spread like wildfire through the town, and a crowd of rabble-rousers gathered outside the jail. William made a mental note of the pegboard beneath the desk where a dozen keys hung, each labeled with the cell it opened.

"Voyeurs," William said. "The whole town has gathered to watch the hostage exchange."

He has no idea how the local militia has fired up the populace in his absence, Caroline thought.

"How is your father?" Caroline asked.

"Happy to be home," William said. "Not too pleased to be part of the formalities." The crowd outside the room's windows doubled during the time it took for them to finish.

"Are the children prepared?" he asked. "The sooner they leave, the better."

"We can depart right after the formal ceremony if you've arranged for Campbell to accompany us."

"We?"

"I've decided to join you," Caroline said.

William opened his mouth to object and then shut it, puzzling the matter over.

"I've sent a note to my mother asking her to arrange for another midwife to assume my duties," Caroline said. "I'm sure there are several young women with adequate skills among the newest arrivals from Massachusetts."

"I've already made the arrangement with Campbell. Returning the three children to the camp on Lake Kejimkujik is a complicated matter of no concern to the officers." William spoke softly so that they could not be overheard. "The sooner we can put distance between the Indian children and Rogers and Scott, the more likely they are to survive."

Caroline once again offered to accompany him. With two horses and the escort of the Scottish guide, she hoped they could make it to Kejimkujik while Rogers was still preoccupied with the governor's visit.

"It's a strenuous journey," he warned.

"I'm always ready for an adventure," Caroline said. "How do you think I ended up in Nova Scotia?"

That settled it. The two watched the lieutenants scurry about the building. A uniformed armed guard stood sentry outside the locked door to the basement. When William told him they were ready to visit the prisoners in their cells, the guard regarded them with suspicion. "Only with the major's authorization," he said.

Rogers was nowhere around. Captain Scott busied himself in a far corner, ignoring their conversation. When Caroline approached the desk, the guard, a lad of no more than nineteen, regarded her skeptically. "This is no place for a lady."

"We have provisions intended for the hostages," Caroline said, holding up the satchel.

William pointed to the pegboard beneath the desk. "If you would, please hand me the key to the children's cell. I'll let myself in. 'Tis my father who was kidnapped, and I am a member of the search party that rescued him," he said. "I don't suppose you want the major to hear that you are shielding the prisoners from my righteous anger?"

"Your name?" Caroline asked the officer, her haughty tone an imitation of Salome's at its most imperious. "I shall report your lack of cooperation at once to the major."

The boy shuffled uncomfortably.

"Let 'em in," Scott shouted from the corner, snickering. He winked at Caroline, pleased to intervene.

William, catching a glimpse of Scott's salacious smile, took his aunt's arm as they passed through the now open door into the purgatory of the basement. "What a horrid man," he said.

"Keep him away from Lucy," Caroline warned.

"Oh, she's over him," William said. At the mention of his sister, he added, "Lucy wants a look at the prisoner. She still insists she met him before the kidnapping."

"The poor girl is better off out of this," Caroline said.

"My thoughts exactly, but she's a stubborn one with a mind of her own."

"The sooner this is over, the better off we'll all be." Caroline walked over to the children's cell. "This man is a friend," she said to Mimi. She could not tell if the girl understood, but the two little ones gladly accepted the food she offered. Even the toddler reached out for a piece of bread. In their clean clothes, they were as close to respectable as they might ever be.

"Mimi here is my worthy helper," Caroline said to William.

Mimi didn't smile back. Pointing at the cell across from theirs where Meuse slept in a damp corner, she said, her voice filled with concern, "*Il souffre.*"

"I've tried to shield the children from the prisoner," she told William. "Their lot is hard enough; they have no need of another's suffering. It is my hope that their release, along with the news of Gehne's and Francis's survival, will strengthen them for the journey ahead. But if they recognize Meuse, if they realize he is a member of their tribe, it will make the situation worse."

Caroline spoke in English, assuming the children could not understand. But at her words, Mimi looked up. Her eyes burned brightly as if a fever had overtaken her. "Meuse?" Mimi asked. *"Il s'appelle* Meuse?" The girl stood at the bars of her cell, searching the shadows of Meuse's cell.

William followed her gaze. It took him several moments to distinguish the boy, his eyes closed, covered by only a burlap bag as he shivered in the corner, his face swollen and bruised, his feet bare.

"I doubt there is much that can be done for him," he said to Caroline.

William approached Meuse's cell. If Lucy was right, the boy was an innocent. Even Parker had refused to condemn him. But while they might rescue the children, he knew he held no sway over the punishment of an Indian who had dared to kidnap a white man, especially a soldier who had fought for the Crown and returned to Nova Scotia a respected man and spiritual leader. This boy was beyond rescue. A pawn sacrificed in a wicked game of chess.

Meuse lay in the cell's corner, soiled, bloody, and damp.

Like a dog, thought William. *A whipped dog.*

In the children's cell, Mimi began to sing, strange Mi'kmaq words, incomprehensible. The song—a lullaby or a prayer?—floated through the dusty air. She stood, grasping the cell's bars, swaying as she sang, her movements like those of a dreamer, minimal and muted. A dancer lost in the dance.

William thought, *He's better off dead.* But just as he concluded he could not help the boy, Meuse coughed with a sputter and opened his eyes with a start. Returning William's gaze, he whimpered.

Caroline approached the cell. "Did the girl's song awaken him?" she whispered.

Mimi continued to sing. With a groan, Meuse pulled himself to his feet and stepped towards them. He tilted his head and listened. On his neck, they saw a necklace of bruises in the shape of fingerprints.

William said, "Lucy must never see this brutality. She would never recover."

William agreed to remain at the children's side until they were officially freed. Campbell would be waiting, prepared to escort them back to

Kejimkujik right after the ceremonial exchange. In the meantime, Caroline could visit the Parkers, update the family on the children's condition, and rest up. "Please keep an eye on Lucy," he asked her, "and tell Salome to keep the girl at home."

Caroline was relieved the children could not understand their conversation. "Let someone remain innocent," she said, her eyes filling with tears.

William nodded, seeking out the boy's eyes once more as the midwife slowly ascended the steps. When Caroline pounded on the heavy door to get the guard's attention, Meuse jumped. William was surprised the boy was still capable of alarm, given his deteriorating physical condition.

This boy did not kill my father, he thought. He had every opportunity to do so, but he did not. Lucy had thought him lonely. Now, like the dog Rogers shot, he lay on the cold ground, helpless. Rogers would use his hanging as a warning to Indians who might consider returning to the area and a declaration of the colonist's power. The whole affair repulsed William. Even his righteous father had expressed dismay at the officer's casual cruelty.

If Lucy were to see Meuse now, what would she see? A defenseless boy who had been convicted without a trial? A helpless native who had lost his hunting grounds, his family, and every strand of dignity? A child without a friend in the world.

"*Aidez le*," Mimi, in her cell, called out. Help him. Meuse startled at the sound of her voice and looked up as if gazing at the heavens and not the dark, stained ceiling. A spider in the corner of his cell dropped slowly, twisting on a glistening thread. He dangled there, looking for a victim for his evening meal. Meuse watched him, licking his parched and bloody lips. Then he too began to sing softly, syllables that sounded like "*Way ha ya yo way.*"

"I'll do what I can," William turned to Mimi. "I *will* help him." Together, they watched in fascination as a fat fly landed on the spider's thread. In no time at all, the spider climbed back up to spin a sticky net around the captive fly.

•••

Parker Mountain, July 1761

Salome spent the morning doing her usual chores as if this was not the day we had all been praying for. When the coast was clear, I tiptoed into the parlor where Father had been resting.

"Father, may I come in?"

Father reclined in his armchair, his legs stretched over the ottoman, leather slippers on his feet and a thick wool blanket over his legs.

"Lucy, my dear one, I thought I might never know such luxury again," he said, yawning and tamping tobacco into his pipe. "What can I do for you?"

"I knew you would come home," I said. "We prayed every day. The Baptists practically lived here before Ma Salome convinced Minister Moulton to take them in. I don't think God had any choice but to let you live."

Father chuckled. "I did some praying of my own."

He seemed in fine fiddle despite his weeks as a captive in the Indian camp. Knowing my time was limited—Ma Salome would call me to help any minute now—I dove right in. I perched on the arm of his chair (a definite no-no in Ma Salome's book) and, encouraged by the lack of a reprimand, asked the question that William had refused to answer. "The Indian boy they are holding in the jail, are they going to hang him?"

"Lucy, Lucy," he said, studying his pipe.

Was that all he was going to say? Would nobody tell me the truth? Frustrated, I asked the other question that needed answering: "Was he the same one you chased away from our field?"

That got his attention. "What?" he said, then stopped to think, "Well, I'll be. You might be right."

He seemed to think it through: the why and where of it all, why he was targeted, who was to blame.

"Father, I have a confession to make." I took a deep breath. "I know that boy."

Father sat up, wide awake now, placing his feet on the floor. His expression was suddenly stern. "Whatever are you talking about?"

"Last fall, when I was working out in the field, he asked me to play a game with him. I think he was a friend of the French girl who used to live here. He showed me a game the Indians play called Waltes. I didn't know the bowl was an object the heathens used to see into the future until Miss Polly told me so. Now I'm afraid I was the one who caused you to get abducted. The boy was looking for me the day you chased him from our fields. Father, I am the one to blame for all you have suffered." *What a relief it was to confess at last!*

"You sweet, foolish child." Father took my face in his hands. "Believe me, this whole sordid affair has nothing to do with you." He sighed, pushing me off the arm of his chair, but gently.

"So, you must tell me. Is he going to hang?" I asked again. "I want to hear the truth. I'm not a child, you know. We've all suffered during your absence. Ma Salome was prepared to be a widow once more, and Sally and I were sisters without a father between the two of us. All I'm asking is what comes next?"

"Only the Lord knows," he sighed.

Just when I thought he might answer me at last, William entered the room. He startled at seeing me standing there. If he had slept, it didn't show. The circles under his eyes were a deep, dark blue. He ran his long fingers through his wavy hair as if that would make him presentable.

"Lucy, Father and I have important business to discuss."

"About the prisoner?" I asked.

"Lucy!" Father said.

Now they were both angry, but so was I. "Father, you are alive because the native didn't kill you. But Rogers and Scott murdered his family, and now they are set on marching that young boy to the gallows. Tell me how that makes sense, Father! You preach righteousness and glory. Tell me how any of this makes sense." Despite my best efforts, my voice cracked, anger and tears competing for my attention.

Father and William stood there, stunned at my audacity. Peeking through the fingers with which I covered my face, I hoped my righteousness might lessen the inevitable punishment that awaited me.

Instead, Father addressed William. "Tell Campbell time is of the essence," he said. "Hurry. As soon as the soldiers leave the jail to attend the governor's prisoner exchange, you must put our plan into motion."

He paused a moment and then addressed me. "Caroline is going to escort Mimi and the children back to the Mi'kmaq's winter camp. Hopefully, the children's family—those that remain—will protect them."

I nodded, grateful for this sign of trust from my father.

But then I noticed an unspoken addendum between William and Father. A meeting of the eyes. There was something more they weren't telling me.

"But I thought William was going with her?" I asked.

"William has another matter to attend to," Father replied.

William nodded. "I'll be gone by the morning."

"Tell the boy I am grateful for his compassion. That the Lord forgives those who see the error of their ways," Father said.

William and my father embraced as men do, stiffly and with a quick pat on the back.

"You mustn't say a word of this to anyone," Father said to me. Then he turned to William and said, "We had better be going. The ceremony begins at three. Give Lucy the package Salome has prepared for the boy." He placed a hand on my shoulder. "If all goes as we have planned, William will instruct you where you can deliver this package. And now I need to get dressed. God help me; the governor is expecting me any minute now."

Father kissed me on the forehead and then took his leave. After he shut the door, William knelt before me and took my hands in his. His expression was deadly serious. "Lucy, not a word to anyone." He handed me the bag. "Hide this for now. Salome will tell you when to deliver it."

And then he, too, was off.

I dusted with uncharacteristic fervor all afternoon, but Ma Salome didn't seem to notice. I mulled over all I had heard, trying to piece together their plan. I couldn't figure out all the details, but I knew that Father and William were my heroes. It surprised me that Ma Salome was involved in it.

As we did our chores, I kept an eye on her. She was in a pleasant mood, humming as she ordered us girls about. After lunch, she baked a spice cake, Father's favorite. At the supper table, we did not discuss the hostage exchange, but I knew we were all waiting for the announcement that Father was officially free.

I volunteered to wash the dishes so that Sally could rock baby Henry to sleep. Now that we had a brother in common, Sally was beginning to feel like a real sister, my one and only. Unless, of course, Ma Salome got pregnant again, which was likely now that Father was home. I supposed it was time I got used to the possibility that there were more siblings to come. If I had to go to church and give thanks for Father's return, I would willingly do so. We were beginning to feel like a family at last. This house was beginning to feel like home.

• • •

Annapolis, July 1761

Parker and William arrived at the fort shortly before noon. A large crowd had assembled outside the gates, awaiting admission to the exchange ceremony where the governor would formally free the children. Atop a grassy knoll visible from the gate, Rogers and Scott paced on a wooden stage, awaiting the governor's arrival. They signaled to the lackey at the gate that Parker and his son should be admitted.

Parker limped up the hill, stiff in the uniform he had not worn since returning to Massachusetts after the Battle of Louisbourg. The jacket was too large for his newly slender frame.

"I will be glad when this is over," he whispered to William as they approached the stage.

William squeezed his father's hand and spoke beneath his breath. "If all goes well, it may be some time before I see you again. But I will never forget the lessons you have taught me."

"I am proud to call you my son," Parker said. "May you walk in righteousness, and may the Lord protect you." Parker inhaled, steeling himself for the ceremony to come. With a determined sniff, he headed onto the stage, leaving William behind.

William watched his father join the officers. How tall he stood despite his ordeal. How resolute his expression. Drawing strength from this image, William headed toward the administration building. The lobby was empty now except for a flustered clerk who had been left behind, too low in rank to join the festivities.

"I've come for the children," William told him, standing tall to assert his authority. He pointed to the keys hanging beneath the desk. "Could you please hand me the key to the cell door? The governor will arrive any moment now."

During the previous night's planning session, William had convinced Scott to delegate this task to him. "Your rightful place is on the stage with the governor," he'd told Scott. "I am only here as Parker's son, but you are an important town official, a key member of the rescue party. Let me do the menial work while you perform your official duties." Although reluctant at first, Scott had conceded. Rogers had nodded his approval.

Now, William accepted the key ring with an expressionless face and a thundering heart. He headed down into the basement of the building, bracing himself for the familiar stench.

"There you are, at last," Caroline greeted him. "I've cleaned up the children as best I can." Mimi wore a gingham dress, a hand-me-down from Lucy, part of the parcel of clothes Salome had packed for the children. The two little ones wore breeches but remained barefoot, eyes wide with fear.

William nodded. "Then we're ready to proceed?"

"As ready as we'll ever be."

"Campbell agreed to meet you right after the ceremony. He understands the urgency of getting these children out of the way."

"And what am I to say if Rogers or Scott asks why I escorted the children to the ceremony instead of you?"

"Tell them the children are skittish and only trust you. You wanted to avoid any delay in getting them to the ceremony on time. Tell them I volunteered to keep an eye on the other prisoner until the ceremony is over."

Mimi watched as they whispered, her comforting arm around the little ones. The prisoners were silent in their cells.

"William..." Caroline said, and then paused as if searching for words that could fill such an ominous silence.

Before she could complete her sentence, they heard the muffled clatter of hoofbeats outside, then the sound of applause as the governor's entourage passed through the gates of the fort.

"Go," William urged her. "Go now, and God be with you." He opened the door to the children's cell.

"And also with you," Caroline said, ushering the children out of the cell and up the damp, dark stairs. At the front desk, the clerk had buried his head in his hands, napping away the monotony of his lowly task.

•••

Meuse's eyes locked on those of Parker's son, the one he called William. All the other soldiers had departed for the exchange. The white woman had gathered up the children, ushering Mimi and the little ones past Meuse's cell, up the stairs and into the lobby. Now there remained only William, standing outside the door of Meuse's cell. Like a dreamer summoned from a stupor, Meuse faced him, unsteady on flaccid limbs and fighting an overwhelming inertia. It was as if he had swallowed a poisonous frog that had deadened his senses and rendered him incapable of movement or response.

"Psst, Meuse," William whispered.

At the sound of his name, Meuse rubbed his bleary eyes.

"Meuse," William repeated. Checking to see that no one was around, he flashed the key cupped in his palm.

Meuse regarded him warily. *Could he trust this man?* He tested his limbs one by one. A startling pain shocked him out of his languor. A sluggish pulse awakened his deadened nerves under protest. Slowly, he regained sensation and the ability to move his fingers and toes.

His legs felt like noodles; he massaged his shoulders with stiff fingers, half numb and clumsy. He approached the cell's door from the spot where he had made his makeshift bed since being shoved into the vile cell. He swayed unsteadily, like a drunk leaving a bar. William watched his slow progress, gesturing for him to approach.

Soon, the two men faced each other with only the cell's bars between them. They stood at about the same height. Meuse was startled by

William's resemblance to his father. But the younger man lacked his father's bravado. Instead, he emanated kindness, even an unveiled sympathy.

"Meuse," William said again. He could not speak the boy's language, but in naming the boy, he acknowledged him.

"William," Meuse replied, the word mushy in his mouth. His English consisted of only a few words, those he had learned during the long nights he had joined Parker in prayer. Since these were the only words he had, he used them now, reciting them as he had with Parker: "Forgive us our sins…"

William's eyes sprang open with surprise. Without a moment's hesitation, he joined in, "…as we forgive those who trespass against us."

In the silence that followed, their eyes met.

"*Nous ne sommes pas*," Meuse said, "*des sauvages.*"

William listened closely, trying to translate the foreign language. "We are… You are not…" he said. And then he recognized the word "savages."

They stood there for five seconds, but it might as well have been five minutes, an hour. The prayer hung in the air like an unspoken negotiation. *Forgive us our trespasses.* This last word named the source of their conflict.

Meuse watched William warily, as, with a finger to his mouth, Parker's son turned the key and opened the door to Meuse's cell.

A tingle of adrenaline flowed through Meuse's extremities. He stretched his aching arms over his head, opened and closed his eyes. His fists clenched. Every bone in his body hurt. Every joint screamed.

"Come with me," William beckoned, an impatient gesture that said, *follow me.*

Meuse studied William's expression. *Was this the moment of his death?* He looked into William's eyes. In their depths, he saw kindness; in William's face, he read compassion. These were not the eyes of a soldier.

Beneath him, his legs wobbled, but his heart beat stronger by the moment, reminding him he was still alive.

William gestured again, urgently now, for him to follow, and Meuse did. In William's shadow, he hurried down a dark corridor to a large door where Meuse had once seen the guards throw out bags of garbage and through which they had dragged the lifeless bodies of deceased prisoners. William flung open this door, reached up over his head, and slid open the rusted bolt of a bulkhead. As he pushed open the wooden door, sunlight flooded the stairs.

"Run," William said. And then in French. "*Cours.*"

Meuse did not need the translation to understand what William meant. At that moment, his body came alive again. He was no longer a helpless boy, but instead, a man propelled by the desire to survive.

In the shadow of the administration building, the two men headed away from the exchange and all its pomp and circumstance. They followed the hoarse call of disgruntled crows in the overhanging trees, heading toward the cemetery on the north side of the fort's property, where generations of soldiers were buried in a tidy graveyard.

With tombstones all around them, they fled, William in front but Meuse right behind him. He ran behind William across the graveyard where the bodies of British soldiers were interred. He followed William into the woods on the other side of the cemetery, his bare feet flying over sharp stones and mucky puddles. It was as if he had awakened from a bad dream only to discover the possibility of freedom.

I am alive, he marveled. *Despite all I have brought upon myself, I am alive.*

And as he ran, he realized William had a plan.

In the shadows at the edge of the forest, William pointed to a dark horse tied to the trunk of a small tree. When the ceremony was over, and the hearty handshakes exchanged, when the "free" children were once more escorted to their cells, where Caroline would prepare to take them home, William and Meuse would be far, far away.

They rode as one on the mare's back through the countryside, avoiding the cart paths and staying in the shadow of towering forests. Soon they arrived on the far side of a cornfield that Meuse recognized. There, William halted the horse, and they dismounted.

William put two fingers in his mouth and whistled, then hesitated as if waiting for a response. Meuse, disoriented, scanned the field where they stood. He recognized the white farmhouse in the distance. Parker's house. They had arrived on Parker's mountain.

Within moments, the girl, Parker's daughter, emerged from the back door of the house, her arms full. William turned to Meuse and pantomimed eating. "Lucy has food for your journey," he said. He held out his hand, and the two men shook.

"May God protect you," William said.

Meuse responded with the word Parker had used to end so many a prayer: "Amen."

With that, William rode off in a cloud of dust.

Meuse watched as Parker's daughter crossed the cornfields by the fading light of the summer sun, skirting the chicken coops. Her gaze was fixed on the woods in front of which Meuse now stood. Her blue eyes were wide. She surveyed the edge of the field. Under one arm, she carried a blanket, in the other, a satchel.

"I know who you are," she whispered in French. "I know you did not hurt my father."

Listening to her earnest yet incomprehensible words, Meuse moved closer to the edge of the forest, woods he had wandered since he was a child. This was no longer a game. How innocent he had been to approach Parker's daughter that first time! How naïve to think they could be friends. This field belonged to her family now. This time, he knew he must leave it for good.

As she came near, he froze. He had seen her watching him the day he had abducted her father. Then, he had felt neither fear nor shame. A warrior might have killed her father, even if it meant taking his own life. But he was not a *smáknisk*, nor a child any longer. He had no use for her guileless kindness. *Let her return to her home and family an innocent child*, he thought. *That is all I owe her father.*

"Meuse," she called out, setting the satchel on a rock near his feet. She stood hesitantly beside it, shivering in the evening air. "I'm sorry, Meuse." She set the blanket on the ground.

"*Merci*," he said, stepping out of the shadows. But he raised his hand as if to stop her, kept his tone cold and his face stern. This was no longer a game. In his hand, he held a smooth stone. Let her decide whether it was a weapon or a warning. Whatever her intentions, she was still the enemy. Despite her family's assistance, he would never forget that his people had been murdered by hers. He had almost died. Mimi had almost died.

"Go away," he said. His words were cold, their meaning clear. He had no time for her confusion. Her good intentions could not save him.

With a look of dismay, Lucy turned tail, like a doe disappearing into the bush. He waited until he was sure she was gone and then picked up the satchel she had left behind. It contained provisions for a long journey.

"Run," William had said when he freed him. But as Meuse watched Lucy flee, he understood. He had been pardoned but not by the officials who had charged him. He had been freed by the family of the man he had wronged. Even so, this was no longer his home.

The defeated boy who had languished in a putrid jail cell waiting to die existed no longer. Meuse might not be hanged on the gallows, but despite his freedom, he would never be welcome here among the white men.

After Lucy disappeared into the house on the hill, Meuse hummed the song Mimi sang that afternoon in the jail, the tribe's gathering song.

Wejkwita'jik niskamijk wula tet nike' a (The spirits are coming, right here now)

Nenmitij na telta'jik, petaqte'ji'jk wtowtiwow. (They know where they are going, the road is straight)

Wejkwita'jik no'kmaq wula tet nike' a (Our relations are coming, right here now)

Pepkwijete' ma'tijik newtitpa'q. Way ha ya yo way. (They will drum all night)

This time, he did not forget to thank his Elders for his freedom. Breathless in the dark undergrowth, he raised his eyes to the sky and gave thanks. To his Elders, but also to Parker, to William, to Lucy, who had aided in his release, and to his Uncle Gehne, who had not abandoned him. To Mimi, who had awakened him with her song. He followed deer tracks down the mountain toward a turn in the creek where he and Francis had long ago stowed a birch-bark canoe in a shallow cave for their summer expeditions. He pulled the oars from a ledge of rock over his head, loaded his supplies, and began rowing.

Upstream, home to Kejimkujik, home to Mimi. Home, where Francis and Uncle Gehne would be waiting. How surprised his family would be to see him, a free man again! In their company, he would decide where to go next. Where he might hide or, better yet, live safely, far from the white men's interference.

With each stroke of his oar, Meuse's strength returned. He knew the Mersey River like he knew the streaks of gray in his murdered mother's hair. Each bend, each rapid was an old friend, providing sustenance. The summer rains propelled the current downstream, but nothing could slow Meuse now. His canoe moved steadily against the current, smoothly cutting through the clear water. He was heading upstream, going home.

With each stroke, he sang: *Way ha ya yo way.*

CHAPTER FOURTEEN

Rogers Reacts to the Escape

Parker Mountain, July 1761

According to Father, Governor Jonathan Belcher's prepared statement lasted for nearly an hour. The governor arrived on the stage only moments after my father had taken his place at Major Rogers's side, saving him from the need to explain William's absence to the officer. Belcher, a college man with degrees in law and mathematics, had yet to speak directly to the major. Instead, before taking his place at the podium, he shook the hands of local barristers, including the squire in whose office my brother Nat was employed. Before Belcher became governor, Nova Scotia had no formally trained law officers. Belcher, like my father, had been raised in Massachusetts, but he had also read law in Middle Temple, London. There, he had been called to the English bar and caught the eye of the king. Father said he enumerated all his degrees in his opening statement and then launched into a blow-by-blow account of how he had successfully negotiated the peace that led to the Burying the Hatchet ceremony and, as a result, this prisoner exchange. His efforts, he said, paved the way for this momentous day. As the governor droned on, Father scanned the fields behind the administration building.

A large man, Belcher exuded a regal authority. He addressed his words to the crowd, appearing to favor neither Rogers on his right nor Chief Étienne Bâtard (who had traveled many miles from his tribe's camp) on his left. When Belcher summoned Caroline and the children to the middle of the stage, he smiled benevolently. "I have three sons of my own," the governor said, touching the chin of the little girl, though certainly he knew the children could not understand what he said. Caroline later told me Chief Bâtard flinched when the governor touched the girl's face. "And a daughter on the way," Belcher said, raising his eyes to Caroline. She said his calculating glance made her shiver. He seemed to be taking her measure.

Major Rogers was restless in his seat. "Will this man ever proceed to the signing of the papers?" he asked my father. Eventually, Major Rogers had enough. He grabbed Father's hand, pulling him to the middle of the stage before the governor had summoned him. Rogers nudged Caroline aside and introduced Parker to Belcher. "Here is the celebrated officer and Christian man who suffered the horrifying indignities of abduction. He was as good as dead before my men freed him from his savage captor."

Scott sidled up next to Rogers. The two stood expectantly, evidently waiting to be congratulated by the dignitary.

Through it all, Father yearned to scan the fort's fields, especially those behind the fort's cemetery, but he didn't dare show his concern. Instead, he kept his focus on the governor. He was sure the celebrated politician had handled more than his share of petty bureaucrats in backwater colonies and watched with amusement as Rogers jockeyed for position. The longer Belcher spoke, the more time William had to accomplish his task. Then, to Rogers's evident dismay, the governor turned his attention to my father. Was he mistaken, or did the governor roll his eyes with a subtle mockery? Chief Bâtard, peace pipe in hand, watched both men warily.

At last, the papers were signed, and the pipe passed. The governor shook Father's hand, declaring him officially a free man. As the assembled crowd cheered the illustrious man's presentation, Caroline ushered the children off the stage, heading for the administration building, where Campbell awaited. Father caught her eye and raised his chin to urge her onward. He said he could barely hear the governor above his pounding heart. The Indian chief left soon after the children, muttering in his strange tongue to the guide at his side as he rode toward the port.

"Nasty business, this," the governor said.

"But thanks to your fair policies, in the end, justice was served," Father assured him, knowing God would forgive him his duplicity. "Do tell me, how were you able to persuade the Indians to sign your treaty?" Over the governor's shoulder, he discreetly scanned the fields behind the administration building. Were those dark shadows he saw disappearing into the woods?

Governor Belcher was more than happy to recap the long process of gaining the Indians' trust. At the same time, he assured my father, the current government had maintained total control over the colony. "With the French no longer in power, Nova Scotia is as strong as any of the British colonies," he bragged. "Our time has come."

"Ah, yes," Father said. "I read the paper you wrote in 1755, in which you concluded the deportation of the Acadians was both authorized and required under the law. Your scholarship and political acumen continue to benefit the region." Flattery, Father told me, is the best way to keep someone talking.

Nat, who had joined Father on the platform, introduced himself. "I also study law," he said, shaking the governor's hand.

Rogers, apoplectic at this high-minded exchange, could hold his tongue no longer. "Where is your other son, William?" he demanded. "Wasn't he supposed to be here?"

"William remained behind, guarding the prisoner," Father answered, never taking his eyes off the governor. "The major neglected to assign that task to one of his officers. Fortunately, my older son generously offered his services." His comment silenced Rogers, whose face had turned red.

"The prisoner, yes," Rogers sputtered. He puffed out his chest and turned to the governor. But Belcher had used this pause in the conversation to signal his deputies and ask them to prepare the horses for his departure.

Rogers saw his last chance to deliver his announcement to the governor slipping away. "We will hang the perpetrator first thing tomorrow morning." He draped an arm over the red wool and epaulets covering the governor's broad shoulders and offered him a cigar. "That, more than any formality, will bring this matter to a close, don't you agree?"

The governor shook off his gesture, although, Father told me, he pocketed the cigar. "Ah, there are my horses," he said. Or perhaps he heard Rogers but chose to leave the sordid part of this whole business to the local authorities. Father said that such subtle evasions often distinguish powerful men. In either case, he bade them both good luck and farewell.

"Tomorrow, Parker?" Rogers watched the governor go, leaving the intent of his words unclear.

Father nodded, committing to nothing. "But now I must take my leave. This has been an exhausting ordeal for us all, and it is time for me to say my prayers and get some much-needed rest. Come along, Nat. Salome and the children await."

Nat excused himself and left in search of his squire.

Father mounted his horse as Rogers and Scott headed toward the administration building. He wanted to be far away from Annapolis when the officers discovered the empty cell.

•••

Parker Mountain, July 1761

Ezekiel arrived home before my father. He was livid. This was to have been the day the Royal Forces recognized his valor, he told Salome in an agitated state. At the governor's side, he had hoped to recapture his father's glory and demonstrate his merit as a foot soldier in the service of the Crown.

Overhearing their conversation, I gathered that had not been the case.

"Eighteen of us crammed up on the stage and Caroline—Caroline!— at the side of the governor," he exclaimed. Salome tut-tutted, as was her wont, but did not comfort him. "Major Rogers didn't even introduce me. I blame Scott. The weasel kept me in the background. After all our family has been through!"

I waited for my father to return. In anticipation of his freedom, I—with Sally's help—had carried the wooden bathtub in from the shed and placed it in front of the hearth. Ma Salome heated water in a large bucket. When he arrived home at last, she evicted us all from the parlor so Father might enjoy a hot bath.

"Not a word of this until your father's done," Salome warned. "I expect all of you to behave. A cozy family supper is in order, and I do not want to hear any more talk of Indians, exchanges, politicians, or soldiers. It's time we put this trial behind us."

I listened to her injunction and struggled not to look smug. Parker was *my* father, mine and William's. And he had chosen to confide in me. He trusted me. Salome knew what William had done that afternoon, but she promised my father she would never discuss it with her own children. When I returned from delivering the package to Meuse, Salome swore me to secrecy. This newfound intimacy with my stepmother thrilled me. Ma Salome continued to rise in my estimation. I wasn't about to let Ezekiel, with his petulant bluster, sully the warm glow I felt from my family's quiet actions.

When Father emerged from his bath, rosy and warm, his damp hair combed back from his forehead, he patted me on the head. "Just what the doctor ordered," he said, fastening his suspenders.

"I made parsnip soup for supper," Salome said. "And pumpkin bread."

"Marvelous," Father said. "My favorites."

I was dying to ask him what he had eaten while living with the Indians, but I bit my tongue. *Later,* I told myself, *I will ask him later.* Perhaps he had eaten squirrel! I heard that was a staple of the Indian diet.

From the far side of the large oak dining table, I regarded my father with admiration. He had trusted me to keep the secret, and I would never betray that trust. Perhaps tomorrow he would confide something else to me, tell me where William had gone. I would keep that secret too, that and any others he wanted to share. I wondered where Meuse was hiding.

As Salome ladled out bowls of steaming soup, a clatter of hoofbeats broke through my reverie. Soon after, a loud pounding on the door disturbed our meal. Angry voices. Men's voices. Above them all, Major

Rogers's. "Where the hell have they gone?" he thundered.

Ma Salome's face went white, all conviviality erased in one moment. Father closed his eyes, as if reciting a prayer. Sally's dark eyes opened wide with alarm. Ezekiel jumped up from his chair, kicking it to the floor, and headed for the door. "It's Rogers," he said. "Something has happened!" I swear he looked happier at that moment than any that had preceded it that day.

When Ezekiel swung open the door, Rogers stormed in, repeating his question. "Where the hell have they gone?"

Father rose to his feet. "Watch your language in front of the children." He walked over to the officers. "Who are you looking for? Whatever is the matter?"

"Your yellow-bellied son and that heathen who tried to murder you, that's who. The prisoner has escaped!"

"Why, Major," Salome said, her voice stern. "Surely you know William was asked to accompany the children you freed today on their trip home. That was always the plan."

"Are you telling us the Indian escaped?" Father asked. His face revealed nothing. "How unfortunate. And with his hanging scheduled for the morning."

Captain Scott stepped forward and stomped his foot. "Gone. The door was wide open, and the key is missing."

Father shook his head as if in disbelief. "What a sad state of affairs." But then, instead of joining the men clustered by the open door, he sat back down at the head of the table and ladled another spoonful of soup. "Close the door." He swallowed as he considered the news. "Would you care to join us?"

Rogers ignored the invitation. I thought his eyes would soon pop out of his head.

"I must admit," Father continued after slurping another spoonful, "both William and I questioned your choice of that young fellow left in charge of the jail. Really, Scott, this was a task that required a skilled officer. I do hope the prisoner didn't overpower the poor chap."

The major's face, red and furious when he had entered, now turned a deep shade of purple. He continued to stand, with his officers behind him. "Traitors, every one of you!" he bellowed.

I looked down at my bowl. Following Father's example, I took a loud slurp of my soup.

"Enough of that, Rogers," Father said. "I am grateful for all you have done for this family, but I refuse to let you disrupt what was, until this moment, a long-awaited reunion. Of course, I have no idea where your prisoner might have gone. When William returns, you are free to interview him, though I doubt he will provide much information of value to you."

Halfway between the officers and the family, Ezekiel's head bobbed. First, he listened intently to Father, and then he turned to catch Rogers's reaction. If I had not been concentrating so hard on following my father's example, I might have laughed. My cocky stepbrother was flummoxed by Father's response, but I knew the truth of the matter. Well, not William's whereabouts. But I knew my brother had not traveled with Caroline and the children. My brother had played a heroic role in Meuse's rescue. The face-off between Rogers and my father was stageworthy. Never had I witnessed such drama, and here in my own home!

"I hope you have no intention of further disrupting those poor Indian children's lives," Father said. The undertone of threat in his voice startled me. I was accustomed to his air of authority but had never known him to threaten another man. "If I hear anything of the sort, I will personally inform the governor of your role in the recent massacre. Like my younger son, Nathaniel, Belcher is a man of law and might find your recent actions objectionable."

At that, Scott reached out to hold the major back. If he had not, Rogers surely would have attacked Father, right there, in front of the family.

"Parker," Ezekiel, caught between the two, abandoned his use of "Father." In a show of loyalty to the officers, he confronted my father as he would a foe. "Major Rogers and Captain Scott are heroes in this community. I have personally witnessed their bravery. They have restored law and order and enforced the governor's decree. How dare you question their actions when they are the very men who freed you from the savages?"

But Ma Salome would have none of it. She put down her spoon.

"Ezekiel, my son…" I studied her, waiting to see where my stepmother's true loyalty lay. "Watch your tongue, lad," she said, her eyes fixed on Ezekiel's face. His anger was apparent, but Ma Salome's simmered just below the surface.

Ezekiel was no match for his mother's determined glare. He turned to the officers. "If there is anything I can do to help, I am at your service." He spoke softly, his tone apologetic.

"Dearest," Father turned to Salome, "I apologize for these officers' untimely arrival at our home. I believe the need to cancel tomorrow's hanging may have embarrassed them, but I, for one, will leave the boy's punishment in God's hands." He sat up straighter, emboldened now. "Ezekiel, sit down. I was promised a family supper tonight."

I watched Ezekiel, his expression now that of a petulant child. Standing halfway between the officers on whom he'd hung his ambitions and his family gathered around the table, he had been humiliated by his mother and intimidated by my father.

"Major Rogers and Captain Scott," Father continued, "if you wish to join the family for our evening prayers, you are most welcome to stay. If not, I would ask you to leave right now. In the days ahead, we can revisit this matter. Now, safe in the bosom of my family, I believe I am entitled to an evening of savoring my return home. I beg you, allow us a night of peace and tranquility."

My father's hair had dried into cherub-like curls that settled on his shoulders. The tall, authoritative soldier who had returned to his family from battle appeared softer this night, more approachable. Perhaps this air of serenity was a consequence of the lessons learned during his abduction, or perhaps I had never really known him. Tonight, I recognized the pastor in him, the man of God, a righteous leader of men.

Ezekiel didn't have a chance. These officers could not intimidate my father. Even Rogers and Scott were silent now, although their fury seethed beneath their reserve.

If only William could have been there to witness Father's impressive performance.

CHAPTER FIFTEEN

Freedom

The Mersey River, July 1761

Meuse followed the stream to the Annapolis Basin by moonlight, skirting the shore as he made his way to the river, hidden from the view of the townsfolk. He paddled all night and did not stop until daybreak was imminent. By the last light of the fading moon, he pulled into a quiet cove to rest. Meuse stretched out in the bottom of his canoe and, lulled by the lapping water, fell into a deep sleep.

He woke to the clatter of horse hooves. He held his breath, slowly pushing his boat deeper into the underbrush. Overhead, crows chased an eagle, who elegantly soared out of their reach. They settled into the highest branches, and their raucous complaint made it difficult for him to determine who approached. The path along the river was narrow and seldom traveled.

Then he heard Mimi's gentle laughter and the lilt of Campbell's brogue. Like him, they had chosen the cove as a welcoming place to take a break from their travels. He watched as Caroline and Mimi took turns caring for the youngest child, wrapped in a tartan blanket. Campbell and the children scrambled onto a cluster of rocks to rest and watch the sun climb into the sky. Meuse backpaddled to keep out of their sight. He listened as Caroline taught the children a song in French: *Frere Jacques, Frere Jacques,* she sang, and they responded: *Dormez vous? Dormez vous?*

Mimi spread the blanket on top of the largest rock and laid out a meal of bread, dried apples, and roasted chicken from a straw basket. Campbell foraged for berries, naming each species as he found them.

Mimi dangled her feet in the water. She wore western dress and must have recently bathed because her dark hair was wet and hung loosely around her shoulders. She cooed at the baby. Ah, how lovely she appeared to him now!

Mimi. Alive. Like him, she was heading home. Softly he sang, *Way ha ya yo way,* not wanting to frighten her but hoping she might hear. When she looked up, he stepped out of the thicket where he had taken shelter and waved. Her face lit up.

"Meuse, am I dreaming? Is that truly you?" Mimi climbed down the rocks to the river, reaching for his hand. "Or are you a ghost?" She hopped down from the last rock. "Or have I inherited Father's ability to summon the spirits?"

He stood before her, placing his hand on her arm.

Like her, he was not entirely convinced this was real. Were they here, together and alive? Or had they taken the shape of two-legged spirits destined to roam Mother Earth like so many in their family? It seemed too much to hope for.

"Come," she said. "Join us." Hand in hand, they approached the picnickers. A wave of relief swept over Caroline's face at the sight of him. Campbell nodded in greeting. The children clapped their hands.

"Welcome," Caroline said. She turned to the Scot. "All must have gone according to plan. The boy is free. Now I only pray that my nephew is safe and that these children will soon be reunited with their family." She offered Meuse a piece of the bread that Salome had prepared for the journey.

Meuse chewed the buttery slice, watching the children eat voraciously, feeling more solid with each bite. From time to time, he reached out and touched Mimi's face. Her flesh was warm. His face was flushed. Soon enough, Caroline reminded them they must move along swiftly. When Meuse's escape was discovered, all hell would break loose.

But even then, Caroline continued talking to the guide. Meuse listened, but the only word he understood was William. The name of Parker's son, the man who had freed him. When the Scotsman noticed Meuse struggling to understand the midwife's words, he translated in surprising fluent *mi'kmawi'simk*. The night Meuse had escaped was William's last in Nova Scotia, he told him. Before the officers under Rogers's command could court-martial him, William had set sail on one of the fishing ships that set out each afternoon from Annapolis. A fisherman indebted to Parker had agreed to take him to the port of Halifax in exchange for forgiveness of his debt. There, William had booked passage on a freighter headed to Boston. In Massachusetts, he intended to offer his services to James Otis Jr. His brother had provided him with a letter of introduction to the vociferous patriot who had impressed Nat with his defense of the city's beleaguered merchants against illegal British search warrants.

Meuse listened to Campbell, who told this tale matter-of-factly, a man who did not take sides. When he had finished his report, Mimi looked up to the sky, expressing her gratitude.

The Scot skimmed a stone across the river. The children watched with fascination.

And then, with Campbell's assistance, Caroline spoke to Meuse. Despite her blue eyes, he sensed he could trust her. This woman had nursed Mimi back to health in a damp, dark cell. She treated the children as if they were her own.

"Until we return the children to your family, you must hide." When Campbell translated her words, he infused them with urgency. "We are under the protection of the governor, but you remain a wanted man."

Meuse asked Campbell to tell her he understood. Loath to leave Mimi's side, he stroked her hand one last time, lifting it to his lips, inhaling the sweetness. They gazed into each other's eyes.

Ma'wiomi weskowa'sit, weltasualtultiek (ah way), Mimi said.

Turning to Caroline, Campbell translated: *A gathering is happening. We are happy to see each other.*

"Perhaps you can teach me your song?" Caroline asked Mimi. But when she attempted to mimic the words, her tongue refused to cooperate, and the children laughed.

Meuse shook Campbell's hand, grateful for his impartial guidance. He thanked Caroline in French. Refreshed by the encounter, he climbed down the rocks and waded back into the river. Pulling his canoe behind him, he jumped in and looked back only once, storing away the image of Mimi and the children laughing on their blanket. Then, with a reenergized stroke, he continued his journey, gliding under the protection of the forest's canopy. His heart was full. As he headed toward Kejimkujik, he heard the children laughing at Caroline's failed attempt to speak their language. Only this convinced him that the encounter had truly occurred and soon they would be together again.

•••

Kejimkujik, July 1761

Meuse watched Francis pace from one side of the camp to the other. His cousin couldn't sit still. His long legs twitched with impatience. His eyes blazed with intention. While the others lolled around the open fire, Francis was on the alert for intruders, wary of invaders.

Caroline and Mimi had prepared a hearty meal of brook trout and greens gathered from the fields. Little remained of the provisions provided by the Parkers. The children, having taken a long nap after a swim in the creek, were famished. Uncle Gehne puffed on his pipe, smiling benevolently at the family that had returned to him just as his Elders had promised. Since Gehne continued to believe Caroline was Anne, Meuse's mother (no one corrected him), he repeatedly thanked the spirits for returning his family intact.

Wela'lioq (Thank you), he said to the sky. *Kesaluloq* (I love you), he said to the trees.

"It's not safe here," Francis whispered to Meuse. They spoke in low voices so that Gehne could not hear. "We're sitting ducks, just waiting to be shot."

Meuse had expected his cousin to be elated when he walked into camp. He had escaped imprisonment and returned to Kejimkujik unharmed. Instead, Francis pounced on him, announcing they should leave for Quebec at once.

Caroline, who had taken the children under her wing, soon informed Meuse that she intended to stay at the camp until she was certain the children were healthy. "It's the least I can do," she said. Francis interpreted her words but added his own. "If we stay here, her countrymen will murder us all."

"Francis, she's one of the good ones."

"No such thing exists."

"Francis," Mimi reminded her brother, sitting down beside them, "if not for Caroline, we would never have gotten out of that horrid jail. We have all suffered, but we are the lucky ones. Think of the generations to come. Don't fall into the same trap Meuse did and let your anger lead you astray." She took Meuse's hand to soften the criticism implicit in her words. He held it, blushing, overwhelmed by gratitude that despite his poor judgment, he was once more among friends.

Francis, the warrior, was having none of it.

"We've got to go. And soon," he hissed. Lisette, he said, languished with her family in a refugee camp in Quebec without his protection. He had already lingered too long. If they left now, Major Rogers's search party would never find them. Nearly one half of the Acadians living in the maritime region had headed up to the territory northwest of Chipoudy Bay, eluding expulsion. Many Mi'kmaq, their livelihoods destroyed and their families starving, were heading north too. He was antsy to join them.

Gehne, oblivious to their discussion, let out an enthusiastic belch. "Ah," he said, "life is good. Anne, dear, would you pour me more tea?" Caroline, who had learned where the brandy had been hidden, prepared another glass of Gehne's favorite libation, which he enjoyed in carefully measured doses. She winked at Mimi, who giggled at her father's delusions.

"*Wela'lin*," he said, thanking her.

"If you go," Mimi said, "I'm going with you." Since his return, Mimi seldom left Meuse's side. "From now on, your journey is mine. But first, we need to replenish our supplies. Francis, you're the hunter here. Instead of fretting and pacing, why don't you and Meuse put your skills to good use? Tomorrow, Caroline and I will watch the children. The two of you can snare us some fish, maybe trap some rabbits. We need to leave enough behind for the children."

This Gehne heard, perhaps because of the mention of food. "Maybe this time, Meuse will kill himself a moose," he said with a chuckle.

Their hunger sated and Francis mollified, they settled on a plan. One day to hunt and rest up. Caroline would remain with Gehne and the children until they could be reunited with members of their tribe. Francis, Meuse, and Mimi would lay low until they were prepared to head north to the Acadian refugee camps. As much as Meuse hated leaving Kejimkujik so soon, he was relieved to have someone else making decisions. His cousin was right. They couldn't remain here, where white men had hunted him down once before with disastrous results. Caroline could shield the children, but Meuse was a walking target.

Francis agreed to stand guard while they slept. And sleep they did, the children warm in Caroline's embrace and Mimi and Meuse on either side of Gehne. Gehne insisted that the couple be separated, telling Mimi that Mi'kmaq tradition dictated that an unmarried woman could invite a suitor into their family wigwam but should sleep separated by a mother and on opposite sides of the fire. Only when they convinced Gehne that Caroline had her hands full had he volunteered to assume the protective role.

Meuse blushed throughout the unexpected discussion, listening respectfully and a bit amused as Gehne related a message from the Elders. (They were always whispering in his ear.) The Elders said that once Meuse had smoked a pipe in a medicine circle to show a lifelong commitment to Mimi, they would permit him to share a blanket with his daughter.

Having received the Elders' approval, Gehne declared that Meuse and Mimi could share his bedroll.

"Father," Francis teased, "if Meuse is to be Mimi's suitor, he owes you compensation. He didn't exactly arrive at our camp bearing gifts. Are you sure he can provide for your daughter?"

Meuse pushed his "cousin" away playfully, happy for once that Francis was not truly related by blood. Since Francis and Mimi were *nic-maq*—extended family—Gehne had no reason to discourage a courtship. Gehne, as the family's chief, gave his blessing. As Mimi's father, he said he approved of Meuse and gave Meuse permission to try to win Mimi's heart.

"My boy will come through for me in the end," he told Francis now. "He learned at your feet and one day will be an excellent hunter."

His competitive spirit aroused, Francis snickered. "I'll believe this when I see it."

"You see?" Gehne said, looking up. Who he was talking to and what he wanted them to see was not clear, but soon he was snoring, and all except Francis joined him in a deep, refreshing slumber.

"I never want to be apart from you again," Mimi whispered to Meuse as she drifted off.

But he did not hear her. His last thought of the day was that he missed Oqoti twitching in dream outside the wigwam's flap. Francis standing guard would have to do.

CHAPTER SIXTEEN

Parker at Home

Annapolis, September 1761

Mercy Baptist Church of Annapolis formally opened its doors two months after Father's rescue. The dedication followed weeks of intensive labor by the congregants: a flurry of activity that rendered the little church shipshape, its walls whitewashed, its floors polished to a heavenly sheen. Experience Baker's husband built pews from trees he cut from the forest behind the little chapel, while Cornelia Eaton's husband constructed a humble altar of ash and birch. On a brilliant Sunday in early November, the entire congregation assembled to witness the long-awaited ordination of my father as their pastor.

Our family sat in the front right pew. Ma Salome, baby Henry in her arms, sat next to Ezekiel, who arrived in full military garb. Nat reluctantly left his clerking duties in the squire's hands, knowing that Father would require his support in William's absence. Sally and I sat side by side, our blossoming friendship sealed by the prestige of being the pastor's daughters.

Behind us, Grandfather Hardy leaned on his cane, and Grandmother

Hardy clutched her prayer book. Cornelia Eaton sat in the row beside them, still convinced she was a family friend, although none of us addressed her when she arrived. Behind the family, a dozen parishioners crowded into the pews, both Congregationalists and Baptists, many of whom had regularly attended the prayer sessions during Father's captivity. I recognized two of the families from the Charming Molly. The children were now taller, their parents grayer. The men wore jackets, the women their best petticoats. Like gulls stalking a fishing trawler, a dozen white bonnets turned to get a glimpse of my father as he walked up to the altar. Our parish had become the talk of the town and Father an exemplar of God's work.

"The Lord be with you," Father said, as he took his rightful place in front of his new flock.

"And with you," they responded.

"From the time I was a boy," Father began, "I stood in awe of the power of divinity, and I have studied the principles of our Christian religion. The rigor of my devotion led me to this day, to the humbling responsibility of assuming this ministry. As you know, I have passed through many trials on my journey here."

A murmur went through the crowd. Now, I could see, they hoped they would hear the full story. Father, still slender and pale, would describe the hardships he had suffered at the hands of a savage Indian. He would condemn his captor, congratulate his flock for keeping the faith. He would thank his rescuers.

But if this was what the congregants had come to hear, they'd be sorely disappointed. Father continued without reference to his recent ordeal.

"At times, the obstacles that faced me seemed insurmountable. I wallowed in the struggles of my mind and failed the challenges put before me by the Lord. After witnessing the horrors of war, I returned committed to peace. I stand before you now, a reverent man. My faith remains unshaken."

Ma Salome sat directly in front of him, her back as rigid as that of her soldier son, her expression serious. From time to time, she nodded in agreement. Here, at last, was the moment she had been waiting for since accepting my father's proposal. She was a pastor's wife, at last, a credit to her husband, a beacon of righteousness in a community of believers he had brought together in a distant land. She sat up proudly and never took her eyes off her beloved.

"We are a new congregation. Some of you will follow my lead and submerge yourself in His spirit. Some may not. I say to you now, choose whatever mode of baptism quiets your mind. Leave behind your troubles and prepare for the calm and undisturbed enjoyment of the gifts we have received from God."

"Amen," called out Cornelia Eaton, the pastor's biggest fan. Father led the congregation in morning prayers with no further reference to his recent ordeal.

The audience's disappointment was palpable, even as they recited the Confession of Faith. Father's lack of drama drained their enthusiasm. I figured Ezekiel was the most disappointed of all. He had begged my father to condemn the heathens, to preach about the abuses he had suffered at their hands, but to no avail. If he had not fled to Massachusetts, William would have wanted Father to question the treatment of the native population and the lot of the Acadians. Only Sally, smoothing her curls and fingering her satin bows as she stared into her lap, was unaware of the congregation's dismay.

I, too, was disappointed. I had imagined a grand moment of revelation when my father would speak of his captor and publicly absolve him. But Father spoke not one word of forgiveness, neither the giving nor the receiving of it.

When I asked him about it later, Father told me that his mission was to bring this congregation together, and this could only be done by avoiding controversial topics. If he were to be a leader among men, he must tread softly and avoid alienating the men and women who looked up to him. They had traveled far and faced many challenges; his role was to offer solace and comfort. To make them feel safe and secure. Discussion of the Indian problem could only exacerbate their anxieties. He had meditated on the matter ever since his return, he assured me. He would not advocate violence, neither would he condemn it. If he played his cards right, he might one day be the instrument of conversion for hundreds of souls.

He would let his actions speak louder than his words.

"It is my greatest desire," he said now, before concluding the service, "that here in this humble church we built with our own hands, we will celebrate many a communion together. We will bring light to a dark world by following the precepts and beliefs of our lord, Jesus Christ. My friends, we are alive and have established a piece of heaven here." He closed with a verse from the Book of Peter, Chapter 2, 1:3: *His divine power has granted us everything we need for life and godliness, through our knowledge of him who called us by his own glory and virtue.*

These soothing verses satisfied the women, and the women being pacified pleased the men.

Following his stoic example, Cornelia Eaton, at the refreshment table, cut the cake while maintaining a stiff upper lip. Experience Baker shook my father's hand and congratulated him on a job well done. Ma Salome walked among them, baby Henry clasped in her arms like the holy mother herself, exuding a faith stronger than the congregants' desire to milk her for a few lurid details of her husband's recent imprisonment.

"Our spiritual community grew today by several dozen," Father said as the family climbed into the oxcart for the ride home. "Today was truly the beginning of a new life in this bountiful land."

• • •

Parker Mountain, September 1761

After Father's disappointing ordination, things went downhill. In short order, the Baptists ruined my life.

With Father safely settled in, Salome assigned me the dreariest of tasks. No longer worried she would soon become a widow, she took it upon herself to teach us girls what she called the "practical skills": sewing, spinning, dusting, and grinding flour for bread. I slogged through these dreary tasks, missing William and envying Nat's apprenticeship at the solicitor's. Our lot, she reminded us repeatedly, was to be the pastor's obedient daughters, chaste in both word and deed, role models for the other girls in the congregation.

I thought I would surely go mad.

Then one day, a horse-faced girl rode up our path. I didn't recognize her, so I figured she wasn't a Baptist. Fortunately, Ma Salome was upstairs caring for baby Henry, so I opened the front door, curious to find out what brought this stranger up our path. She looked me over as thoroughly as I did her and then told me she was inviting all the girls in the township to a "constitutional" the next day to be held at her home at the bottom of the mountain. Her name was Amy, and she had recently moved here from Massachusetts.

"Do you like to dance?" she asked. "My brother plays the flute. If we ask him nicely, I bet he will accompany us." Amy had a bright smile, and her enthusiasm was contagious.

Her invitation thrilled me. My heart leaped at the prospect of an afternoon socializing with other girls my age. But I knew I would have to get Ma Salome's permission to attend. That afternoon, as we dusted the woodwork, I conveyed the girl's invitation to Sally, and her face lit up in response. "But can we?" she asked, timid as a dormouse as always. I told her about the constitutionals I had attended in Massachusetts when Father was away soldiering. But Sally said she had never danced. Her mother strictly forbade it.

"Let me talk to her," I said. "In the meantime, if you like, I'll teach you to waltz." Sally's eyes grew wide, but she didn't protest. At last, I had something to do besides the drudgery of "practical" tasks.

With what I thought was admirable skill, I set out to convince Ma Salome that having spent our days perfecting housewifery, Sally and I now needed a chance to practice the social graces required of women of our social standing. Ma Salome had been resting in her bedchamber while we worked and now lay in her bed with a cool cloth draped across her wide forehead. As I caught a whiff of stomach upset, it occurred to me she might be expecting again. But I plowed ahead anyhow, explaining about the invitation and the benefits I saw in attending the constitutional. She heard me out and then removed the cloth and handed it to me. "Dear, would you mind refreshing this cloth?" When I had done so, she asked me if I had finished my chores. I wasn't at all convinced she had listened to my request, but I interpreted her response—after all, she had not said no—as permission granted, and this is what I told Sally. "We can go!" We hugged in excitement. As we completed our chores, I showed her dance steps, and we completed our tasks in record time. This gave us the opportunity to rifle through our bureau, looking for suitable outfits for the party. I laid out my black bib and apron and shined my pompadour shoes, which I had not worn since leaving Massachusetts. Sally debated between a cap with blue ribbons and a red cape, which we decided was too showy for an afternoon tea.

But when Father came in from the fields, he took one look at our outfits and put his foot down. "Absolutely not," he said. "I forbid it." He directed a stern look of disapproval my way.

"It will just be girls," I pleaded. "In Massachusetts, Mother allowed me to join the other girls for an afternoon's entertainment."

"Baptists do not dance, even with members of their own sex," he snapped. Apparently, now that he was pastor, dancing, like alcohol, had been added to his list of mortal sins.

Sally and I had moved the hooked rug aside, intending to practice the minuet. As Father and I argued, she rolled it back over the oak floor, not wanting him to accuse her of collusion.

"Lucy, I'm afraid I may have indulged you in the past and created a wrong impression," Father patted my head. "But I expect you to understand, our family must now set an example, even to those who do not share our faith. The time for childish games has passed."

"But Mother let me…"

"Salome is your mother now. It would behoove you to follow her esteemed example."

I stood there, speechless.

After the events of the prior year, I thought my father had changed, but now I saw I had been sadly mistaken. For all his talk about freedom, he allowed me none.

All afternoon, I pictured the neighboring girls dancing in their elegant dresses. What would have been the harm? In my anger, I included Amy's brother in my daydreams, imagining him playing the flute as we performed minuets in Amy's parlor. In my mind's eye, he was as handsome as William, whom I missed terribly. If only Father had allowed me to attend! Surely, even a good Baptist occasionally needs companionship.

Sally and I returned to our tasks. She didn't complain, but I simmered with resentment. Salome resumed her role as supervisor, her strict adherence to routine barely disguising her obvious nausea, which confirmed my suspicions. Despite her pregnancy, she set out to teach us how to make candles, soap, and starch, determined to turn us into industrious housewives. Every time her mother looked as if she were about to vomit, Sally ran to her side, a look of penitence imprinted on her guilty face. It was clear from my stepsister's demeanor that she held me responsible for my father's reprimand. She stopped short of telling Salome that I had lied to her, but her silent stoicism only worsened the monotony of our chores. Father may have noticed my discontent because, after supper, he allowed me a second piece of apple pie, but I thought it a poor consolation and refused to thank him.

Once she admitted she was expecting, Ma Salome reverted to doe-eyed devotion to Father's pronouncements, calling him "Pastor" when congregants visited and sometimes at the dining table when only the family was in attendance. After Sally and my dalliance with the sin of dancing, she watched me like a hawk, alert for any further signs of sinful behavior. She slipped into a feigned passivity more infuriating than her insistence that I make my bed and that of Nat and Ezekiel every morning before breakfast. Oh, how I missed Caroline and our spirited discussion of a woman's role in society! And to think, I had considered calling Salome "Mother" as Father had asked. Now, I decided that Ma Salome she would remain.

The worst part was Father expected me to be just like her.

The next morning, Salome asked Sally and me to sit down with her at the table.

"Girls," she said, "as the pastor's daughters, you must be on your best behavior at all times." She droned on and on, encouraging us to take advantage of the consolations of religion, to live our lives with spirit and propriety. According to her, women must bear their sorrows in silence, putting on a serene and cheerful face even when our hearts are heavy. A righteous woman must restrict her life to the domestic sphere and eschew contact with the outside world.

Where had Salome's gumption gone? Where was the woman who was prepared to be a widow again and who had helped an Indian boy escape persecution? The woman I admired had disappeared as surely as my aunt and brother.

To illustrate her point, Salome showed us a pillow on which she was stitching Milton's description of Eve:

Grace was in all her steps. Heaven in her eyes,

In every gesture, dignity and love.

Sally, ever her mother's defender, said she thought the verse was divine. I bit my tongue. Clearly, the embroidered lines were nonsense, but I chose my words carefully.

"Why, I believe those words perfectly describe my Aunt Caroline," I said. *My mother, too,* I thought, but I knew better than to say that.

Salome sighed. "A woman's place is in the home," she said. She pursed her lips and directed her remonstration at me. "Your father has done you no favor, girl. Exposing you to matters that should have been none of your concern." She stood up, still clutching the embroidered pillow over her stomach. As she headed toward the stairs, Sally tugged at my hand, correctly interpreting her mother's action as the end of our conversation.

CHAPTER SEVENTEEN

La Chasse a Mort

On the St. Johns River, August 1761

Meuse, Francis, and Mimi paddled up the St. Johns River for three days, stopping only to relieve themselves and search for food and water. Meuse took the lead, pleased to show off his paddling skills to Mimi. With each stroke, the muscles in his arms grew stronger. When he tired, Francis took over at the helm, and Meuse sat down next to Mimi. She rested her head on his shoulder; he stroked her blue-black hair. Basking in the late summer sun, they headed north, quickly putting miles between themselves and the Annapolis waterfront. Sometimes Mimi sang, but often they traveled in companionable silence.

Soon, however, they learned that no distance was far enough. The voyage they had undertaken was dangerous. British troops scoured the countryside, looking for Acadians evading deportation. When exhaustion overcame them, they sought shelter with a band of Mi'kmaq who had set up a camp along the Atlantic shore. But far from welcoming them to a safe haven, their kin were in the process of packing up their belongings, preparing to leave their camp. "The rangers say our friendship with the Acadians is suspect," the weary migrants said. Even this far north, Mi'kmaq were not safe.

As they paddled into Chipoudy Bay, Francis instructed Meuse to steer the boat toward the shore. There, he had spotted a raggedy group of Acadian refugees and wanted to ask for news of the LaFleurs. As Francis stepped out of the canoe, the French refugees eyed the travelers' supplies hungrily. Meuse and Mimi relieved themselves behind a pine tree while Francis asked the refugees if they had encountered the LaFleur family during their trip north.

The Acadians on shore were a hardy but mean set of characters. One wore a hat decorated with lace taken from a British soldier's uniform. Another carried a firelock and cartouche box inscribed with the insignia of Knox's Forty-Third Regiment. They said they did not know of the LaFleurs but happily retold tales of search and destroy missions during which they had resisted the British the only way they knew how: using stealth, ambush, and terror. An elderly grandfather, his wrinkled skin red and flaking from exposure to the elements, told Francis theirs "was a true *chasse a mort.*" What choice did any of them have, he asked, except to become vigorous hunters of the English? He bragged about the exploits of an Acadian named Broussard, a skilled resistance fighter and intrepid warrior who had killed no fewer than one thousand English. "That crazy bastard," the old man said with a wheeze, "cannot hear a Yankee name pronounced without being seized by a kind of frenzy."

Francis asked where he might find Broussard.

Mimi and Meuse stood on the shore and listened to the Frenchman's overblown stories. Meuse recognized the man's tone: angry, violent, and set on revenge. He put a protective arm around Mimi. If only he could shield her. His protective instinct competed with his weariness.

Francis strutted on the shore, bragging to the Acadians about the men he had killed.

"My brother is like a cock ready to enter the ring," Mimi said. "Any moment now, we will see feathers flying."

"That is not the purpose of our journey." Meuse assured her he had no interest in joining the Acadian resistance. He spread a blanket on the beach, and they huddled there for warmth while Francis smoked with the Acadians. Overhearing the men's hyperbole, Meuse questioned the wisdom of their journey. He had hoped to leave the horrors of Nova Scotia behind. Quell his anger. Find peace at last. Violence, he had learned, provoked only responses in kind.

As if to illustrate his thoughts, a young man whose bloodshot eyes and stinky breath betrayed a weakness for liquor launched into a description of a refugee encampment where women and children had been brutally murdered. As he surveyed the bodies, he said he had stumbled on a note attached to a stake. Signed by a ranger from New England, it said: "What you have begun, we shall continue."

Meuse walked over to the men and tugged on Francis's sleeve. "We should get going," he said.

Francis shook his gesture off, enthralled by the rebels' passion.

Meuse knew that if it were not for Francis's pursuit of Lisette, Francis would have joined the resistance then and there. How much longer would the lure of Lisette keep his friend away from the incessant call to battle? One week into the journey, Francis no longer spoke of Lisette. Instead, he was obsessed with revenge, fueled by tales of the dastardly deeds of the rangers.

The sun was setting when he finally convinced Francis to climb back into their boat. "The starving season will be here before we know it," Meuse said, watching the sun sink to the west as Francis pushed their canoe off. The summer days were growing shorter. "If we want to locate the LaFleurs' camp, we need to do so while the days are still warm."

Reluctantly, Francis agreed. "The rangers say that at Miramichi, the closest port, refugees are already running short on food and supplies. Any day now, they will head inland. If we don't go now, we may never find Lisette or her family."

• • •

They continued north. Each time they passed a southbound boat, Francis flagged down the occupants to inquire about the LaFleurs. With each day, more families told them they were returning south rather than dying of hunger. Hollow-eyed oarsmen, their families huddled miserably around them, regarded the trio with suspicion, shrugged their shoulders, and paddled on without answering Francis's entreaty. Francis grew impatient.

Finally, a stringy fellow who had worked on the dikes said he knew of Lisette's uncle. He told them that a group of Acadians had retreated to the peninsula's northern shore. A French schooner had picked them up there and ferried them to Baie des Chaleurs. If the LaFleurs were lucky, they might have traveled up the bay in the hope of surviving the winter by making a camp in the remote northern interior territories, where they could live off stray livestock and wild game. If Francis wanted to find the LaFleurs, he would need to abandon the canoe and continue inland by foot.

Determined to do so, Francis was concerned their supplies were running low. On their last day on the river, he insisted they anchor more often so that he could steal provisions from the unmanned boats tied up on the shore. At first, he armed himself with only a knife, but after returning from an expedition carting a bag of potatoes, he brandished a rifle he had "liberated" from a patrol while crossing a bridge. "We'll need this in the interior," he said. Meuse knew his friend spoke not of hunting game but of defending themselves from their enemies.

"Don't look at me like that," Francis said. "This is a battle for survival now."

True, thought Meuse. But Francis was not traveling alone. Neither Meuse nor Mimi shared his thrill at the prospect of battle. Francis might identify with the killers, but Meuse had narrowly escaped being among the killed.

Nevertheless, he held his tongue. Francis had always been the fighter. Even when the two of them were boys, Francis longed to be a hunter, pursuing squirrels with his slingshot, stalking chipmunks in the woodpile. He had never questioned his place on the food chain. Although Gehne taught both boys to treat prey with honor and compassion, Francis watched his victims die without blinking. And because Francis had been older, stronger, and Gehne's only true son, Meuse had never challenged his friend, no matter how uncomfortable his actions made him.

In this unfamiliar world, nothing had changed.

"If you continue to follow my brother's lead," Mimi confided as they hid in the underbrush, waiting for Francis to return from his latest foray for provisions, "we'll all end up like those refugees. Starving, or worse, dying far from our family."

"What choice do we have?" Meuse asked.

"Choice is all we have," she said. Mimi no longer smiled shyly when she spoke to him nor reached for his hand when they stepped in or out of the boat. "I would never have left my father behind if I thought you didn't understand that." Her dark eyes probed his. "My father always told me that every decision I made would affect the well-being of the next seven generations. I was certain I still had a future with you, despite all the horror we have witnessed."

Her words sent a chill up Meuse's spine. He had lost so much; he could not lose her now.

Mimi continued. "That day on the Mersey River, I was overjoyed to see you freed from that awful prison. When you planned this trip with Francis, I decided I never wanted to be apart from you again. And I agreed with you that 'going to something is better than running away.'"

Meuse reached out to embrace her, but she shook off his hands.

"Francis's determination to find Lisette was a commitment to hope. It inspired me to do the same, to follow you. But what began as a quest has turned into a fool's errand. Can't you see that?"

Meuse suffered her condemnation with a sinking heart. Mimi was right. Francis's bluster could easily lead to a lonely death in a distant land far from their tribe and family. He had barely recovered from cruel imprisonment and longed for respite. With each tale Francis brought back from his forays among the refugees, Mimi had become more fearful, drawing into herself. She seldom sang anymore. In cramped corners of dreary campsites, the girl who loved to dance rarely stretched her legs. She'd spent most of the day curled up on the boat's floor, cowering under a blanket.

When Francis returned, Mimi stopped talking altogether. Meuse asked her what was wrong, but she refused to answer. Meuse stared into the distance, his stomach cramping. Hunger had become as familiar as the rocking of their boat, but her despair triggered in Meuse a physical pain far worse. He felt as if he had lost a limb. He loved her more every day, but he feared he was watching as she disappeared.

This he couldn't abide.

"Francis," Meuse said, backpaddling to stop the boat.

They had been paddling for hours without making any visible progress. He chose his words carefully, gauging his cousin's response. "It's almost September. We're not any safer now than we were on our own lands."

"Our lands?" Francis waved his hand, dismissing Meuse's concern.

"We have to turn around." Meuse was determined that his cousin would listen to him this time. Mimi said she had joined him on this voyage because she thought they had a future together. "At least if we starve to death in Kejimkujik, we will lie down next to our ancestors. Here, we will die among strangers."

Francis reached for his oar. "If you're just going to sit there whining, I'll take the helm," he said.

"You will not." Meuse met his friend's eye. "If you continue northward, that is your decision. But this boat is turning around. If you are not joining us, get out."

His words echoed over the water, fierce. He waited for Francis to respond.

Francis's grip on the oar loosened, but he did not let go. "Little brother," he said, "we have come so far. What sense does it make to turn back now?"

"Get out," Meuse said. "Go find your Lisette. But Mimi and I will not accompany you any further. We have talked it over, and our decision is final. I love you, Francis. You are like my brother, but I will not follow you on a journey that leads only to starvation and certain death."

Meuse had been through so much. He had survived dark days, but he had learned many lessons. He tapped into them now, reminding himself that pride was not righteousness, and every man must take responsibility for his actions. Could he stand up to the cousin who had always led the way?

The sight of Mimi huddled on the floor of the boat strengthened his resolve. *Here they were again*, he thought, *no better than prisoners, except their jailer was one of their own this time.*

It was time he took his life into his own hands.

•••

They traveled no further that day, neither upstream nor down. Sullen and not speaking, they pulled into a quiet cove and tied up their canoe in a harbor. From their docking place, they could see a delegation of Acadian leaders assembled on the town green.

"What are they up to?" Francis asked a fellow traveler fishing off a pier for his dinner.

"They've raised the white flag of surrender," the fisherman replied. A dispirited crowd watched from a grassy knoll. "They traveled seven hundred miles down the river from Quebec only to swear the oath of allegiance they had refused to sign at home." He pulled a flailing fish from the water and smashed its head with a rock. "Everywhere I fish, Acadians are giving up," he explained.

Francis, already frustrated by Meuse's intransigency, fumed at the sight of the cowardly Acadians. Raising his arm as if holding a hatchet, he bellowed: "If we are now in a war that has made you Acadians miserable, remember it was your priests who were the cause." A willing disciple of Father Le Loutre, Francis had never before disparaged the Catholics, especially in their presence. But in his fury, he turned his back on the crowd. Pointing to Meuse and Mimi still seated in their canoe, he said: "We are Mi'kmaq. We have lived on these lands for generations. We have escaped across the woods and exposed ourselves to a thousand dangers. Unlike you cowards, we will never give up."

The desperation in his cousin's words startled Meuse. Francis, forever the warrior, would never surrender, but now Meuse heard a reservation in his declaration. Their voyage had accomplished nothing, and yet he persevered, set on surviving despite all odds. He was not here in pursuit of his mademoiselle. Did he still believe this was a battle they could win?

"Enough of your nonsense. Let's get going," Francis ordered Meuse. "As you pointed out, time is short."

Meuse froze. They had been on the water for weeks now. His arms ached; his legs were numb from the cold. He was hungry and longed for a full night's rest.

"No," Meuse said. Mimi sidled up to him.

"Francis, we're going home," she said. "I want you to join us. But if you are determined to continue north, you're on your own."

"We've had enough," Meuse said. For once, his voice was firm with conviction.

The Acadians watched the two boys spar, one intent on heading out on a suicidal mission, the other with his eyes turned to the sky. As Francis hesitated, Meuse raised his oar, prepared to backpaddle and turn the boat around. He had not yet given up on survival.

Francis stood with one foot on the shore and one resting on the side of the boat. Mimi watched her brother silently, but her eyes filled with tears. An icy drizzle soaked her now-ragged dress. "Where can we travel without provisions?" Meuse asked Francis. "How can we escape from an enemy who will cross ice to murder us?"

They had reached an impasse. Neither was ready to back down. Rocked by gentle waves, Meuse looked again to the sky for guidance. Francis followed his gaze. If only it were that easy, if, like his father, he could consult with his Elders. But this was not his way. His eyelids grew heavy. He was cold, wet, and miserable.

"Francis, your father needs you." Looking down, Meuse said the only words that could bring Francis back. Words he had spoken so many times as a young boy, summoning his adventurous friend back to their tribal camp.

"How could you possibly know what my father needs?" Francis asked, emphasizing the word "my."

Meuse gazed out at the dark water and thought of the nights he had prayed with Parker in the wigwam, of the man's faith and his own decision to let his hostage live. He remembered the damp floor of his jail cell. He recalled William's face when he saw his father alive because of Meuse's restraint, the bravery of his compassion when he freed Meuse from jail.

Even at the worst of times, mercy had saved him, often unexpectedly.

How could he explain this to his cousin? Had they come this far only to give in to desperation? Had he come to love Mimi only to watch her disappear? Now, he gave the gift of mercy to his friend.

"We need you to protect us," he said. "Please don't abandon us now. Think of Lisette, your wife. Of what she would want you to do."

Mimi added, "Come home with us, Brother. We are fools to continue. I'd rather die on the open sea than starve to death among strangers. Let's go back to where we belong."

Francis stood tall, stiff, and defiant as the Acadians dispersed, defeated and downtrodden. Meuse could see the conflict in his face, muscles twitching as he chewed over the dilemma. Francis searched the crowd for an ally, but today there were no rebels to incite him nor allies to take him in.

"Francis, I admire you. You are the warrior I've always wanted to be. But this is not our war. You said it yourself. If we are going to survive, it will be as Mi'kmaq. Go find your mademoiselle if you must, but I'm taking Mimi home before winter arrives and kills us all."

Francis sighed, looking one last time to the heavens. He narrowed his eyes and snorted like a restless stallion.

With a glance back at the forlorn Acadians, he stepped into the boat and took the second oar. As a boy, he had beat his cousin in every foot race. But in a battle of words, Meuse always won.

As night fell, Mimi sat at Meuse's side. He was overjoyed to have her upright once more. Under her breath, she sang.

Francis cradled his rifle in his lap. "Cowards," he muttered. But he and Meuse headed south, rowing in unison. They let the river's current carry them, coaxing the canoe through the dark water until the river deposited them into the open sea.

Mimi hummed as if serenading the spirits that took them home. For the first time in days, she sang *Way ha ya yo way.* Perhaps she heard her father's voice calling. Perhaps her own spirit animals kept her company as the waves whipped them onward.

For the second time that summer, Francis declared: "This isn't over."

But he said it with less vehemence, and when he saw Meuse's eyes closing, he offered to man the oars. With confident strokes, he propelled the boat south without further comment.

Perhaps, Meuse thought, *after such a long journey, Francis's mademoiselle no longer calls him. Perhaps, in the weary, defeated faces of the Acadians, he finally realized the futility of his search.*

Whatever the reason, each of them arrived at the same conclusion. More than anything else, they wanted to go home.

Ironically, Francis soon learned from a French family that the LaFleurs were also on their way back to Nova Scotia.

A beret-bedecked father of four told them the Planters of the Annapolis Valley had discovered that the dikes that made their farmland so valuable were crumbling. The summer Nor'easter that had trapped Meuse in the wigwam with Parker had slammed into the Bay of Fundy, producing a tidal surge that breached the dikes and inundated the fields with salt water. Only the Acadians who had worked on the dikes knew how to repair them.

Governor Belcher had devised a scheme to allow nearly two thousand Acadian refugees to return to Nova Scotia to work on the dikes as laborers on land they had previously owned. Although the returning French would continue to be prisoners, the Planters would provide them with support and subsistence if they repaired the dikes to preserve and recover the marshlands.

Lisette's father was among the first to volunteer his services. The family had sailed in August and might already have arrived in Chignecto.

Buoyed by this good news, Francis joked with the beret-ed Acadian, smoking and drinking with him and inviting him to join them at a camp along the river for a good night's sleep. With haste no longer a priority, the travelers took their time now, joining other refugees at the abandoned camps they spotted along the shore. The local tribes had moved inland, where the British could not find them. Francis continued to play the role of provider, his hunting skills now augmented by thievery and trickery. Meuse and Mimi, relieved to be heading back to Nova Scotia, no longer questioned his methods. When Francis told his French friends that he was returning to the dikes to work with his father-in-law, Meuse and Mimi laughed, happy to hear that he was no longer determined to join the resistance.

CHAPTER EIGHTEEN

Parkers

Parker Mountain, September 1761

I had pulled up my quilt and was drifting off to sleep when angry voices downstairs startled me awake.

"My father didn't die so you could piddle away your time scribbling at the squire's office." I recognized Ezekiel's sarcasm and listened for Nat's defense.

"Without just laws, the sacrifices of our fathers will have been in vain."

I could hear their argument through the floorboards and pieced together the dispute. Nat's squire had asked him to deliver an order the town's board had received. In it, the governor stated that all efforts by the local militia to recapture the Indian boy must cease immediately. The governor, who took his orders directly from the Crown, said there were more crucial issues facing the colony, and these were to be given priority.

Upon reading the document, copies of which had already been delivered to Major Rogers and Captain Scott, Nat and Ezekiel got into a terrible row. Even when they closed the parlor door behind them, their voices carried throughout the house. It was a wonder baby Henry slept through it all. I was certain Ma Salome must also have heard the heat in their voices. Ezekiel declared that Governor Belcher was a traitor. "We will only achieve lasting law and order if a rigorous campaign to rid the island of heathens is completed!" he shouted. "If we allow prisoners to run free, all hell will break loose."

At that, Father intervened. "The Indian boy's capture is none of your concern." He had forgiven his captor and wanted to hear no more about the matter. In his solemn pastoral voice, he said the boy's fate was in God's hands now.

"Well, I, for one, am not willing to settle for that," Ezekiel said. I pictured my stepbrother standing there in his military attire, pounding his chest with a white-gloved hand. "The authorities sentenced a criminal to die on the gallows. Whoever assisted in his escape should be tried and called to account. Using the hostage exchange as cover for undermining a lawful arrest? I fear for the future of this community if we tolerate such deception."

"I beg to differ," Nat said. "Order will be established once we have passed just laws, not by vigilantes and self-appointed raiders such as the band of men you have befriended. We are not outlaws but civilized men, I hope. This is why I study the law. And, I must say, I agree with the governor. We have shed enough blood in Annapolis. Now is the time for hard work and rational debate."

"Bull," Ezekiel said. "My father died for this country. And I intend to honor his memory."

"Boys, boys," Father spoke over them. "There are children sleeping in this house."

At that, the volume of their discussion dropped, although the argument continued late into the night. Neither Nat's lawyerly discourse nor Father's placating pleas were audible, but Ezekiel's enraged shouts rose above them both, despite their attempts to quiet him.

"We're in a battle for the future of civilization!" he proclaimed at one point. "The British summoned us to cultivate these lands, and I, for one, take this responsibility seriously. Father's abductor cannot be permitted to get away with his outrageous crime."

Listening to them argue, I thought of Father calling my desire to dance a sin. Who decided what was a sin? Or, for that matter, a crime? Ezekiel insisted that the Indian boy was a criminal, but if William were here, I know he would have countered that there were crimes committed on all sides. If I had been a boy, I might have gone down to make the assertion myself. I was convinced Father would agree with me.

But Ma Salome had reminded me repeatedly that such issues were not a woman's concern, so I laid there, biting my tongue. The anger I heard in Ezekiel's voice was more adamant than Father's faith, more insistent than Nat's scholarship. The aftereffects of my father's abduction continued to haunt the house, keeping the family awake long after we all should have been fast asleep.

Ezekiel left after midnight, slamming the front door in a final thunderous display that shook the house to the rafters. Nat and Father spoke for some time more, but by then, I was fighting to keep my eyes open. In the morning, when I descended the stairs, I found Nat asleep on the couch, still wearing his clothes from the office. He had spent the night instead of returning to his room above the squire's office. Someone had covered him with a blanket.

Ma Salome never mentioned the argument, even when I tried to provoke her by commenting that it had been difficult to sleep through the noise. The matter might not have been a womanly concern, but I noticed Salome asked Bertha to care for baby Henry so Father could sleep in, saying only that "the pastor was up late last night." Ma Salome avoided my eyes over breakfast and closed the parlor door so Nat could sleep undisturbed on the couch. Then she sat in the parlor while Sally and I finished our breakfast alone in the kitchen. Ma Salome could not hold down breakfast so early in the morning. Ezekiel was her eldest son, her treasured tie to her late husband, and no matter what she said, I was certain she found the argument unsettling. Even the child in her belly must have sensed that something was not right. We couldn't speak about it, perhaps, but the fallout from the past six months would surely linger long after this baby, and the next, was born.

• • •

Nat and I rode side by side in the carriage to Grandfather's funeral. Father broke the sad news to us last night, telling us that Grandfather Hardy had died as he had lived, working in his fields. What more could an honest man desire? In his life, my grandfather had been a teacher, a soldier, and, in the end, a farmer, and he was never happier than when he was working his land. One day he was twisting his impressive mustache as he admired his fields, and the next, they were placing his body in a tub full of ice to slow the decomposition. Now he lay in a six-sided coffin in front of the altar of Mercy Baptist Church, where Father would preside over his last rites. Grandmother Hardy had asked that all his grandchildren be present to bid him goodbye.

As the cart passed over the rutted road, it occurred to me that this would be the last time that we, Maggie's children, would gather as a family. By all rights, William should have joined us. But in his last letter, he had bragged he would soon enroll at Harvard College, for which he had qualified by reading the Old and New Testament in Latin and "resolving them logically," whatever that means. Despite this admirable feat, he assured me that, unlike many of his classmates, he did not intend to enter the ministry but instead aspired to outsmart the loyalists and contribute to the colonies' growth and prosperity. A noble undertaking, I am sure, but not one I could share. Massachusetts was so far away! He assured me that one day soon he would ask me to visit, but the possibility seemed increasingly unlikely. Soon Salome would have another baby, and she counted on me and Sally to help take care of the little ones.

Our carriage turned the corner and approached the front stairs of Mercy Baptist Church. How long it seemed since those early days in Nova Scotia when I had dreamed of running away to live with my grandparents, when all I wanted was to escape Salome's dominion. More and more, I was happy I had remained on Parker Mountain, where life was often full of joy and activity. How lonely it would be to live with my grandmother now, especially since Caroline no longer lived in the colony. As we approached the church, I craned my neck, hoping to see Caroline among the crowd clustered in front of the door. Surely Caroline would abandon her Indians to attend her own father's funeral? I had not seen her since the day she left with the Indian children, although Campbell, the Scottish guide who had befriended her, periodically brought the family news of her and assured us Caroline was content caring for her new charges.

Grandmother Hardy greeted me from her perch on a wooden chair in front of the open door of the church. "Every day you look more like your mother. Let an old woman take one last look." As if I were the one to be buried! She had made this observation before, and it made me shiver. I had studied my face in the hand mirror just that morning, wondering if I truly resembled my birth mother. Grandmother had sprouted a wispy beard, her eyes were cloudy, lost in puffy red lids, and her breath smelled of yeast. "One by one, I'm losing everybody," she sobbed. Behind her back, Nat rolled his eyes.

"I love you, Granny," I said, handing her the mourning ring Ma Salome had helped me to purchase from the local jeweler. Gold, with a lock of Grandpa's hair and trimmed with white enamel.

"It is all our loss," Grandmother insisted, grabbing Nat by the chin before placing the ring on her finger. She held up her hand and examined the craftsmanship. "First your mother and now my dear husband. Nova Scotia is calling us home one by one." Nat grimaced and reached out to free my hand from Grandmother's clinging grasp.

Experience Baker took my place at my grandmother's side, stroking the old lady's back kindly as she admired the ring. Outside of the church, Mr. Baker and his son Benjamin put the last touches on the community grave-yard. The younger man waved shyly when I looked his way, causing me to blush. Lately, I had noticed the boy watching me in Sunday school, and I was fairly certain he fancied me. But now was not the time for flirtation. Despite Mr. Baker's invitation, Grandpa Hardy would not be the first congregant buried behind the freshly painted picket fence. Instead, Grandmother had insisted he be buried in Nictaux next to my mother, his beloved daughter.

The service was blessedly short. Thank God the colonists spurned the Catholic rites of the French and believed in keeping the ritual simple. One by one, members of the congregation walked to the front of the room to affix a message or verse to the bier. Later, Cornelia Eaton, as church secretary, would gather these and place them into a book for Grandmother to keep as a memorial. Eaton had also coordinated the funeral feast the previous evening at Grandmother's house, assigning dishes to the ladies of the parish and guarding the serving table from a few of the menfolk who had drowned their sorrow in the ample supply of rum hidden in the barn out of sight of their pastor. These same men, I noted, now sat in the pews, gray and full of remorse, if not mourning.

As Father presided over the gathering, wearing the funeral gloves Ma Salome had made him for the occasion, I searched once again for Caroline but saw only Grandfather's cronies, the prosperous Planters who had left Massachusetts behind to call Nova Scotia their home. Graybeards every one and now pallbearers for her grandfather. The younger men, the underbearers, prepared to carry the bier down the aisle while the older men picked up the pall to spread the cloth over the coffin. A fitting end to the long voyage Grandfather had made, which had started with us on the Charming Molly and ending here in Annapolis on a gray afternoon. Many of the mourners had taken this voyage with us. Now, they were the patriarchs of families thriving on the peninsula. Their children aspired to become the town's doctors, squires, soldiers, and teachers. Nat and I sat among them, the next generation, inheritors of all these brave men had claimed.

I had written a verse for Grandfather's bier.
Together, we planted an apple tree.
Now you have gone to heaven,
I will water this tree in your memory
And plant the seeds to nurture your eternal life.

I was quite proud of the verse and had shared it with Nat on the ride over. With a gentle smile, he tugged my braid, which was as close to a compliment as I was about to receive from the future squire. Now I walked down the aisle and attached the parchment to Grandpa's bier. I whispered goodbye, letting him go, letting all of them go.

Standing there in front of Grandfather, I mourned the loss of my mother, of William, and, most of all, of Caroline. All of them were now memories from a life I had left behind. Father had been granted Parker Mountain, but the family who would join us that night at the dinner table had been transformed. Families, by nature, grew and changed. In the end, only those buried in the graveyards remained.

After the service, a second band of pallbearers loaded the casket onto an oxcart for the long trip to Nictaux, where they would bury Grandfather between Mother and a second plot reserved for Grandmother Hardy.

Nat and I chose not to attend the burial, but we assured Grandmother we would attend the arval at her home that evening. Cornelia Eaton assured Father she had emptied the rum barrel and let it be known that there would be nothing to drink at the arval but tea. Grandfather had requested a Baptist burial, and his friends and family owed him a righteous remembrance. She would brook no opposition to his desires.

Before the arval, Father, Nat, and I returned to Parker Mountain together to rest up for the evening's activities.

"Father," I asked him, "when I die, will they bury me with Grandfather in Nictaux?"

"No, my darling," my father said. "I have already arranged for a family parcel in the new community cemetery in the shadow of Mercy Baptist Church. One day very, very far in the future, you will join us there, perhaps in the company of your husband and a family of your own." Exhausted by the day's emotions, I let out a satisfied sigh. This was exactly where I wanted to be, at my father's side, in my family home, even under Salome's protection and surrounded by too many siblings to count. The afternoon of Grandfather's funeral made that clear. I belonged at Parker Mountain now. In the bosom of my new family, part of the growing Annapolis community, I hoped I would blossom just like the flowers on the tree I promised to plant in my funeral verse.

•••

Father embraced his new vocation. Whenever the Baptists summoned him, he ran out at once, his flock taking priority over his family. I hardly knew him for the man who had returned after being abducted. Then he had been skin and bones with dark circles under his eyes. Now he was all sermons and vigor, restored to health by Ma Salome's copious cooking and the adoration of his flock. When he was home, he was solicitous to Ma Salome, insisting we girls take over the household chores as Salome's stomach once again grew large with child. Even Father soon recognized the burden this placed on us children. When her apron could no longer cover her stomach, he cleaned out a shed next to the cornfields, explaining that it would now house a full-time maid to help around the house. Once it had been suitably appointed with a bed and bureau, he drove to Annapolis and returned with a Negro woman, Bertha, who had recently arrived from the West Indies. He explained that the woman had agreed to work for us in order to earn her freedom.

As grateful as I was for Bertha's help, I couldn't help thinking once more that Father was willing to free everybody but his daughters.

Not that I didn't like Bertha. I did, from the moment she arrived. She winked at me when Ma Salome issued her "instructions" and saved sweets for us girls as rewards for assisting her in the day's work.

Bertha didn't mind when I complained about my chores, but she told me I should count my blessings. "Life is hard, sweetie pie," she would say. "But your father is a good man. I've seen worse." Her accent charmed me. "Salome is a gentlewoman who has taken on a lot," she would say, and I would repeat it to myself, trying to catch the Caribbean lilt. One day, as we were boiling linens, she described being sold to a cruel master at the age of six. "I lost my mother too," she said. "The last time I saw her, she was standing in chains as I was being loaded onto a slave ship."

When Bertha told us her stories, Sally never said a thing, but later we would speculate on how Bertha had escaped from slavery. How she had arrived in Nova Scotia, and how my father had secured her services.

As the months passed, Massachusetts seemed farther and farther away. If my dear mother returned from the dead, I doubted she would recognize me in my apron, doing menial labor alongside a black woman from the West Indies. No matter how hard I tried, I could no longer hear her voice or recreate her scent. Nor could I imagine the French family who had lived in the house before us, thinking it was theirs. Their ghostly presence faded by the day, along with the memory of the Indian boy who had asked me to join him in playing Waltes and then abducted my father. Some days, our growing family created such a racket that I was lucky to hear the migrating birds singing as they crossed the vast blue sky. Little by little, I accepted that these were the cards I had been dealt, and they weren't so bad after all. In Father's words, my life had been preordained. If the world seemed unfair, this was as God intended.

With that revelation, I decided to put aside my nightly journal, the one I had maintained every day since leaving Massachusetts. I tucked it under my mattress, where I suppose I will forget it. Instead of writing every night before I go to bed, I now offer prayers of gratitude for God's gifts. I pray for William in Massachusetts and Caroline and all the children she helped bring into the world. I thank God for not selling me into slavery or slaughtering my family. I pray for my growing family, the love of Father, and the comfort of my loving home.

CHAPTER NINETEEN

The Serpent Dance

Kejimkujik Lake, October 1761

"Think of yourself as a rattlesnake," Mimi said. Despite her best effort to teach Caroline the Serpent Dance, the midwife kept stumbling over her own feet. "Little steps," Mimi counseled. "Let your body find the dance. Step lightly, and let the rhythm lift you."

The steady beat of Meuse's drum, the tap of his stick against the birch bark, filled the dark woods. A bright fire lit the camp. Hidden from the routes traveled by white men, the family had set up camp in an out-of-way clearing on the opposite side of Kejimkujik Lake, a day's paddle from the family's traditional winter camp. It was a spot they hoped would be safe, where they could survive the approaching winter.

Gehne stood at the center of their circle, a smile of contentment on his ruddy face. When Caroline threw up her hands in frustration, he chuckled loudly. "As if Anne hasn't danced her whole life," he said to his Elders. Meuse had long ago given up trying to convince his uncle that Caroline was not his mother, returned from the dead. If the delusion brought the old man comfort, what harm was there in his confusion?

Mimi shushed Gehne. "She'll get it, Father." They began again. Mimi led the dance, her small, shuffling steps echoing the beat of his drum, her eyes half-closed, and her body swaying. Caroline followed, imitating as best she could.

"The snake is waking from his winter sleep," Mimi explained. In her shadow, Caroline studied Mimi's feet. Her tiny steps seemed to go nowhere and yet moved her forward. They walked around the circle three times. By the third revolution, Caroline's feet caught on. When Mimi turned her back on Gehne, still dancing, Caroline did the same. Facing the forest, they circled around Gehne three times. Caroline relaxed and let the dance carry her. Then the two dancers turned their backs on each other and continued three times around the circle. Changing direction, they retraced their steps in the opposite direction until they had completed twelve revolutions.

"The serpent wakes up now," Mimi said. Never missing a step, she sidled aside, leaving an opening for Gehne to join in the dance.

"The serpent leaves his hole," Meuse said. He pounded the drum louder, filling the woods with rhythms that had echoed there for thousands of years. Each tap a heartbeat, pulsing life through their dancing bodies.

"Siss." Gehne imitated the serpent, twisting and turning his wiry body, consumed by the momentum. In one hand, he grasped a horn filled with small pebbles, which he rattled with every step. "Siss. Chuga chuga," Meuse chanted under his breath. The women moved around him in a constantly changing orbit, making smaller and smaller circles until they coiled around him. When Gehne reversed the direction of the dance, the snake uncoiled. The line of dancers, the serpent, slithered back toward the fire.

Now Gehne stood alone, and the dancers dropped away, breathless. Gehne's chant filled the camp. Caroline watched, her face filled with awe. She nodded at Mimi, swept away by the magic. The two women swayed. The drumbeats filled their hearts. The children watched, their sparkling eyes reflecting the life of the fire. They were home now, thriving in the loving embrace of family. Their feet firmly on Mother Earth, they prepared for a joyous occasion.

While Meuse and Mimi had been away, Caroline had nursed Gehne back to health, patiently deferring to the Elders who still had his ear. Now that Meuse and Mimi had returned, she encouraged Gehne to resume his duties as chief, father, and beloved uncle. Restored to health, he gave his blessing to the couple. With typical joviality, he teased Meuse about his manhood, insisting that he would preside over the upcoming marriage ceremony, though a bull moose had yet to cross his path.

Meuse has set out each morning to gather adequate provisions to sustain the family during the dark days that were fast approaching. Each morning, he set traps, speared fish in the roaring streams, and hunted small animals with his bow and arrow. Mimi smoked the meat from the animals he killed and buried root vegetables deep in the earth to preserve them. Like any Mi'kmaw man who desired to marry, Meuse knew his uncle expected him to demonstrate his ability to provide. He might never have slain a moose, but he would protect his family in the winter ahead. In the evenings, which arrived early now, he sat at Uncle Gehne's side and listened to his meandering stories with newfound respect.

In the meantime, Mimi prepared her regalia. She dug up minerals from the soil and painted her tunic with elegant red and yellow ocher designs. She used the last of the summer flowers to distill a brilliant blue dye. She sewed colorful trim to the sleeves and hem of her dancing dress, attaching tinkler cones she crafted from copper. From the remains of small game, she collected teeth and claws that would add sound and movement to her step.

Francis and Lisette would arrive any day now from Digby, where Francis and his father-in-law were building a house. But tonight, the family danced. "When Francis arrives," Gehne announced, "we will celebrate by holding a smudge ceremony." Few relatives remained to witness Meuse and Mimi's marriage—a pity—but their absence only made the significance of the celebration greater.

"You'll stay until after the ceremony?" Mimi asked Caroline that afternoon, as they stripped the fur off two rabbits Meuse had caught in his traps.

"I'm in no hurry to leave," Caroline said. "I came to Nova Scotia as a favor to my sister but never felt I belonged in the British colony. On his latest visit, Mr. Campbell assured me a competent midwife from Massachusetts had taken over my duties in Annapolis."

"I didn't know you had a sister," Mimi said.

"She died in childbirth," Caroline replied. She hadn't spoken of Maggie since leaving her parents' house. "I was her midwife, but I wasn't able to save her."

"Sometimes I forget that we are not the only ones who have experienced heartbreaking loss," Mimi said. She took Caroline's hand in hers. "I'm so sorry to hear about your sister. And now your father has also passed away in your absence. You must miss him."

"I do. But Mr. Campbell has graciously agreed to deliver my letters to my mother and return with her replies. The letters I receive from my mother, and those from my niece Lucy, are filled with news of the family. At least my mother is not alone. I am grateful to my brother, who has asked her to join his family at their farm. He has so many children by now, she will soon forget me altogether.

"I doubt that," Mimi said. "But you know, here you also have a family."

"Your friendship is much appreciated," Caroline said. "I will never forget what you suffered at the hands of my people. Every time I see your father's eyes go blank, I remember who is responsible."

"But you, too, have suffered."

Caroline smiled. "Yes, but I have benefited from your family's kindness. Your father, you know, is an amazing man."

Gehne continued to call Caroline "Anne," as if in doing so, he could restore Meuse's mother to the family. Caroline rather liked it. She hadn't refused the items of clothing he had discovered when they moved the family's winter belongings to the new camp. When she held the tunics up, she realized that not only had the two women been nearly the same age, but they were also similar in stature. No one in the family objected when she wore Anne's tunics. Meuse seldom mentioned his mother, but he complimented the food Caroline prepared and did not complain when she asked about traditional Indian remedies and incorporated them into the treatments she had learned as a midwife. The children in her care treated her as their mother. "Indian style," Meuse said. "There's family, and then there's *family*."

Mimi, more than any of the others, valued her company. Caroline imitated Mimi's effortless movements as they continued stripping the rabbits of their skins. The fur would come in use to keep the children warm in the winter. For now, they set it aside.

"We would certainly understand if you chose to return to Annapolis County with Francis and Lisette after the marriage ceremony," Mimi said.

"But who would take care of Gehne?" Caroline loved Mimi but doubted that Meuse and Mimi, so young and newly wed, would know how to treat the old man's failing health or monitor the children for trauma. Who would heat water for chamomile tea to warm the family when the snows set in?

What she didn't say was that she no longer felt she had a home to return to. She had no desire to test the hospitality of the Parkers. Nathaniel had Salome at his side and would have surely recovered from his ordeal by now. She felt some guilt about deserting little Lucy, but she supposed that her niece would soon be absorbed by her growing family. Indeed, the letters Campbell delivered indicated that the strong-headed girl was adjusting to her new lot in the thriving Planter community. There was always Boston, of course, but the idea of returning to a city on the verge of revolution appealed to her not at all. Let William represent the family in that quagmire.

Instead, she would learn to dance. And maybe, just maybe, she might stay through the winter. Continue to care for the family and this strange man who spoke to his Elders and never told a lie. She had much to learn from the family *sagamore* who had weathered tragedy with a grin on his face and who treated her with warmth and an affection she had never received from her own father. Where else might she share a home with a wise man who spoke to the spirits with breathtaking facility? Certainly not in the company of the Baptists whom Parker had chosen to lead. If

Gehne could be an uncle to Meuse, why couldn't she become the family aunt? She was convinced they needed her.

A Mi'kmaw Auntie. The idea appealed to her. The bottom line was she was happy here.

As she and Mimi danced, the earth below their feet joined them. Gehne was the head of the snake, and she only one segment of the serpent's body, twisting and turning with the others in unison. She was learning the ancient dance as a novice, but they taught her patiently and effortlessly, with a generosity of spirit she didn't deserve but treasured enormously.

• • •

Francis and Lisette arrived by canoe from Church Point in Digby. By the time they arrived at the family's camp, they had walked many miles from the river, and Lisette was weary. Heavy with child, she clutched Francis's arm with one hand and shielded her stomach with the other. Her elegant features were offset by her enormous belly, which seemed out of place on her slender frame. Her fragility contrasted with her husband's sturdy build and heavy step. "Bonjour?" she called out in French as they emerged from the forest. The proud papa positively strutted as he presented irrefutable proof of his virility.

Meuse was out checking the traps, so Caroline was the first to see them. "*Pjila'si*," she said. "Welcome. Your father will be so happy to see you." She led Francis to the family's wigwam, where Gehne was taking a nap. Francis gawked at the white woman in native leather attending to the fire. But he, too, had been transformed. He wore a white shirt and vest and was proud to present himself as an Acadian farmer, although he had decorated his straw hat with feathers he had collected during their journey.

"In Digby," he bragged to his father as Gehne blinked awake and Caroline poured tea for the visitors, "we were invited to join a colony of exiled Acadians." With *Monsieur* LaFleur's help, he was building a wooden house with two windows. According to the terms of the most recent peace treaty, exiles had been allowed to return to British territory. Of course, their former lands had been ceded to New England Planters, but a surveyor from the Irish county of Clare had carved out a large chunk of rocky land on the southern peninsula that was isolated and infertile and thus disposable enough for the returning Acadians.

"The LaFleurs were given land for a homestead and a hundred-acre woodlot. Our land is rocky and wooded and dotted with bogs, but if farming doesn't pan out, we'll try logging or fishing. If all else fails, I can always join my father-in-law on the dikes."

Gehne laughed, delighted as always at his son's bluster. "You building dikes?" he said. "That'll be the day." But he beamed with pride at this tall son who'd strode into the family shelter like a returning hero. Here was a man who knew how to resurrect himself. Gehne poked Lisette's belly as if testing bannock to see if the dough had risen. What a wonder! He was about to be a grandfather! Francis translated his father's excited words into French for Lisette, omitting the comments his father attributed to the Elders. Soon enough, his wife would realize what she had gotten herself into.

When Meuse returned, he handed the day's catch to Caroline and then hugged his cousin before standing back to take in this new version of Francis. Gone was the warrior, the revolutionary, even the thief. Francis in his beret seemed gentled, a horse who had accepted the bit. The adversary who had declared "This is not over" had, for the moment, stepped away from the battle. And although Meuse doubted the change would last, he was glad for the respite.

"Mimi and I are delighted you could make it," he said. "In traditional fashion, our celebration will last four days. Settle in," he said. Lisette smiled shyly, understanding nothing. For once, his cousin let Meuse take the lead. "I hope you've taught Lisette the serpent dance," he said.

"I will," Francis said, "as soon as you learn *français.*" Francis spoke in French to his wife. She blushed, and he laughed, miming the movement of a snake through long grasses.

Soon the traditional games began. Francis's competitive instinct resurfaced at once. "What shall I beat you in first?" he taunted Meuse. "*Tooad ik,* lacrosse, or *madijik*? Or are we simply going to stay inside and play Waltes? It's been a while since I've had a chance to humiliate you."

The men headed outside, jostling against one another, each proclaiming their superiority. Caroline asked Lisette if she knew how to make bannock. The women set to work preparing the wedding feast. Now that their guests had arrived, there was much to be done.

The next morning, the entire family assembled in the wigwam for the smudging ceremony. Gehne had prepared the herbs: sage to drive away the bad spirits, cedar and sweetgrass to carry their prayers to the creator, tobacco to clear their vision. With atypical solemnity, he lit the herbs and fanned the tiny spark into a flame, extinguishing it when smoke curled from the bowl. He rubbed his hands together and directed the smoke toward his face and over the top of his head. He prayed that the unseen powers would cleanse his spirit. He bathed himself and, eagle feather in hand, walked to each of his guests in turn and repeated the motions, channeling the smoke where they needed healing the most.

When his uncle approached him, Meuse closed his eyes, overcome. The last time he had performed this sacred ceremony, he had been filled with rage. He had performed the cleansing ritual for his captive like a charlatan. He had been unworthy, a foolish boy playing with fire. All that ensued had taught him the fallacy of his foolishness. But today, his heart was open. As Gehne directed the smoke at his chest, tears filled his eyes. Without shame, he let them fall.

As his tears dampened the dirt floor, he heard the voices of his Elders calling him. In chorus, they chanted the many names he had been called on the journey to this moment: a fatherless boy, an unwanted usurper, a savage, a coward, a criminal, a wanted man, a condemned prisoner, a man on the run, a refugee in exile, and now a man on the eve of his wedding.

In their language, every word was an action. Everything he had become shaped the world he would live in.

"I will be worthy," he whispered. To Gehne, to his elders, to Mimi, who would be the mother of his children, he made a promise. To the seven generations that would follow.

"*Wantaqo'ti*," Gehne said. Peace. The tiny laugh lines around his eyes crinkled with pride. The sweet smell of sage surrounded them.

After the smudging ceremony, Gehne placed the Waltes bowl in the center of the wigwam. The men had played the dice and bowl game the previous evening. Francis had won, of course. "The more you talk to the dice, the better they roll," he said. Before they had gone to bed, Gehne had filled the sacred wooden bowl with water from the stream. The hardwood had deepened in color, the veins of the wood now a map he studied with great intensity. As the others watched, he examined the grain of the wood.

"Ahh," he said, looking up at Meuse, a fond smile on his face.

"Mimi, my love," he said, "you have chosen well."

He ran his fingers along the rim of the bowl and held them to his nose, inhaling deeply. He cocked his head as if listening. He examined the wood's grain again. This time, his brow furrowed. His lips pursed. Whatever he saw, it did not please him.

"My son," he said, at last, not raising his eyes, "Francis, you were born a warrior. I always knew this. A warrior must protect those he loves, act to preserve his family." He continued to read the bowl as if looking for another end to this story. "But," he cried out, "sacrifices come at great cost. Oh, Great Spirit, I beg you, protect my boy!"

Francis regarded his father with dark eyes. Fierce eyes filled with recognition. At his side, little Lisette clenched her fists. She watched the old man's face, trying to decipher his message.

"There are dark times ahead," Gehne said. Was this steady drone his uncle's voice or that of another speaking through him? "I see our people banished to unwanted lands. Children taken from our sides to be taught another's beliefs. I see darkness and hunger and…." His voice broke, and he spoke no more. He shrunk from the vision, becoming older and smaller before their eyes. All his usual vitality disappeared. Even his laugh lines dissolved into dark crevices etched onto his weary face.

"What is he saying?" Lisette asked anxiously. She took her husband's hand. "Tell me. I don't like this at all." When Francis did not respond, she turned to Caroline and said in English: "I'm afraid."

Caroline, who followed little of what Gehne had said but intuitively understood his warning, answered the frightened girl with words she had often used to calm a woman in labor.

"There may be hard times ahead that will test our fortitude, but we will face them together." As she carefully framed Gehne's vision in a way that would not frighten Lisette, a breeze rustled the wigwam's flap, blowing it briefly aside. An errant ray of sunshine pierced the darkness. The faint light permeated the smoky space and illuminated the remnants of smudge and smoke with a ghostly luminescence.

"But this is Meuse's wedding day," Gehne declared, an impish grin reclaiming his face. "The bowl tells me we shall survive. For this, we are grateful. We must protect those we love, and that includes the animals that nurture us and Mother Earth, who protects us. Everything is interconnected. We know this because, after all we have been through, today Meuse will take a wife. And my daughter," he beamed at Mimi, "will become a woman."

At his words, Mimi blushed, embarrassed by her father's lascivious giggle. Gehne embraced her, holding her tightly, recited the traditional prayer of the seven sacred teachings.

•••

Kisu'lk wela'liek wjit wla Na'kwek kisi Iknmuiek.
Wela'liek wjit wla kis tli Mawita'nen, aq etamulek piskwa'n ta'n eymek,
klaman kis tliatew
ta'n tel-mnueken.
Iknmuinen Nsituoqn, klaman kjijitutesnen ta'n
koqoey Kelu'k wla wksitqamu'k.
Iknmuinen Ksaltultinen klaman kisi siawa'tesnen ksalsuti msit tamiaw.
Iknmuinen Kepmite'sultinen, klaman Kjijitutesnen ksalsuti msit tamiaw.
Iknmuinen Mlkitelsultinen, klaman ma' wen
nutajite'lsik lukwatmn wla tett.
Iknmuinen menaqajewo'ltinen, klaman ma'
wen ewlek kisna ewla'lat wen kikmanaq.
Iknmuinen Penoqite'lsultinen, klaman ma'
wen kisi aji espite'lsik aq wikma'jl.
Aq Niskam, Iknmuinene Ketleweyuti klaman

*waqme'ktital Nkamulamunal aq njijaqmijinaq
ta'n tujiw nmu'lek elmi'knik.
Na tliaj*

Creator, thank you for this day you have given us.
Thank you for allowing us to gather here today and we ask you to enter where we are, so that your teachings will work in us.
We ask for wisdom, so that we will know what is good in this world.
We ask for love, so we can spread your love everywhere.
We ask for respect, so that we will know that everyone comes from one place... from you.
We ask for bravery, so that we will not be afraid to do your work here.
We ask for honesty, so that no one will lie or harm anyone of us.
We ask for humility, so that no one will be superior to another.
And lord, we ask for truth, so that we will see you in the future, on the last day with clean hearts and spirits.
Amen

•••

Francis, under Gehne's critical eye, had constructed an arbor at the edge of a field, an intricate archway of dried branches. The maples were bare now, having laid down a carpet of red and golden leaves. The oaks burned golden in the sun. The men sat on a blanket, sharing bannock and berries, telling stories of Meuse's boyhood.

"He followed me everywhere," Francis remembered, "this fatherless boy with the wide brown eyes. If I threw a stone, he threw a stone. If I farted, he farted."

Gehne laughed, clapping his hands in delight. "Even then, he was your brother."

Meuse punched his cousin in the arm. "You liked that you could beat me in every game we played. My clumsiness showed off your prowess."

"Perhaps, but you were the one that reminded me that nothing is promised. Every day is a gift from the Creator."

The women appeared on the other side of the field, readying themselves. Caroline adjusted Mimi's white moose-hide robe, straightening the vertical strips of ornamental leather so that the red, blue, and yellow ocher stripes hung equally on each side. She placed the peaked hat on her head and adjusted it so that her earrings—long strings of wampum, shells, and porcupine quills—hung freely. Mimi played nervously with the bracelets adorning her wrists.

"I suppose we had better take our places," Francis said. Meuse and Francis walked arm in arm to the opposite side of the field, still joking, still jostling. The young children, wide-eyed and silent, toddled behind them. Gehne skipped along the path in defiance of his arthritic limbs; the feathers on his headpiece danced. "Watch it, old man," Francis said. "We have a long day ahead of us."

The dry grass in the field rattled. The arbor stood empty, ready.

The men began to beat their *ji'kmaqn*, birch-bark boxes they held in one hand and beat with a stick. The women slapped layers of split ash against their hands as they surrounded Mimi and marched from the south, the women's door. They giggled, self-conscious in their finery. Their silver jewelry tinkled in the breeze, the glitter of their regalia glistening in the sun. Even Lisette had decorated her modest smock with a string of sparkling beads. Mimi's long braid was entwined with flowers. The pungent pepper of juniper berries and the sweetness of rose hips surrounded them. The women walked to the arbor and turned to wait for the men.

The men came from the north, the men's door, pounding their *ji'kmaqn* with great excitement, still laughing. Meuse led the way, grinning at his bride, a bright red sash around his waist. He had painted his face for the occasion, a joyful pattern of red and black. Gehne held his head high. Today, he was the Elder, secure in his rightful place as the family's *sagamore*. They marched in unison, eyes fixed on the women who preceded them. For the ceremony, Francis once again wore traditional garments: feathers in his hair and a supple leather breechcloth decorated in tribal colors. They joined the women under the arbor.

There they stood, laughing. Displaying themselves like turkeys fanning their feathers in the springtime despite the blazing color of late fall surrounding them.

At Gehne's signal, they sat down on colorful blankets on the short grass under the arbor. Gehne lit his pipe with a smoldering stick from the fire. He puffed and exhaled with pleasure. "Like me and my pipe," he said, "marriage is a lifetime commitment. We are here, not to show off our splendor, though I must say we do look fine, but to witness the uniting of Meuse and Mimi." He inhaled again and then handed the pipe to Meuse. In turn, each member of the wedding party shared the pipe.

"Now, my children," Gehne said, "make me the happiest man on earth." Meuse helped the old man stand up from his seated posture. That done, he offered Mimi his hand, and she rose to stand beside him.

Everyone was quiet. Gehne extracted a knife from his sash and cut a lock of Meuse's hair. He held it up for all to see and then handed it to Mimi. She placed the glossy strands of black hair in a pouch around her neck. Then Gehne cut a shiny blue-black lock of hers, which he handed to Meuse. He, too, put it into a pouch he wore on a leather strap around his neck.

The grasses rattled. The wind danced in the trees. Gehne wrapped a blanket around the bride and groom. The family hooted and cheered. The heartbeat of their drums filled the air. In the excitement of the moment, no one in the wedding party heard the hoofbeats in the distance. No one, that is, except Francis, always vigilant, who waited for the wedding party to assemble for the serpent dance before retrieving the gun he had secreted in a thicket upon his arrival. The same gun he had bought up north and had carried ever since. Just in case. As the others took their places for the dance in jubilation, he slipped into the forest, ready to protect them at any cost.

"I've got your back, my brother," he whispered to the wind. The tall trees offered him cover.

The dancers formed their sinuous line. At its head, Meuse beamed, not catching his friend's words but feeling his love. Gehne sighed as his son disappeared.

The newlyweds danced. The snake slithered.

In the dark forest, Ezekiel approached on a powerful steed. The hooves of his horse stirred up dust and kicked aside leaf litter. Too soon, the wedding party heard what sounded like a crack of thunder in the distance.

CHAPTER TWENTY

A Letter to William

Parker Mountain, December 1761

My dearest brother William,

I hope this letter finds you well. How timid I feel, addressing a fellow of Harvard College! I try to imagine you in Boston. Do you wear long robes and hold your hands behind your back as you perambulate? I, your lowly sister, can hardly compete with the likes of James Otis and John Adams. What high-minded conversations must now fill your days! From my perch on Parker Mountain, the Massachusetts colony seems like another world. I spend my days minding babes, doing housework, and weeding the kitchen garden. You write of strolling through the Common with the greatest intellectuals of our age.

And yet, life on Parker Mountain is far from uneventful.

Undoubtedly, you have heard by now that Ezekiel is no longer with us. He died a horrible death. Despite Father and Nat's frantic attempts to discourage him, he set out in the middle of the night in pursuit of that Indian boy who escaped from the Annapolis jail.

Ma Salome discovered his empty bed and a note declaring his intentions. You would hardly have recognized her as she read his note aloud, her face as pale as bed linen, her hands shaking in despair.

Father, hoping to deter Ezekiel, left at once to retrace the path that his rescue party had followed up the Mersey River. For days, we heard nothing of either of them. Ma Salome, Sally, and I performed our daily chores with ears cocked for the sound of hoofbeats. Nat stopped by each evening to offer solace and an assessment of the legal implications of Ezekiel's actions, which the local government had already condemned.

Three days later, Father returned. We ran out to the porch in great excitement as he approached. His drawn face made his expression unreadable. To my great surprise, behind Father rode Caroline, with Ezekiel slumped in front of her. He was hardly recognizable, with clothes stained reddish brown, skin pasty white, and mouth contorted in pain.

"My son," Salome ran to his side. Her sobs drowned out the thud of Father dismounting.

"He's been shot," Father said to me. "Caroline has kindly agreed to care for him." He looked over at Salome as if considering his next move. Then he told me, "I have business to attend to downtown. Please tell Salome I will be home soon."

Before the dust of his retreat settled, Salome and Caroline asked for help carrying Ezekiel up the steps, into the house, and into the front room, where he collapsed onto a chair. Ezekiel, usually so full of vim and vigor, muttered incomprehensibly and didn't seem to recognize us. His skin burned with fever. His clothing was stained with more blood than I have ever seen, even during childbirth.

William, how wise you were to flee! No good can come of this conflict. All evening, I longed to ask a million questions, but I bit my tongue. You know I felt no love for Ezekiel, but seeing his torment, not to mention Ma Salome and Sally's, I did my utmost to assist them.

For two days, we nursed him. After the first, he no longer opened his eyes. He didn't even seem to know his own mother. On the third day, Salome asked us to leave them alone. He passed soon after.

Caroline had not slept in days, and I urged her to lie down beside me in my chamber. But still she did not sleep, her eyes focused on the ceiling.

"Who shot him?" I whispered when I could no longer be silent.

She turned to me in surprise, unaware she was not alone.

"A friend of the Indian who abducted your father," she said after a long pause. I had never seen my aunt so weary; her words were barely audible. "Ezekiel shot him first, but the other man shot back before dying."

She witnessed it all, our beloved Aunt Caroline! I ventured only one more question. "Are you an Indian now, too?"

She sighed, a sigh so deep it sounded like a sob. "No," she said. "As much as I have come to love them…"

I've imagined so many ends to this sentence she never completed. No, I've come home. No, my mothers need me. No, I prefer births to death. *But instead of asking her what she intended to say, I spooned her quaking body, hoping my warmth would ease her pain.*

Father, it turned out, had ridden off in search of Chief Bâtard, the tribal chief who had attended his exchange. Nat told me this later, but I can hardly imagine the conversation that took place between that stone-faced man and Father, who sought his assistance in relocating the Indian family that had taken Caroline in. How he located the chief or where the family has gone, I will never know. Father refuses to speak further of the matter, and Ma Salome looks askance at me whenever I try to bring it up.

So, dear William, you must see how strange it is for me to read about your attendance at an oration by the great patriot James Otis at the State House and your political discussions with John Adams about the arbitrary claims of Great Britain. I only pray the revolution you foresee is one that takes place without loss of blood. That liberty and justice can be achieved through peaceful means. I urge you, if you have any say in the matter, to remind these illustrious men that their vision will be just only if it provides equal benefits for all.

But then, who am I to weigh in on such intellectual matters? I'll leave this up to you. If the past few years have taught me anything, it is that the decisions made by the great minds of our time affect families of every background and creed. As Father often preaches from his pulpit, justice resides in the hands of God but is only visible when implemented by us, his lowly servants.

Excuse my ramblings, but I miss our talks.

As always, your affectionate sister,
Lucy

EPILOGUE

What Gehne saw in the Waltes bowl was a tale of two families.

He saw Francis waiting for Ezekiel, musket in hand. Standing erect, muscular legs spread defiantly. This was the moment Francis had prepared for his whole life. He would defend his family or die trying. Without his bravery, they would all perish. He would stand up to the enemy, whatever the cost. Lisette would try to stop him, tug at his sleeve, but Gehne knew she would not prevail. The two men would engage in mortal combat as Meuse and Mimi escaped once again into the forest.

He saw blood. Blood and the painful sight of warriors dying. He saw Caroline cleaning up the mess before Major Rogers discovered what had befallen his most loyal sycophant. Francis shot only once, but his bullet lodged in Ezekiel's belly, a wound that would fester for days. Gehne saw the wound reflected in the bowl, nauseating and graphic. Unlike Ezekiel, Francis would die immediately.

He saw Chief Bâtard arrive five days after Meuse and Mimi's wedding had turned into a funeral. He watched the tribal chief arrange the survivors' safe passage to an isolated settlement on Cape Breton. There, they would settle and raise three children, poor but surrounded by other displaced Mi'kmaq. In the mid-1800s, their descendants would move with a dozen other families to the newly chartered reservation at Eskasoni, where life continued to be hard. Meuse and Mimi's offspring remained faithful Catholics but schooled their children in their Mi'kmaq roots.

Three generations later, in the 1930s, he saw their great-grandchildren removed from their family. At the Shubenacadie Indian Residential School, they were allowed to speak only English, forced to do manual labor, and beaten when they misbehaved.

When the Department of Indian Affairs introduced a policy in 1942 to centralize native people, he saw Eskasoni named one of two reserves in the province. Although the government promised aid and housing, they did not provide enough resources for the influx of people that crowded onto the reservation.

Gehne's heart soared when he saw, in the sixth generation, the Eskasoni band council elect as tribal chief Meuse's great-great-great-grandson, Elias, and when, in the seventh, Elias's son Matthew enrolled at the University of Cape Breton to study sociology. There, Matthew fell in love with a teacher at the reservation's immersion school, became a Star Trek fanatic, and played video games in his spare time.

Gehne saw all this, and more.

He saw Caroline return with Parker to Annapolis, reluctantly nursing the injured Ezekiel but unable to slow the spread of his infection. Despite her ministrations, his wound wept and oozed putrid pus. After Ezekiel's death, she went back to her work as a midwife, choosing life over death but never having children of her own. He saw Parker's ministry thrive, even after the white man buried his stepson.

He saw Parker, the first of three generations of Baptist ministers in Nova Scotia, sit with eighteen children around his dinner table. Even with the help of a string of black maids, his wife Salome could hardly keep up with the endless chores of raising children, maintaining a home, and fulfilling her obligations to Parker's congregation.

He saw Lucy marry Benjamin Baker, the son of a Planter whose grandfather had crossed the Atlantic on the Mayflower.

He saw Lucy's great-great-great-grandson move to Washington State, where he opened one lumberyard, then another, and became wealthy and influential in local politics. The businesses required more and more lumber—there was never enough for the rampant construction taking place on the new frontier. Over the next generations, he watched Parker's descendants clear-cut the forests of the Olympic Peninsula to satisfy that demand, leaving only a narrow band of trees along the sides of the interstate to camouflage the barren tracts of land.

He saw seven generations of Parker women, bright and educated, stay at home to support their husbands. With each generation, they drank more: cocktails with lunch, vodka while cooking dinner. They were a little bit nasty and often discontent. In the seventh generation, Lucy's great-great-great-great-great granddaughter, a rebellious teenager, dyed her hair bright yellow and moved to a commune in Vermont, where she tried to live off the land, read about epigenetics, and licked stamps laced with LSD. For a while, she taught history in an elite Massachusetts college, but repeating the lessons of her forebears grew tedious. Each year, another species was declared extinct. The planet's air and water, lifelines for its inhabitants, were sacrificed to industry, victims of corporate greed.

He saw all this and then looked up to the sky for guidance, hoping the verdant forest might shelter them from all the damage yet to come.

•••

SOURCES

Calnek, W. A. (William Arthur) (1987). *1822-1892: History of the county of Annapolis, including old Port Royal and Acadia [electronic resource] : with memoirs of its representatives in the provincial parliament : and biographical and genealogical sketches of its early English settlers and their families / (Toronto : W. Briggs; Montreal : C. Coates; Halifax [N.S.]: S. Huestis, 1897), also by A. W. Savary (page images at HathiTrust; US access only)*

Candow, James E. *(1995). "The New England Planters in Nova Scotia," ed. John Thomas, Planter Notes 6, no. 2.*

Conrad, Margaret, Laidlaw, Toni, and Smyth, Donna (1988). *No place like home. Diaries and Letters of Nova Scotia Women 1776-1938.* Formac Publishing.

Eaton, Arthur Wentworth Parker, 1992. *The History of Kings County, Nova Scotia, Heart of the Acadian Land, Giving a Sketch of the French and Their Expulsion, And a History of the New England Planters who Came in Their Stead, with Many Genealogies, 1604-1910.* Mika Studio.

Gespe'gewa'gi Mi'gmawei Mawiomi (2016). *Nta'tugwaqanminen: Our Story: Evolution of the Gespege'wa'gi Mi'gmaq.* Fernwood Publishing .

Longley, R.S. *(1988). "The Coming of the New England Planters to the Annapolis Valley," In They Planted Well: New England Planters in Maritime Canada, edited by Margaret Conrad Fredericton.* Acadiensis Press.

Mackey, E. (2016). *Unsettled expectations: uncertainty, land and settler decolonization.* Fernwood Publishing.

Moody, Harry (1995). *"Growing Up in Granville Township, 1760-1800," In Intimate Relations: Family and Community in Planter Nova Scotia, 1759-1800, edited by Margaret Conrad (Planter Studies 3. Fredericton:* Acadiensis Press.

Paul, D. N. (2021). *We Were Not the Savages, First Nations History: Collision between European and Native American Civilizations, 3rd edition.* Fernwood Publishing.

The Planter Studies Series *(2001):*

Margaret Conrad, They Planted Well: New England Planters in Maritime Canada

Conrad, Making adjustments : change and continuity in Planter Nova Scotia, 1759-1800

Conrad, Intimate relations : family and community in planter Nova Scotia, 1759-1800

Margaret Conrad and Barry Moody, Planter links : community and culture in colonial Nova Scotia

Stephen Henderson and Wendy G. Robicheau, The Nova Scotia Planters in the Atlantic World

Planters Study Center, Acadia University. Acadiensis

Rawlyk, George A. *(1973). Nova Scotia's Massachusetts: A Study of Massachusetts-Nova Scotia Relations, 1630-1784.* Montreal: McGill-Queen's University Press.

Wilson, Isaiah W. (1900). *A Geography and History of the County of Digby, Nova Scotia,* Holloway Brothers

Websites and cultural organizations:

http://www.muiniskw.org/

Simply stated, this site was created in order to give people a reliable place to find accurate information about the Mi'kmaw people and their culture, their history, and their spirituality.

https://native-land.ca/wp/wp-content/uploads/2018/06/Mikmaq_Kekinamuek-Manual.pdf

https://www.historymuseum.ca/cmc/exhibitions/aborig/fp/fpz4inte.html "Arrival of Strangers," as retold by Stephen Augustine, from an original by Silas Rand in Legends of the Micmacs, 1894.

https://www.mikmaweydebert.ca/home/wpcontent/uploads/2015/06/Pg_42_DOC_MikmawPrayer.pdf

ACKNOWLEDGMENTS

Many thanks to the depth of information and generosity shown me by members of the Millbrook Cultural & Heritage center and Eskasoni First Nation. They helped me on this journey, but I could not have completed it without the support of the Amherst Co-housing Friday Writers, Caren McVicker, Gemma Lury, my husband, and Lucy, buried in my family tree, who wouldn't stop talking.

ALSO BY KATHRYN HOLZMAN

Real Estate, a Novel

Holzman's accomplished prose propels her beleaguered characters through tragedies and watershed moments. There's much to enjoy in this well-constructed sketch of people constrained by their family and their choices.

—Publishers Weekly

Great Book Club Pick!

Our book club gave "Real Estate" high marks. It is a fun and interesting read about two families who move to Santa Clara CA in the early 1960's as Silicon Valley begins to emerge. The changes they experience are viewed through the eyes of Harriet, the daughter of a Japanese war bride with a Navy pilot father, and her next-door neighbor Bobby, a computer whiz who has little interest in the financial success he achieves.

We particularly enjoyed the way the author set the scene. She took us back in time with an array of throwback music, magazines, TV shows and political events. There is plenty to discuss about family expecta-tions and how they shape our lives, the freedom to follow one's own path, and the experience of Japanese war brides.

Kemmerer Library Harding Township

ABOUT THE AUTHOR

Kathryn Holzman is the author of two collections of short fiction, *FLATLANDERS*, Shire Press 2019 and *MIGRATIONS*, Picaflor Press. Her first novel *REAL ESTATE* was published by Propertius Press. In the Fall of 2020, she received the Grand Prize in the Eyelands International Short Story Contest. More information and links to her work can be found at kathrynholzman.com.